"Promise me, Cordelia," her father had said to her that day. "Swear to me you will never tell anyone about the monsters we keep here."

If people knew how many monsters Cordelia and her father were keeping, they would be afraid. They would demand that the monsters be kept in cages, or shipped off to some foreign place or even killed. Perhaps they would want Cordelia and her father to be arrested.

They didn't understand that everyone needed saving sometimes. Everyone needed someone to care.

Even—perhaps *especially*—monsters.

ALSO BY
LAUREN OLIVER

Before I Fall

Broken Things

Liesl & Po

The Spindlers

Panic

Vanishing Girls

Replica

Ringer

Curiosity House: The Shrunken Head

Curiosity House: The Screaming Statue

Curiosity House: The Fearsome Firebird

THE DELIRIUM SERIES

Delirium

Pandemonium

Requiem

Delirium Stories: Hana, Annabel, Raven, and Alex

FOR ADULTS

Rooms

THE
MAGNIFICENT
MONSTERS
OF
CEDAR STREET

LAUREN OLIVER

Quill Tree Books
An Imprint of HarperCollinsPublishers

Quill Tree Books is an imprint of HarperCollins Publishers.

The Magnificent Monsters of Cedar Street
Copyright © 2020 by Laura Schechter
All rights reserved. Printed in the United States of America.
No part of this book may be used or reproduced in any manner whatsoever
without written permission except in the case of brief quotations embodied
in critical articles and reviews. For information address HarperCollins
Children's Books, a division of HarperCollins Publishers, 195 Broadway,
New York, NY 10007.
www.harpercollinschildrens.com

Library of Congress Control Number: 2021936718
ISBN 978-0-06-234508-0

Interior art by Ethan M. Aldridge
Typography by Catherine San Juan
21 22 23 24 25   PC/BRR   10 9 8 7 6 5 4 3 2 1
❖
First trade paperback edition, 2021

To Normandy Itzhak and West Lester:
For the Adventures ahead
And the Magic inside
And the Love everywhere

A SHORT GUIDE TO THE MONSTERS REFERENCED IN THIS BOOK,

EXCERPTED FROM

A GUIDE TO MONSTERS AND THEIR HABITS, BY ELIZABETH CLAY

Alicanti (*sing.* Alicanto). The alicanti, or *Aeriol complainus*, are closely related to harpies, and may have evolved from the same prehistoric ancestor. The *Aeriol complainus* are known for their piercing shrieks, loud enough to pierce an eardrum, likely due to their preferred mountainous habitats, which require the mating alicanti to call for mates across vast swaths of distance.

Atlantic Firr (sing. same). Like the sloth, to whom they are closely related, the Atlantic Firr are sweet, slow-moving herbivores, although they have been known to eat insects for dessert or on special occasions. Known for a ferocious scowl that long made them an object of fear, the Atlantic Firr are actually quite easy-going. The directional pull of their wide, nearly toothless mouths is an expression of biological and not temperamental traits: due to years of sipping nectar and moisture from canopy leaves, their mouths are simply pulled into permanent frowns. Though once found across a wide range of habitats, from the jungles of the southern hemisphere to the rangy woods of Northern Europe, during the Middle Ages the Atlantic Firr were hunted to near extinction, when it was thought that consumption of their kidneys would keep a person safe from the plague. In fact, it is the Atlantic Firr's salivary glands that produce chemical compounds nearly indistinguishable from today's strongest antibiotics.

Baku (*sing.* same). The baku are an unusual variety of feathered mammal, once uniquely found in tropical regions. Due to their legendary sweet tooth, the baku's habitats grew more diverse as a result of the explosion of the sugar trade, and the ships that often inadvertently carried stowaway baku in the cargo hold as they navigated the world. They are loosely related to a particular variety of Amazonian spiny tree rat, which likely resulted in the feathering that serves as camouflage when they are roosting—or hunting—high in the tree canopy.

Bogeys. Like the specter, the bogey cannot actually fly but only coasts on air currents, scanning for prey. Some have suggested a connection between the two, but this has been impossible to verify, given the difficulty of collecting meaningful living or fossilized specimens of either. It is likely, however, that bogeys are related more closely to succubi—their nourishment comes from a form of parasitic attachment that requires epidermal (skin-to-skin) contact, much like the succubi's. It is worth noting, however, that bogeys do have a standard shape, although their biology is spread so thinly across a vast surface area that they are rendered translucent and nearly invisible to the naked eye. Given its lack of eyes, ears, mouths, or appendages, the bogey's sensory apparatus was for years a mystery. Early nineteenth-century research, however, discovered that bogeys excrete a slimy, sticky substance from all over their bodies, with which they bond to host creatures, leave tracks for other bogeys, and perhaps attract their mates. Their Latin name, *Mattahorn salivus*, roughly means "drooling Mattahorn," and comes from that of the unfortunate scientist who discovered this feature by volunteering as host for a bogey.

Bullieheads have the head of an ox and a small, burly build like that of a bulldog; they are herbivores and quite shy. They are herd animals closely related to the *Capra aegagrus hircus*, or domesticated goat, and do very badly when separated from the pack.

Carbuncles. So-named because of a stippled, knobby hide that resembles the painful dermatological condition, the skin of the modern carbuncle is a *deliberate* evolutionary adaptation in response to a shrinking habitat. The hide of an adult carbuncle is actually one enormous, striated callus, made as a result of long and painful exposure to volcanic or mountainous elements. Much like tree rings, the fine layers of a carbuncle's hide may be separated and counted as a decent estimate of age. Ranging from just a few ounces to the size of a small raccoon, the carbuncles are often mistaken for rocks—until they shriek, show their teeth, or blink one of their dozens of heavy-lidded eyes.

Chupacabras. Variously described as resembling a dog or a large, scaled reptilian creature, the chupacabra has characteristics of both. It is indeed a carnivorous reptile, descended from a prehistoric genus of reptiles known as pareiasaurs, roughly the size of a large wolf. It is thought that chupacabras may have emerged as a distinct species due to a catastrophic environmental change, which might have also necessitated their move away from an herbivorous diet. Although associated in popular imagination with drinking blood, especially that of livestock, chupacabras are primarily scavengers. Because *drought,* however, is the chupacabra's primary source of environmental stress, Monsterologists have previously observed mixed communities of chupacabras and zuppies, a cooperative relationship due to the zuppies' ability to go without water. It is theorized, then, that chupacabras drink blood either for the limited hydration it provides or, more interestingly, to collect it for the zuppies in their pack, as zuppy teeth are too small to penetrate an animal hide.

Cockatrices. Described in mythology as an aberrant winged monster with a dragon's tail and the head of a rooster. Advances in paleontology have discovered the quite obvious connection between the modern cockatrice and its ancient ancestor, the pterodactyl. Like other members of the order Pterosauria, cockatrices are flying reptiles, and have close relatives in various species of flying gecko.

Diggles are small, sociable, and do better in "stands" of three or four members. Covered in scales made of a ridged calcite, they are extremely sharp to the touch and look, superficially, rather like English roses, but with razor blades instead of petals. They molt their skins annually by exploding, and may be softened through regular application of warm milk-baths. Despite being terrible swimmers, they have relatives in the *Paracentrotus lividus*, or sea urchin, species.

Dragons. Almost innumerable species of dragon once existed, and there are still likely undiscovered species living in remote and jungle areas. Direct descendants of pterodactyls, dragons originally evolved in underground caves, likely as a result of an environmental or atmospheric disaster that wiped out most other dinosaur species. It is the retreat to subterranean caverns that is responsible for their definitive trait: fire-breathing. In the absence of oxygen, dragons became selectively aerobic, meaning that they do not require oxygen to live, and can instead metabolize other gases, like methane, commonly released by bacterial growth and hot springs underground. In the presence of oxygen, however, the methane in their metabolic tracts becomes an agent of combustion. When the dragon breathes fire, he is actually regurgitating gas; the motion of the dragon's highly textured tongue adds just enough friction to generate a spark.

Dungaroos are so-named likely because of their resemblance to miniature kangaroos. This is a classic example of taxonomic confusion, related to the early naturalists' habit of using recognizable and physically obvious traits to classify species, often erroneously. Dungaroos are in fact amphibious creatures and are related closely to the *Lithobates catesbeianus*, or bullfrog. Full-grown dungaroos reach thirty-five pounds on average, much of their weight concentrated in the musculature of an enormously powerful set of hind legs, which allow them to spring more than eight feet in any direction. Dungaroos have a peculiar method of ensuring gender equality: after gestation, the female lays two to three eggs directly in the "pouch" of the male, who will then hatch them over the course of thirty to forty-five days.

Fairies evolved around fifty million years ago from the very first species of flying bat. Although often imagined as tiny winged humans, the resemblance collapses up close. Their cranium (skull) is quite large, the rest of their facial features look much more feline, and their arms, legs, and hands—though elongated and hairless—show structural similarities to rodents. Importantly, they are a diurnal species—and, in fact, famously early to bed and late to rise—an important distinction that no doubt pushed their evolution away from the many species of bat. This no doubt influenced their dietary evolution, too—fairies feed on plants and nectar, and often build communities close to human gardens. Although in legend they can converse fluently in our language, in reality they are only mimics—much like certain species of parakeet, the advantage is in bond formation with the humans whose gardens and communities they have long depended on.

Filches are amphibious in nature, with tapered snouts, coarse fur, and an anatomy similar to that of a chimpanzee, to which they are closely related. They are, however, swamp creatures, and eat a varied diet of mud, grubs, and small fish, which gives them a famously identifiable stink. While known for "farting" regularly, these regular expulsions of gas are actually an important feature not of the filches' digestive tract, but of its sensory mechanisms. Filches have poor eyesight and only decent hearing, but excellent depth perception and incredible mobility as a result. Recent studies have suggested they "see" in part by expulsions of gas particles, whose particular passage into space, or onto obstructing objects, is then detected through scenting.

Gnomes are not a singular species, but a genus, *Ignomia*, which includes more than forty different species and exists almost everywhere in the world. Their evolutionary divergence from other Hominoidea likely began roughly five million years ago, between the Mesozoic and Cenozoic eras. Ironically, despite a population of gnomes thought to number one billion globally, we have almost no fossil or skeletal records to guide us. All species of gnomes are characterized by a great capacity for camouflage and are thought to cannibalize their dead as a sign of respect.

Goblins are, along with trolls, a member of the *Homo* order diverged from humans roughly one to two million years ago, and still capable, in some cases, of reproducing with them. It is a broad family designation that includes multiple species, some of them nearly identical to humans: the *Cobalus viridi, Cobalus silva,* and *Cobalus urba* are three such examples. In humans of mixed goblin ancestry, the traits that express vary from individual to individual, and may even skip generations. One interesting feature of all goblins that have historically mated with humans: the physical development of traditional goblin features, such as emotional states tied to changes in skin color, a unique "three-ring" dental structure, and the decorative warts long associated with beauty and health in goblin communities, rarely show before adolescence. It is thought that this is a defense against early abandonment or attack by their caretakers.

Gremlins are a single species of carnivorous marsupials distantly related to the family Dasyurida, and most closely to the species *sarcophilis harrisii*, or Tasmanian devil. Unlike their Tasmanian cousins, however, gremlins are enormously widespread, comprising more than two hundred breeds, each with distinctly different personal traits and physical characteristics. Among the more populous gremlin breeds are the *burrowers*, solitary scavengers who make their dens beneath the floorboards or between the walls of human homes; the *leonines*, known for their tawny facial hair and sharp, curved teeth; and the shrills, the smallest-known gremlin breed in the world. Roughly the size of a rose blossom, their custom of affixing crowns of mushrooms and leaves to the tops of their heads makes for excellent camouflage.

Growrks are thought to be a North American relative of the sub-Saharan rhinoceros, although the exact evolutionary connection is unclear, and some have argued that in fact growrks might instead be more closely related to muskrats. They bear a superficial resemblance to wolves, except for their legs, which are short and jointed, like those of an alligator, and their tails, which are controlled by a complicated diamond-matrix of musculature and cartilage, giving them enormous flexibility and incredible strength. Despite their appearance, domesticated species make for loving and loyal companions.

Hippogriffs. Described in early literature as having the head and wings of an eagle and the body of a horse, and represented in mythology as a four-legged creature with a vast wingspread, the hippogriff and hufflebottom, to whom they are closely related, likely share the same prehistoric origin: a large, feathered reptile that lived somewhere between the Paleozoic and Mesozoic eras, with two powerful hind legs and *four* functional wings. One pair of wings is believed to have gravitated down the shoulder blades over time, as a changing climate meant the hippogriffs no longer had to migrate south in wintertime. Modern hippogriffs, though quite rare, share a diet similar to North American deer and use their wings only to escape detection, avoid predators, and enact mating rituals.

Hufflebottoms are found exclusively in northern climates. Like bears, they hibernate for roughly six months; unlike bears, their period of hibernation occurs from April to October. Their enormous girth is ill-proportioned for the four jointed "flippers," evolutionary proof of their original wings, that in combination with their hind legs allow for clumsy locomotion on dry land, and much faster and precise speeds over snow, ice, and swamps. The hufflebottom's dietary staple is the common snail; its long snout is exquisitely well-suited to sniffing out hibernating snails in wintertime and prying, sucking, or dislodging them from their hideaways. The period just before hibernation is known to monsterologists as "the frenzy," a period in which the males court the females with snail shells they have collected all winter long. The female selects a mate by gorging on his offering. This is important, as she will gestate her baby during hibernation and give birth immediately upon waking up. It is thought that this mechanism allows mothers to rid themselves of the excess weight that limits their mobility; baby hufflebottoms are extremely playful, inexhaustibly excited, and difficult to wrangle.

Lionfish are, despite their name, not fish at all, but amphibians related to the bullfrog, like their cousins, the dungaroos. Their designation likely comes from the appearance of a colorful "ruffle" that appears during mating season, or in times of fear or challenge. This, in combination with a powerful, sustained "roar"—actually the motion of their hind legs, vibrating to form an almost mechanical rhythm—may be responsible for the "lion" in their names. Like many modern frogs, lionfish hatch first in water and pass through developmental stages similar to the growth of tadpoles. The development occurs over a much longer period of time, however, resulting in an adolescent mixed state in which the ruffle often emerges a few weeks before the legs have begun to nub. In this state, they are slow and cumbersome swimmers, and vulnerable to being fished. This is likely how the misunderstanding of their true biology began.

Mordrum live deep underground, near thermal springs that allow the refreshing of fungal growth thought to be a part of their diet. Little is known about these subterranean creatures, and fossil/skeletal evidence has provided competing indications about their evolutionary origin, as they have prominent biological characteristics of both bats and snakes. The mordrum have no eyes and see by echolocation. A fascinating tubular appendage is filled with thousands of ropy scillia for powerful harmonic expression. The sound of a mordrum in distress, for example, is often confused for a baby crying; a mordrum announcing a new food source, however, sounds very much like music.

Phoenix birds. Once so plentiful that almost every early human civilization had similar records of these majestic birds, phoenixes are sadly thought now to number somewhere between 1,000 and 1,500 globally. Although phoenixes are capable of spontaneous regeneration through a poorly understood process of combustion—it is thought that the act of dying might trigger a powerful release of flammable chemical agents, and that the fire somehow reverses biological damage to—and even aging of—the bird's cells. It was not until the early 1800s that it was observed that the biological process relies on the composition of the bird's *feathers*; tragically, the loss of vast herds of phoenixes is due almost entirely to humans, who for centuries trapped and plucked the birds alive, believing (incorrectly) that their feathers had healing powers similar to those of their tears.

Pixies. Like their fairy cousins, pixies likely evolved from the first species of flying bats, roughly fifty to sixty-five million years ago. Unlike their fairy cousins, they are a nocturnal species, and are covered in a fine fur known as pixie-silk; they are, as a result, more widespread, and more capable of withstanding the cold. Famously, the two species loathe one another, and fossil evidence indicates historical wars between them that culled hundreds of thousands of individuals on both sides. Pixies, too, are dependent on humans, in that they are scavengers. But perhaps due to their furry bodies, and to facial features much closer to the common bat, pixies share an uneasy relationship to humans and have resisted domestication. This is perhaps why pixies are known for being such troublemakers. The passage from adolescence to adulthood is marked in pixie communities by the organization of an elaborate raid on a human home. Tasks may range from stealing individual socks from a sock drawer, to emptying milk bottles or hiding a pair of reading glasses.

Sea Behemoth. The iconic image of the Sea Behemoth is a vicious, many-tentacled oceanic monster, squeezing a schooner in its ferocious grip. This is a warped portrait of the *Gargantuan oceanus*—a majestic, shy, and deeply intelligent species—and a reputational hattrick perpetrated on the sea behemoth's memory by the same people who tragically hunted it to extinction. The ancient Greeks, in fact, trained sea behemoth to tow their ships in times of adverse or windless weather. But several millennia later, its associations with the Ottoman Empire were to prove its undoing: the sea behemoth was, according to the Church, a maritime representation of the devil, and the Church declared open season on the creatures.

Slints are pack animals, found in forested regions of North America, South America, and Europe, with only slight variations in the species. Though averaging only eighteen to twenty pounds, and sharing many characteristics of a badger, to whom they are closely related, they develop an armored "shell," similar to a turtle's, in the first six months of their lives. Made of a secretion of calcium deposits, the shell enlarges their size by double or even triple, and additionally allows them to confuse predators (and monsterologists!) into mistaking them for rocks. Unlike their badger cousins, however, slints are extremely social and live in multigenerational packs—likely a result of their primary defense tactic, a rarely spotted phenomenon known as the "tuck and roll," and also known as "bowling."

Sloozes, Latin name *Bilious caterpillarus*, are an extinct species of gigantic caterpillar, the largest of which may have weighed nearly one ton. Whether the sloozes molted like a vertebrate or invertebrate is still hotly contested. It is not known whether their natural habitat was oceanic or simply amphibious, as there is fossil evidence to support both claims.

Specters are composed primarily of vapor, and are loosely bound together by a transparent membrane. They inhabit wet, damp places and are often mistaken for mist. Long considered one of the smartest species of the monster kingdom (Prodigia), their method of communication—or even thinking—is poorly understood. Recent findings suggest that all specters may, in fact, be a *single* body, spread out across the globe, and collecting, interpreting, and sharing data by a pattern of vapor transfer. In the 1850s, in fact, a controversial research project suggested that every ounce of rain is at least 25 percent specter.

Squelches have webbed feet and closely resemble ducks—at least during summertime, and from a distance. Their biannual pattern of growing fur just before wintertime, and feathers in spring, is unique and poorly understood. They are amphibious mammals, thought to have some connection to the Australian platypus. Their wide-ranging diet includes various species of insects, vegetation, and even small reptiles. They have flexible necks that can, when extended, reach four or five feet; these, in combination with a wide, shallow bill, allow them to scoop fish, frogs, and insects from the water. Despite their innocent appearance, they are one of the most dangerous monsters in the world. When they are confused or threatened, a small gland in the back of their throat releases a five-foot spray of poison.

Squinches, despite the similarity in their names, are entirely unrelated to the squelches, and in fact come from a different taxonomical order altogether. They are gliding mammals with relatives in both bats and species of flying squirrel; their spinal cords, however, and in fact all their bones, are made from a flexible tubing we have not yet identified. The squinch at rest resembles a small, furry globe, "plumped up" by a normal circulation of liquid through the flexible tubing. In this state, squinches move primarily by bouncing, often reaching heights of twenty feet and more. At that point, the squinches "shed" water, expelling liquid from the structural tubing that keeps their shape intact and flattening to the shape of a disk. This has two advantages: now weighing only a few ounces, the squinches coast easily on the wind, directing their movement by very small adjustments of their outer taper, or edge. Additionally, the liquid shedding leaves a residue on their fur that is particularly repellent to birds and owls that might snatch them.

Succubi are, in legend, demon spirits that take the form of women; in reality, they are small river-dwelling monsters that feed by attaching to an animal's back via the suction of their oversize mouths, and slowly draining their "host" of nutrients. It is unclear how the association with females came to be, especially since succubi are one of the few large vertebrates that reproduce asexually and have no gender assignment at all. Although attacks by succubi on humans are rare, given their tendency to gravitate toward sparsely habituated places, they do occur. In the Middle Ages they were far more common, and it is likely that women, who were charged with washing linens and dishes, and often did so outdoors, in rivers or local watering-holes, were the great portion of victims. It is easy to see how over time the legend might have confused the victim for the predator.

Trolls have, until recently, been classified as members of the *Homo* genus and ancestors of the Neanderthals. For a long time after divergence from Homo sapiens, troll-human pairings were quite common, as suggested by fossil evidence. But there have been few, if any, provable modern examples of mixed troll ancestry. Nonetheless, we know that troll communities do exist, although the indications are rare and infrequent. Trolls are thought to have migrated into cold, mountainous regions more than two million years ago, due to a warming planet. As a result of the organization of human communities and advances in toolmaking and weaponry roughly 100,000 years ago, trolls began to "burrow" into camouflaged mountain hideaways, their habitat to this day.

Vampire bats are not to be confused with the subfamily of bat known as Desmodontinae, which share their name. They are not, in fact, bats at all, nor are they the undead of popular imagination. Likely descended from pterodactyls, and sharing features of their modern cousins the vultures, vampire bats were an important ally of early human communities. Carnivorous scavengers, vampire bats subsist off decaying animals: the gas triggered by the animals' death is necessary to successful digestion. Before fire allowed for better weaponry and safer food consumption, humans were scavengers as well—but greatly at risk of consuming tainted meat, whose effects would prove fatal to many. Vampire bats served as important "testers" for our earliest ancestors. The safer the meat, the more gaseous it would make the vampire bats. The less they burped, the more dangerous it was. Over time, this early intermingling blended the communities more and more, until vampire bats began to take on humanoid traits, like walking upright and communicating with grunts and whistles. After the advent of fire, the species diverged, but the vampire bats, legendary mimics, organized communities of their own. Their understanding of tool use and fire slowly made fur unnecessary, and their wings superfluous, especially as humans began to herd animals and organize into bigger cities. Their language evolved into one as sophisticated as modern English. Some people claim, in fact, that Latin was originally the language of vampire bats. Today, although vampire bats still exist, they are indistinguishable from humans. They are not immortal, or undead, although the strength of their immune systems does give them lifespans of two hundred to two hundred fifty years.

Wailers are a deceptively harmless-looking species of reptile and resemble incredibly wrinkly gecko. Their skin flaps, also known as trumpets, serve two purposes. When individually "tufted" or raised through controlled breathing—the wailer's "lungs" are in fact a complex system of interior valves and shutters—they function like sails, and help the wailer skim over the water at staggering speeds. But their primary purpose—and danger—is defensive. The wailer can inflate the trumpets by the simple act of holding its breath. The trumpets are so closely stacked that their trembling—a natural result of oxygen deprivation—creates an intolerable, rising, continuous note that soon reaches decibels so dangerous to humans it can lead to vertigo, memory loss, and even paralysis.

Werewolves are greatly misunderstood and have long been imagined as humans "infected" with a disease that transforms them into bloodthirsty animals at will. In fact, the truth is exactly the opposite. Werewolves are one of the most fascinating species that exists, with a collection of traits found in snakes (skeletal rearrangement, as of the jaw and spine), octopus (powerful ability to camouflage, by changing color and shape); and certain species of bird (mimicry, language). As a result, their evolutionary origin is still a mystery—some monsterologists have even proposed that werewolves do not exist as a separate species from the morpheus, and may in fact be traced directly to the kingdom Prodigia, from which all monsters originate. They are solitary hunters, and widespread across the globe, which perhaps explains the evolutionary necessity of shape-shifting camouflage. Although werewolves do occasionally, and briefly, take human form—often an exact replica of a human they have recently observed or interacted with, which explains where the legend might have started— humans are by no means their only, or even favorite, assumed shape. Werewolves camouflage themselves as sheep, deer, bears, and even large, domesticated breeds of dogs—any mammal, in other words, that shares a rough body mass equivalent. There is no connection between werewolves and the full moon, other than for mating purposes. A common mating ritual involves a series of rapid transformations, a kind of "talent show," that will result in either mating or rejection. Unsurprisingly, this occurs by the light of the full moon, so the visual display can be appreciated.

Zuppies are often known as "zombie puppies," although that term is misleading, in that it suggests all puppies might be turned into zombies, or the walking dead. Even the idea that the zuppies are, in fact, *dead* has for years been the subject of debate, although what is known is that the zuppy has no working heartbeat, circulatory system, or need for oxygen, water, or food beyond blood—or, in a pinch, carrion. The zuppy is actually derived from a single domesticated canid species nearly indistinguishable from that of *Canis lupus familiaris*, but thought to have diverged from them 60,000 to 100,000 years ago. It is thought that as some wolves began to be domesticated, others remained distrustful of humans, leading to the emergence of dogs and wolves. Evidence suggests, however, that a third class of wolves *wanted* to become domesticated, but were rejected both by human communities and wolf packs. It is likely that many of these wolves were the weakest, or even prone to sickness and injury. Because zuppies could not find protection in a pack, and were too weak to hunt successfully and too unattractive for human companionship, they developed into scavengers. This, too, was dangerous, especially as humans exploded across the globe—they were often associated with trash and filth, and trapped or put down. Interestingly, the zuppy is the only species whose defense mechanisms include dying. Other species may mimic death, but the zuppy actually dies—sometimes, of course, due to injury or sickness, but other times voluntarily, to avoid periods of starvation or to deter predators. It is thought that reanimation, which becomes possible only because of deliberate care and feeding, permits the zuppy to "survive" via dependence on its caregiver. In other words, the blood provides the chemical nutrients required to animate, given that many of its essential needs *before* death—such as scavenging, biting, chewing, escaping, finding shelter, digesting, regurgitating, etc.—are no longer required, nor are the biological processes or organs they depend on. The zuppy, in other words, now requires only the brain, and only certain parts of it. The rest of its organs are thought to decay into a kind of sanitation system, which passes blood directly into the rest of the brain, after "digesting" it into the necessary chemical components.

CHAPTER
1

Squeak. Squeak. Squeak.

"Cordelia." Dr. Cornelius Clay spun around, and the lantern attached to his forehead bobbled slightly. In his oversize goggles, which were misted slightly from the drizzle, Cordelia thought he very closely resembled the species *Cavorticus poison*, otherwise known as the lionfish—a monster Cordelia had only ever seen in illustrated form, on page 432 of *A Guide to Monsters and Their Habits*, Cordelia's favorite book.

Cornelius's eyes darted nervously behind her. He had

been anxious all night. "What have I told you about wearing your mother's boots? I can hear you coming from a mile away."

"Sorry." Cordelia wrestled the boot off her right foot and, balancing on one leg, allowed the moisture to drip out of its toe. She shoved her sodden sock back in the boot and wiggled her toes experimentally. Better.

Blue Hills Park looked very different at night than it did during the day. During the day, hikers huffed red-faced in the cold along winding hiking trails; children hunted the marshes for frogs, losing the occasional mitten, and even boot, to the sucking mud along the estuary; and fishermen returned again and again to the same fishing holes, breaking through the morning ice to drop their lines. It was a beautiful place, crowded with dogwood trees and lady's slippers, herds of white-tailed deer, copperhead snakes. But during the day, even the wildness seemed tame, almost deliberate, as if it had been made specifically for the enjoyment of its visitors. The hills and woods, the marshes and the ribbons of streams that fed them—all of them had been named, surveyed, and bounded, and their outlines appended to new maps of the Greater Boston area. Tamed and flattened, like a dead butterfly pinned beneath glass, and now property of the newly formed Metropolitan Park Commission.

But at night, Blue Hills wasn't a park at all. It was a vast, strange, wild thing, alive with insects and movement. It watched Cordelia and her father with yellow eyes, winking in the grass. It tracked them by their echoes, bouncing news of their progress to great geometries of bats that passed back and forth overhead. It swept in on gusts of wind and touched their necks to make them shiver. It carried news of their skin into a thousand different corners, whispering warnings of intruders.

At night, it was very obvious: they belonged to Blue Hills, not the other way around.

At the beginning of a steep pathway that wound up and through the hills, Cordelia's father stopped. He squatted, his lantern swinging slightly, and brushed his fingers to the damp grass. Then he straightened up.

"Look, Cordelia." He extended his hand to her. His fingers were streaked with black.

"Ash," Cordelia whispered.

Her father nodded solemnly. "We must be on the right track."

Rector Cushing's wife, Mary Cushing, was the first person to have spotted a fire. On an evening stroll with her husband, a rhododendron bush had, quite without explanation, burst into hearty flames, nearly frightening her out of her skin. For several days afterward, there had been a steady stream of visitors to the spot, claiming to see in the blackened husk of the bush various saints and spirits. Her husband had even declared that portion of Blue Hills Park sacred ground, and Mrs. Cushing had enjoyed several days of fame, though many accused her of being overly imaginative, and the minister of a rival church, Mr. Buchanan, had even suggested that witchcraft was involved.

Then Miss Finch, who worked as a schoolteacher, and whom no one would ever accuse of having an imagination, had spotted another bush—this time, an ugly pricker—go up in flames. This had provoked a roaring debate. Was Blue Hills haunted? Was it blessed? Was it cursed, and harboring demons? Were the events, as the scientific community declared, merely a product of a bizarre chemical reaction stemming from various alkaloid concentrations in the soil?

Only Cordelia and her father knew the truth.

The fires had a different cause altogether: an injured, and possibly dying, dragon. "We must go very carefully from here on out," her father whispered, selecting a pair of dingle clips—like handcuffs, but with flexible openings, meant for restraining dragon wings without injuring their delicate membranes—from his rucksack. After a slight hesitation, he switched them out for a slightly larger pair. "The fire-sites suggest that the dragon is mobile, though of course it can't have the use of its wings, otherwise it would—"

"—have retreated at the first sign of humans, I know." Cordelia's palms were sweating. Five years earlier, when she was just seven years old, she and her father had once treated a dragon. Digbert, as they had come to name him, was ancient: a withered creature, roughly the size of a couch, whom they had found after locals complained of mysterious bonfires on the beach. His eyes had been clouded by cataracts so solid, he could no longer navigate—and even the eye drops Cordelia's father had prepared, a special tincture of chicken blood and crushed lily pads, had done little to help. They could do nothing but keep Digbert in the living room and make sure he was comfortable until the end. The rug and sofas still bore large, singed holes as proof of his existence. Patching them would have simply been too sad.

Digbert had been one of Cordelia's favorites. He loved to be tickled on the chin, where several silvery whiskers had grown, and to be stroked on the leathery-soft joint behind the wings. When she came in from the moors with her fingers crooked from cold, he used to warm her hands by exhaling on them.

But not all dragons, she knew, were so gentle.

They moved up the narrow dirt pathway. This was

where Cordelia was happiest: in the deepest, blackest portion of the night, under a great sweep of stars and a rolling fog, like the touch of velvet; walking with her father while the rest of the world was asleep. Out here, she didn't have to think about Sean O'Malley, who hurled stones at her whenever she passed and had started the rumor that Cordelia and her father were vampires; or Elizabeth Perkins, who giggled behind one gloved hand when she spotted Cordelia in the street, and whispered *freak* when Cordelia passed. She didn't have to think about Hard Times, and the money dwindling in the pantry, and the marchers in the streets.

Then her father spoiled it.

"I heard about your scuffle with Henry Haddock," he said, and Cordelia's heart plunged into her boots. She'd been sure, when her father had said nothing after Cordelia returned home with a scraped knee and swollen cheek, that she would somehow avoid getting into trouble for her latest fight.

"He told everyone that you were bonkers," she said. "He told everyone that we keep locked rooms full of eyeballs." Henry Haddock had said plenty more besides that, over the years. That was not why Cordelia had punched him. But just thinking about what had really happened made her skin tighten with rage, and her fist throb, as if it wanted to punch him again.

"That's no excuse," her father said. "The boy had an eye as swollen as a tomato. He was terrorized."

"He deserved it," she muttered, shoving her hands into her pockets.

Dr. Clay kneeled so he was face-to-face with Cordelia. The lantern lit up the crags and hollows of his cheeks, and the web of lines around his eyes. Cordelia experienced a sudden shock: her dad was growing old. "I know things aren't always . . . easy for you," he said quietly. "I blame myself for that. If you hadn't grown up among so many monsters—"

"I love the monsters," she interjected.

He smiled. But his smile didn't reach all the way to his eyes, and once again Cordelia had the impression that he was anxious about something. "I know you do," he said. When he was very serious, the Scottish accent that had trailed him all the way from Glasgow grew warmer and richer, rolling his vowels and consonants together. "But people can be cruel. They are afraid of what they don't understand." He put two fingers under Cordelia's chin. "You're too old to be brawling in the street. At St. George's—"

"I'm not going to St. George's," Cordelia said, for what felt like the hundredth time.

Even the mention of St. George's filled her with a vague panic, an image of coffin-like rooms and a

7

thousand girls, all of them as cruel as Elizabeth Perkins, all of them laughing at her.

Her father shook his head, but he let the subject drop. "You have to learn to control your temper, Cordelia. That's part of growing up."

"Maybe I don't *want* to grow up," Cordelia fired back.

She expected her dad to yell at her, but instead he just sighed again. He stood up slowly, wincing, as though even his bones hurt.

"We all grow up, Cordelia," he said, in a strange voice. "The world changes. We have to change along with it."

She knew he was talking about more than her fight with Henry Haddock, but before she could ask him to explain, he was walking again.

The wind sounded like distant voices, howling and whispering and sighing by turns, and the rain felt like a fine spray of glass against Cordelia's skin. At one point, she was sure that she heard footsteps behind her and turned, hefting her lantern. A man with glittering shark eyes, a sharp beak of a nose, and neatly parted hair was moving through the mist.

Cordelia started to call out to her father, but then the man turned down a bend in the path and was gone.

Cornelius Clay was unusually quiet. Normally, when

they were on the trail of a monster, he told Cordelia stories about the world when it was young: a time when the hills of Scotland, where Cornelius had lived until he was twelve, had been packed so densely with werewolves it was death to go out after dark; when phoenix birds warmed their feathers by the high noon sun; when magic and monsters were everywhere. But now he responded to her questions with a grunt, or not at all. She wondered whether he was angry with her.

For an hour they traveled in silence, their lanterns casting twin circles of light on the rough and rocky ground ahead of them. Cordelia was aware of the faint fizzing sound of the rain against the hills, and of the rustling of the underbrush as unseen animals scurried about their business. She was aware, too, of the smells on the air: wet grass and rotting leaves, and the smell of her father, like lint and tobacco.

Cordelia's father had taught her long ago that monsters—who liked the dark and knew all about skulking in the shadows—could be identified not just by sight, but by sound and even by smell. The mordrum smelled a little bit like burnt toast; the filches let out rumbling farts that smelled like rotten eggs. Cordelia had once found a diggle caught in a ditch, its hind leg twisted at a hopeless angle, because of the sudden and overwhelming smell of freshly baked gingerbread cookies.

Which was why, when halfway across the foothills that rose like gentle waves toward the moon, Cordelia smelled the faintest wisp of acrid smoke on the wind, she knew that they had found their dragon.

Her father was walking ahead of her, head bent, lost in thought. "Dad—" she started, to call him back to her.

But she didn't finish her sentence. Just then a large tangle of briars at her left elbow burst into lively flame, and Cordelia was knocked backward by a sudden *whoosh* of air.

CHAPTER
2

Cordelia didn't even register hitting the ground before she was rolling, rolling, away from the still-crackling flames, moving by instinct.

"Cordelia!" Her father was running down the path toward her, sliding a little on the slope. She fumbled in her rucksack for her goggles and the nubby thick gloves, made of fire-retardant material, that her father had made her. Stupid to have been caught without them. She slipped on the goggles, and then the gloves, just as her father reached her.

"Are you all right?" He pulled her to her feet. She nodded shakily. "I'm all right."

The fire—which had burned hot, in a sudden explosion of blue and pink flames—was already shriveling. As the briars turned black and curled into smoking nothing, the flames withered and died, leaving the air heavy with the smell of bitter smoke.

"Stay back," he commanded her. He pushed into the thick tangle of growth, parting hedges and yew branches with his gloved hands, his lantern swinging. But Cordelia took a deep breath and plunged after him.

It was even darker once they were off the path, and the moon, barely peeking through the storm clouds, was eclipsed by tall, overgrown sycamores and tangles of vines.

"Where are you?" Cornelius muttered.

As though in response, there was a low hiss from just ahead, and suddenly the scene was lit up as another low-hanging bush burst into flame. Cordelia caught a quick glimpse of a pair of glittering eyes and felt her stomach drop. A dragon. Then the eyes were gone, and her father was frantically clapping out the fire before it could spread.

Cordelia saw a sudden movement to her right—a flicker, a slight shifting of the undergrowth.

"Cordelia!" her father cried, but she ignored him, parting a curtain of hanging vine, ducking under a magnolia branch. Her heart was pounding so hard, it was a constant thrum. A dragon, a dragon, a dragon.

A twig snapped. She froze, listening. The wind lifted in the trees, carrying with it the sound of her father's urgent whispers—"Cordelia, get back here, wait for me"—and the smell of singed bark and leaves. Nothing else stirred. The dragon had once again faded away into the darkness.

Just then her father plunged through the growth behind her, panting, a streak of ash painted from cheek to chin. "Do you want to get yourself killed? Dragons are very aggressive. If we don't approach carefully, we'll end up roasted like—"

"Look out, Dad!" This time, Cordelia had seen the first spark, the two winking eyes. She hurled herself at her father, knocking him out of the way just in time. They rolled several feet, crashing through a mulberry bush, as another portion of the forest turned to flame.

Cornelius lost his head strap to a clutch of bushes. His lantern went out with the faint tinkle of shattered glass. Cordelia's goggles were knocked off her head, and she landed with her nose planted directly in a soft pile of dirt. She sat up, sneezing.

And came nose to snout with the wrinkled, wizened face of the dragon.

A very, very small dragon.

It was roughly the size of a kitten. Its wings, when

fully extended, were the size of an eagle's, but full of leathery folds, collapsible as a paper fan. In the illumination of the flames reaching for desperate purchase across the wet and leafless winter branches, its eyes were the color of polished moonstone, and when it opened its mouth, Cordelia could see a row of small, sharp teeth, some of them no bigger than a pencil tip.

"It's a baby," she said wonderingly.

The dragon drew back its gums, as though it was trying to smile. . . .

A rough hand seized Cordelia by the collar and jerked her to her feet as the dragon released another burst of flame, incinerating the spot where her nose had been only a second earlier.

"Baby, yes," her father said. His goggles were hanging crookedly from his nose. "Harmless, no. Did you bring the tuber root?"

Cordelia nodded. Her cheeks felt hot, as if she'd received a bad sunburn.

The dragon hopped back a few feet, hissing, passing out of the small square of moonlight that filtered in through the trees. The storm was finally passing. Now Cordelia could barely make out the soft thrush of its wings dragging against the ground—one of them, Cordelia saw, was hanging crookedly, obviously hurt.

Cornelius touched a finger to his nose, and then

pointed to the left. Cordelia nodded again to show she understood, and watched him slip off into the darkness in a rustle of leaves. She had never understood how her father could move so quietly; soon he was nothing but a shadow.

Cordelia fumbled in her bag for the tuber root—a favorite among dragons, especially growing ones—but could feel nothing in her thick gloves. She hesitated for a second—take the gloves off, and she risked having her fingers turned to toasted marshmallows. But time was running out; if the dragon passed into the shadows again, they might lose it.

She shook off her gloves, letting them fall into her rucksack, and almost immediately her fingers closed around the narrow jar of tuber root. She popped the lid with one hand and shook a bit of the dark, flaky substance into her palm.

The dragon hadn't moved. She could still see it, just barely, its wings fanned across the carpet of leaves and mud. She could hear the whisper of its breathing when it inhaled; faint curlicues of smoke emerged from its nostrils.

She didn't know where her father was.

She took a careful step forward and the dragon scuttled backward, baring its teeth again. Cordelia hesitated, one hand extended.

"It's all right," she whispered, even though she knew the dragon couldn't understand. "I'm here to help you."

Slowly, slowly, so slowly she felt as if she were sinking through a heavy vat of molasses, she lowered into a crouch. The fires were smoldering now, into bare embers. The dragon's dark eyes watched her, reflecting the miniature swell of a nearly full moon. Now Cordelia's bare hand was only six inches from the dragon's nostrils—close enough to be burned.

Close enough to be *smelled*.

The dragon advanced an inch, so that once again the moonlight fell over the ridged peaks of its long snout; over the hard knob of skin between its eyes; over its velvet-dark nostrils, quivering slightly.

Come on, Cordelia thought.

Another inch. Now the dragon's snout was only a centimeter away from her fingertips. Her pulse was going crazy. It could take her hand off in one gulp, or fry her like bacon. She felt the electric heat of its breath every time it exhaled, and had to force herself to stay still, to stay calm.

Where was her father? What was he doing?

Suddenly the dragon moved, and Cordelia nearly fell backward, yelping in surprise.

At the last second, just as the dragon nudged its head into her hand, she managed to right herself. At a slight nod from Cordelia, it hungrily gobbled the tuber root from her hand, avoiding nipping her skin.

Cordelia wanted to laugh out loud. Her blood was singing. A baby dragon was eating from her palm, its jaw working against her fingers, its hot breath stinging her skin. The dragon smelled like damp leather, and fresh wind, and fire.

"That's a good boy," she whispered. Up close, she could see the small knob on the back of its head that distinguished it as a male. She noted a tear in its left-wing fold, and a place where the bone looked crooked. She felt a surge of pity for the monster. Who knew how long it had been earthbound, or when it had last eaten?

She hoped that it had not yet developed a taste for human fingers.

Cornelius appeared behind her. He kneeled to slip a large muzzle over the dragon's snout. "Gotcha!"

Instantly, the dragon went still. The muzzle, secured in place by means of several leather straps and made of the same fire-resistant material as Cordelia's gloves, included soft leather blinders meant to impair its vision. Dragons were extremely dependent on their eyes, and easily confused without use of them. The constant flow of flame through their nostrils meant that their sense of smell was practically negligible, and their ears were comparatively small and unreliable. That was why Digbert had been so miserable when his eyes began to fail.

For a moment, both Cordelia and her father sat there over the now-subdued dragon, breathing hard. At last, Cordelia's heartbeat began to normalize. A sense of wonder invaded her whole body. The dragon had touched her. It had *licked* her.

Cornelius removed his goggles, resting them on the top of his head, wiping sweat from his brow with the back of a palm. "All right, Cordelia. Fetch your lantern. Let's see what's what."

She stood up and hurried back the way they had come. Her knees were wet and the wind reached cold fingers down her back, but she barely felt it. She was full of a profound joy: love for her father, love for the shadows and the forest, love for all the strange and wild things that lived there.

She found her lantern lying in the dirt where she had dropped it. She soon managed to get the wick lit and returned to kneel at her father's side.

"Let's see, let's see," Dr. Clay murmured, as he did a careful visual inspection of the dragon for injuries. The lantern illuminated delicate colors threaded through the dragon's wings: seams of gold and purple and blue and green. "The dingle clips won't do. Put them back in my bag, will you, Cordelia? It looks like the femur is broken, poor creature. And see where the membrane has ripped away? I don't want to worsen the tear."

He was all business now. He indicated the injury with the tip of a pencil, tracing the outline of the wings in the air, and Cordelia tried to absorb and memorize everything. "He'll need stitches, too, but that will have to wait. A splint might work, but I'm concerned the trauma is too deep." He frowned, obviously deep in thought. Then, rousing himself, he replaced the pencil in his jacket pocket. "Better to be safe than sorry. Cordelia, get the rigiwings from my rucksack, will you? The smaller size should do."

Once again, Cordelia hurried to obey. How often had she knelt with her father in the thick darkness, tending to a sick or injured monster? How often had he called her to his side, or ordered her to fetch bone splints and cough drops, heart-pumps or tentacle creams? Countless times. Measuring tablets and tinctures, patching wounds, selecting instruments, sweating in the darkness— all of it was familiar to her, as familiar as the sound of her father's footsteps or the smell of her mother's perfume, which she could still perfectly recall.

And yet—for a moment, kneeling beside her father's rucksack, digging through the jumble of tools and medicines—she was assailed with a certainty as sudden as fear: this was the last time, the very last time, that she and her father would ever save a monster.

Immediately, she dismissed the idea as ridiculous. As long as there were monsters in the world that needed saving, Cordelia and her father would be the ones to do it.

The rigiwings were not actually wings, but a series of interconnected mesh plates that somewhat resembled a waffle iron. This, Cornelius eased carefully over the entirety of the dragon's injured wing, tightening each plate carefully, so that the wing was entirely immobilized. Only then did they risk moving the dragon itself. Cornelius had anticipated they might have to return home for the wheelbarrow, but given the dragon's size, decided it was unnecessary. Instead he removed his jacket, and they bundled the dragon carefully inside it.

It was unlikely, Cordelia knew, that they would be spotted. Still, the fishermen would stir and the bakers would start kneading their dough, even before dawn. And her father had told her a million times: no one must be allowed to see or know about the monsters.

"Why?" she had wailed as a young child, when after telling a story about naughty pixies, she had been promptly lashed by Mrs. McDonough—the final and shortest-lived of all her tutors.

"Most people," her father had said very slowly, "want the world to look like what they know already. They are afraid of seeing the face of the unfamiliar. That's why your mother was so determined to . . ."

He had trailed off, his eyes brightening with tears. Years after her death, Cornelius still struggled to speak his wife's name. But Cordelia understood.

Elizabeth Clay, a naturalist, had devoted her life to monsters. She had seen her work on the origin of monsters discredited, ridiculed, even slandered as diabolical—all because she had set out to prove that monsters belonged to the world just as much as people did, that they had evolved just like Mr. Darwin had proved other animals did.

In the end, she had even died for it—absorbed into the jungle on her final trip to recover a specimen she was sure showed evidence of a branching evolutionary path definitively relating the monster and animal kingdoms.

She had never returned. Her book had never been completed. And her work would remain forever unfinished.

"Promise me, Cordelia," her father had said to her that day. "Swear to me you will never tell anyone about the monsters we keep here."

If people knew how many monsters Cordelia and her father were keeping, they would be afraid. They would demand that the monsters be kept in cages, or shipped off to some foreign place or even killed. Perhaps they would want Cordelia and her father to be arrested.

They didn't understand that everyone needed saving sometimes. Everyone needed someone to care.

Even—perhaps *especially*—monsters.

From a distance, the home Cordelia's grandfather had purchased on Cedar Street after emigrating to America with his wife and twelve-year-old son, Cornelius—and earning a small fortune selling wagons and supplies to westbound prospectors—looked as stately as it must have a hundred years earlier, when it was first built. There were four chimneys, a sweeping front porch framed by a grand balustrade, and a total of forty-eight windows studding the redbrick facade.

The impression of wealth began to fade, however, as you approached, like a mirage that broke apart before you could reach it. Up close, it was obvious that at least half of the forty-eight windows displayed major cracks. Three were missing altogether, and the holes had been hastily patched with plywood. Mortar decayed by decades of Boston snow and rain had slowly loosed dozens of bricks from the facade, giving an impression of pockmarked skin. Shutters hung crookedly, beating an erratic rhythm in the wind, and briars grew so thickly over the porch and balustrade that Cornelius and Cordelia had long avoided it altogether. Only the kitchen door was still in use. There, a wooden placard—once polished to a high sheen, now stained so much from wind and rain it was nearly illegible—welcomed visitors (who hardly ever came) and customers (who never did) to the Clay Home for Veterinary Services.

The inside wasn't much better.

The great room, which had once seen dinner parties and dances, was the baku's preferred spot for napping: the twelve-foot-high shelves, spongy with moss, no doubt reminded him of a treetop habitat. Piles of feathers lay in drifts over the carpet—a natural result of the hufflebottom's periodic molting—and no matter how often Cordelia scrubbed, she could not fully get rid of the smell of hay and wet chicken.

Four of the bedrooms were homes to monsters in various stages of recovery: a diggle healing from a bad laceration below one of its eyes; a squinch just now getting over the flu; a goblin suffering from bouts of melancholy. A lionfish made its home in the cast-iron tub in the larger of two washrooms; Cordelia and her father shared the other.

The office, where Dr. Clay had long ago greeted clients and examined their sniffling German shepherds, their bleary-eyed Labrador retrievers, or gassy tabby cats, had been completely taken over by a family of pixies rescued years earlier from an overflowing gutter, in which they had been drowning. Now they had rooted in the leather armchair, ripped the paisley wallpaper to shreds, and built a nest out of old receipts, bills, and veterinary reports, so that entering the room gave the impression of stepping into a snowstorm of paper.

Many years ago, the veterinary office had received actual, paying clients, and the slew of injured, sick, and recuperating monsters were kept carefully locked away upstairs in case a friend or neighbor should stop by. Eventually, the clients had become tired of the Clays' erratic hours (monsters were, for the most part, nocturnal; Dr. Clay's office began to open later and later, until it was open only from five p.m. to seven p.m. on weekdays and five thirty p.m. to seven p.m. on Saturdays), just as they were afraid of the unexplained creaks and groans and growls emanating from the upstairs rooms.

Still, Dr. Clay had kept a handful of old clients, enough to buy milk and cheese and eggs, and enough to buy Cordelia a new pair of boots every year and the occasional surprise of a box of chocolates or a new tool for her own collection.

But that was before the Hard Times. The change to forty clients from sixty, then twenty clients from forty, then to ten clients from twenty, then nine clients from ten, then eight, then five, had happened over so many years that Cordelia hardly noticed it until her father's stack of client records was so thin it hardly counted as a stack.

Then Mrs. Durling's Doberman had finally been put down. Four. Then Mr. and Mrs. Brodely couldn't afford to keep their two beloved retrievers anymore, and had to give them to a wealthy cousin in New Jersey. Three. Then the Culvers' tabby cat wasn't eating, and Cornelius found a suspicious lump, and the suspicious lump turned out to be a death sentence. Two. Then Mr. O'Reilly lost his job and had to pick up and move to New Hampshire, where his brother had found him work at a steel mill, taking his two Yorkshire terriers with him. One.

Cordelia remembered, with a certain wistfulness, their very last client: Mrs. Allan, a robust woman with a gray topknot, who had brought in her fluffy Persian cat for an annual examination. Mrs. Allan had been threatening to take her business elsewhere for the ten years she had been coming as a client. The waiting room was too cold or too hot. There was a strange smell. You might think they would at least offer her some tea. Her beloved Persian, Ophelia, was her primary obsession, and she seemed to blame Cornelius anytime he suggested that she might need to lose a pound or two, or require medication for worms—as if he weren't diagnosing a problem, but causing it.

"There's nothing wrong with little Fee," she would

say. "She's *perfect*." Cordelia wondered why she bothered coming at all.

That day, she was especially offended. There was a smell, most certainly. Ophelia was very sensitive to smells, and she was *very* upset. There had been strange fur caught in the welcome mat—not a very nice welcome at all, was it? And had she heard something growling upstairs? Because Ophelia did not do well around dogs, especially violent ones . . . see how upset her little princess was . . . ?

Cornelius had just managed to wrangle the enormous Ophelia onto the table with Cordelia's help. "No need to be upset," he said cheerfully. "Probably just the floorboards. Old houses do have a tendency to—"

CRASH.

A thunderous noise trembled the ceiling, sifting plaster into the room, and Ophelia broke out of Cornelius's grip and launched, screeching, for Mrs. Allan's arms. She landed instead on her face, and toppled Mrs. Allan, screaming, to the ground.

Upstairs, more than two dozen monsters decided to respond. Grunts and wailing, screeches and nattering, thuds and crashes and screams—the sound was so loud it shook the walls and crashed Cornelius's university diploma from the wall.

It was perhaps the only time Cordelia was sorry to

see Mrs. Allan leave. Luckily, since she was sprinting, Cordelia barely had time to regret it.

That was several years ago now. At the same time, Mrs. McDonough, Cordelia's final tutor, quit after a two-week-long campaign of harassment by the pixies, who pulled her hair and put pepper in her tea when she wasn't looking, and once, when she dropped off to sleep, inked her eyebrows together. By then, Cornelius could hardly afford to hire a replacement.

So Dr. Clay had shut down his veterinary services— at least, he'd shut them down to *normal* animals. Slowly, the collection of monsters grew, until the third floor, and then the second, could no longer contain them. They had three griffins alone; two bullieheads; four phoenix birds, two squelches, six squinches, two werewolves, eighteen vampire bats, three wailers, two chupacabras, four cockatrices, one baku, a lionfish, a filch, the extended family of pixies, a hufflebottom, a baby growrk and one adolescent that was growing alarmingly fast, dungaroos, a stand of diggles, a carbuncle, and even a bogey.

Every morning Mr. Clay would scour the newspapers for news that might lead them to an injured monster: unexplained howling in the woods; sightings of a monstrous, limping wolf that might, in fact, turn out to be another growrk; fishermen's tales of strange fish with human eyes. Every few months, he and Cordelia would suit up and head out in pursuit of some poor creature. Sometimes they returned home empty-handed.

Often, they brought home another monster.

Each new monster was supposed to be only a temporary addition. But somehow, the monsters stayed. Out in the world, they might be shot or trapped, caught in nets and gutters, choked by soot, or run over by carriages.

There may have been occasions that Cordelia resented living in a home where the tub was occupied by an adolescent lionfish, still nubbing its legs; where the heavy bedroom curtains had to be sealed continuously to keep sunlight off the delicate skin of the bullieheads; where her best friends had extra eyes, or sharp teeth, or wings, or all of the above. But if there were times she longed for *normal* playmates, for the orderliness of a house in which carpets didn't shake themselves and turn into hippogriffs, and pixies didn't rattle the kitchen pots all night long, she no longer recalled them.

She loved the way the hufflebottom curled its soft black tongue around her wrist whenever she fed it carrots, the proud strut of the cockatrices, and the way the baby growrk whimpered in his sleep. She loved her father's patience and kindness, and the way even the most dangerous and difficult monsters would eat vitamins from his palm. She loved the big, drafty rooms, the sifting snow of wallpaper and plaster, the smell of leathery hides and hay and feathers.

Most of all, she loved the feeling that she and her father lived together in their own little world, a place of secrets and magic. The attic was the North Pole, where the heat-loving baku migrated in summertime and the cold-loving hufflebottoms lived in the winter. The third floor was a continent of different habitats—marshy bedrooms where the ceiling leaked rain onto moldy carpets, and mushrooms grew in corners for the wailers to eat; stifling linen closets, where burrowing diggles loved to snooze; the old conservatory, flooded with light and filled with a jungle of overgrown plant life, where the diggles and the bullieheads often chattered late into the night. Cornelius's bedroom, on the other hand, was perfectly normal. No one would ever guess that only a single wall divided it from a riot of squinches—unless, of course, they started bouncing.

The second floor was a series of interconnected islands, rooms with walls broken or crumbled away to allow passage between them, a constant, fluid flow of the more social monster species. Between them was a parlor they had converted into an aquarium, now full of enormous glass tanks and oceanic sloshing (the dungaroos surfed their bathwater on the floor whenever they wanted attention). Even these were connected to the rooms on either side, although outraged screeches erupted whenever the lionfish was caught in the tub with its ruffle down.

Only the walls of Cordelia's bedroom were intact, except for a small hole in the wall the pixies had tunneled so they could play tricks on her while she slept. This, however, had been blocked by an armoire.

The ground floor was a vast city, full of bustle and energy, especially during the rush hours of midnight to four a.m. The great room was the transportation hub, where monsters slid, flew, bounced, or tumbled on their way to different places. The sitting room was a public garden, a colorful landscape of different nests, a wilderness of fur and twig and mud and leaf piles, mulchy with shredded newspaper, its walls honeycombed with miniature burrows. The kitchen, the old veterinary office, the corridors, the pantry, the root cellar: all of these were different countries, regions, landscapes on the map of her world. Every day, Cordelia traveled the globe. Every day, she journeyed from one end of the world to the other, leaving no territory unexplored, no landscape unmapped.

Except for one.

Except for *the* one.

There were nineteen rooms in Clay Manor. And then there was *that* room.

The room on the first floor, at the end of the corridor, at the edge of the world: her mother's library, her mother's study, *her mother's* world.

Cordelia imagined that it must look exactly as it had the last time that Elizabeth Clay, PhD, had shouldered her travel bag, dimmed the lights, and closed the door firmly behind her, although she had been inside it only once since then. The mahogany desk and the old leather blotter, the row of pens gleaming dully in their stands of ink, the floor-to-ceiling shelves and the stairways of books that climbed them, her mother's unfinished manuscript, its hundreds of pages like leaves slowly withering: none of it had been touched, or even cleaned, since her mother's fatal journey. It was as if Cordelia and her father had, without ever discussing it, agreed that Elizabeth Clay's study be kept waiting for her—as if she might thus be tempted to return.

So, one day, he had locked the door, and it had never since been opened.

And slowly, slowly, their house began to fill with life, and their lives began to fill the rooms, until the rooms became their lives—all of them grown around the single, quiet center of a closed door.

But Cordelia was happy in Clay Manor with her father. She knew very little about the world, but she knew enough to know she wasn't missing anything.

Out in the world, bad things happened: mothers went

on voyages and never returned from the jungle. People broke promises, lost faith, turned traitorous. Out in the world, it wasn't the monsters you had to worry about.

Cordelia knew from experience: the monsters people name are not the real danger. They are never the real danger. It's the monsters who name themselves that you really have to watch out for. Problem is—you can never tell just by looking at them.

CHAPTER
3

B y the time Cordelia and her father made it back
to Beacon Hill, the sun was just breaking over the
Boston Harbor, like the yolk of an egg spilling
over the wide bowl of the sea. In the morning light, Clay
Manor—rising to the sky, vast and stately, surrounded
by a wild nest of tangled growth, like a large ship sail-
ing through a froth of dark waves—struck Cordelia as
very beautiful. A single light was burning in the kitchen
window, and it looked like a fire seen from a distance,
across a dark plain.

Cordelia hopped over the large cracks in the paving
stones and dodged the brambles that were reaching out

to snag her jacket, taking the crumbling stone steps in one easy jump. It took several tries to get the door open. Everything at Clay Manor was just a little bit crooked. For a time, she and her father had done their best to keep up with repairs. But there were too many monsters, and never enough money, especially now that they had to Tighten Their Belts.

Inside, Cordelia and her father were greeted with a quiet chorus of thumps, bumps, growls, and snuffles.

"Not again." Cornelius sighed as they passed inside, directly into the snug warmth of the kitchen. Several jars had been smashed on the floor, and a large puddle of what looked—and smelled—like fish oil was seeping out from underneath the old wooden table. Two pixies, both females and coated in heavy brown fur, were perched on the woodstove, chattering excitedly, and a diggle was sleeping in the corner, its spikes rising and falling gently with its breath.

"Out of here! Out of here!" Cornelius shifted the dragon carefully into the crook of his left arm so he could shoo away the pixies. They took flight, still chittering, and disappeared into the darkness. "You too." Cornelius nudged the diggle with the toe of his boot. The diggle stretched, yawned, and continued sleeping.

"It's okay, Dad," Cordelia said quickly. "I'll clean up. You take care of the dragon."

Cornelius patted her on the shoulder. "I think a

few stitches and a splint ought to do it." He grabbed a matchstick from the mantel and used it to light a new lantern. "I'll be in the office if you need me."

Hefting the lantern high, he set off down the hallway. Cordelia watched the light fade, like a star into the darkness. After a minute, she heard a muffled curse, and then another burst of happy chittering. She repressed a smile. Pixies. They were always causing trouble.

She had just finished sweeping up the glass and disposing of it in the dustbin, when the ancient bell above their door gave a weak jingle. At first she barely spared it a glance, telling herself that the wind must have set it dancing. No one ever came to the house besides creditors, demanding payment for overdue bills—and creditors, she knew, didn't bother ringing the bell. They pounded on the door. They screamed and pressed their red faces against the windows, like gigantic blowfish.

Ring-ring-ring. This time, the bell rang more insistently. Cordelia was so surprised, she dropped her dustpan with a clatter. *Ring-ring-ring.* The ancient bell jumped on its string.

There was no denying it. Someone was ringing the bell.

Cordelia debated going to her father, but she knew he hated to be disturbed when he was operating. Instead she hefted herself onto the wooden counter so she could peer through the windowpanes. She swiped at the smudgy glass with a sleeve; even so, she could barely see through the clutter of withered wisteria growing outside.

Standing outside her door was an enormous, overgrown mushroom.

She soon realized she was merely looking down at the top of a floppy hat. Whoever had rung the bell must be even shorter than she was, so she could make out no individual features: just the hat, and a lumpy coat, and a bit of straw-colored hair protruding around a pair of large ears.

Ring-ring-ring.

She knew she wasn't supposed to let strangers into their home, but curiosity won out over caution. Quickly, she hopped down from the counter and shooed the sleepy diggle out into the hallway, closing and locking the door to the hallway once the monster was safely out of sight. She tidied the kitchen as best she could, shoving anything mysterious or unusual—her father's dingle clips, the jars full of exploding phoenix feathers, a large glass filled with frothy pink hufflebottom milk—into the pantry. She glanced at her reflection in the bottom of a copper pot, combing a few leaves from her hair, then took a deep breath and opened the door.

The boy standing on the stoop was indeed several inches shorter than Cordelia, though he looked to be about her age. He was as dark as she was fair, and she knew him at once for a street urchin—likely, from the reek of shoe polish he exuded, one of the many orphans who made their living blacking boots for the lawyers, doctors, and merchants of the North End. His clothing was filthy and seemed to have come from a variety of eras and styles. He wore too-large boots with a hole in one toe, a too-small jacket with patches at the elbows, a striped undershirt that could only have come from a fisherman at the docks, and a pair of bow-legged riding pants. In his arms, he carried a puppy wrapped in a blanket.

"Are you the vegetarian?" the boy asked, as soon as she swung open the door.

This was a decidedly strange beginning to the conversation. But the boy didn't seem the slightest bit embarrassed. "What?" Cordelia said.

"Are you the vegetarian?" he repeated patiently.

Cordelia realized he must mean *veterinarian*. "My father is," she said.

"I need to see him," the boy said, lifting his chin, which was quite pointy and gave his whole face the look of an inverted flame. "It's urgent."

"He's busy right now," Cordelia said. She added, "Can I help you?"

"It's my dog," the boy said, and angled the bundle he was holding into the light for Cordelia's inspection. "I think he's sick."

It was clear, at first glance, that the boy's dog was worse than sick. His eyes were glassy and unseeing. A stiff black tongue protruded from his mouth. His whole body was rigid, his tail ramrod straight, as if he'd been frozen in place in the middle of running after a squirrel.

"I'm sorry," Cordelia said gently. "My father's a vet. He's not a miracle worker." She started to close the door.

The boy jammed a boot in the doorframe before she could get it closed. Cordelia yelped and jumped backward. The boy was starting to irritate her.

"I'm not an idiot," he said. "He's not dead, even if he looks it. Here. See for yourself." And he shoved the bundle into Cordelia's arms.

She started to protest—the dog was freezing cold, like a block of ice—but then she felt, to her absolute surprise, that the dog was *breathing*. Underneath his skin, his ribs were expanding in and out. She heard, too, the faintest whimpering sound. There were dim points of red light barely shining in the center of his eyes, like dying embers.

Cordelia was so stunned, she nearly dropped the puppy.

"See?" the boy said.

"Where—where did you find it?" Cordelia croaked out. She knew now that what she held in her arms was extraordinarily special, and extraordinarily rare. Not a puppy. A *zuppy*.

A zombie puppy.

"Him," the boy corrected crossly. "His name is Cabal. And it's none of your business where I got him." There was that chin again, quivering proudly in her direction. "The question is, can you help?"

Cordelia hesitated. The zuppy was very sick—anyone could see that. He had likely only just died, and it was safe to assume that the boy had no idea how to care for a recently turned zombie puppy. If she didn't help, the zuppy would suffer greatly; eventually, he might die again, this time for good.

On the other hand, it might be irresponsible to treat the zuppy and then release it back into the boy's care. Although zuppies were distantly related to regular dogs, the mechanism that allowed reanimation made them completely dependent on a human caretaker—and came with whitening of the zuppy's fur and the reddening of its eyes. The boy couldn't hope to keep Cabal concealed for long. And then what? The zuppy might be killed. Or hauled into a scientific laboratory for experimentation, poked and prodded with needles.

People are afraid of what they don't understand.

Could she contrive a way to keep the zuppy here, at home, where he would be safe?

As if sensing the direction of her thoughts, the boy spoke up. "Please," he said. This time he spoke quietly, earnestly, and his pointy chin began to tremble. "He's a friend. He's my *only* friend."

Cordelia felt a wrenching twist of pity. She knew better than anyone what it was like to have only monsters for friends.

"Stay here," she told the boy, and retreated into the kitchen, latching the door behind her, just in case the boy got it into his head to follow her. She would have to move quickly, before her father finished repairing the dragon's wing and came to find her. She was sure Cornelius Clay wouldn't allow her to return the zuppy to the boy's care. He would tell her it was far too dangerous—for the boy, but mostly for the zuppy.

Fortunately, Cordelia knew just what to do. She had read all about zuppies in her mother's book, *A Guide to Monsters and Their Habits*, whose publication had launched Elizabeth Clay to prominence in the monster-ologist and naturalist communities. She had even, a year after its publication, been the first woman invited to lecture at Harvard University.

Then, suddenly, scathing articles began to flood the prominent newspapers. Elizabeth Clay was a sham, and her methodology was sloppy. Elizabeth Clay was an anarchist, bent on the destruction of the natural order.

Elizabeth Clay wanted to normalize monsters, wanted monsters in our parks and forests, in our gardens and even in our homes. She wanted monsters stalking our playgrounds and schools. She had more interest in protecting monsters than in protecting people.

Then death threats came, in a trickle, and then a flood. The book was pulled from the shelves, and her second book contract was canceled.

Even so, Elizabeth Clay had only been more determined to prove that there was nothing monstrous about monsters at all. Two years later, deep in the work of a second book she was sure would redeem her to the scientific community, she set sail for the jungle, and vanished.

By now, Cordelia's copy of *The Guide to Monsters and Their Habits* was so old and worn that the yellowed pages had come loose from the binding, and the whole thing was held together by ribbons. It didn't matter. Cordelia had read it so many times, she had practically memorized the whole thing.

For the first several weeks of the zuppy's new life-after-life, Cordelia's mother had written, it is critical that its diet be regular and uniform.

Which, Cordelia knew, was a fancy way of saying that newly turned zuppies ate one thing, and one thing alone.

She placed the zuppy on the kitchen table. His eyes flickered, just barely.

"Hang on, little guy," she whispered. She went to the ice chest and dug past frozen hunks of meat and jars of rare ingredients, labeled in her father's neat script: praying mantis eggs, sap milk, tails of electric eels. At the very bottom of the ice chest, she found several vials filled with a rich, purplish-red liquid, each bearing identical, handwritten labels.

Blood.

Cordelia warmed the vial by rolling it quickly in two hands, then reversed a little into a pipette, used most commonly to give eye drops to the filch, who suffered frequently from infections. With one hand, she eased open the zuppy's jaw, revealing the stiff black tongue. With the other hand, she squeezed several drops of blood into the zuppy's mouth.

For a minute, nothing happened. The zuppy didn't stir.

"Come on, little guy," Cordelia said, and brought the pipette once again toward the zuppy's open mouth.

All at once, he blinked. In one fluid motion, the zuppy sat up, latching onto the pipette so fiercely he nearly tore it from Cordelia's hand. She laughed out loud as the little zombie puppy began to wriggle. He wagged his tail. He blinked at her expectantly, and then pawed her hand. "Not too much now," she said, as he drained the eye dropper entirely. "You'll make yourself sick."

A sharp red gleam had returned to his eyes, burning bright as coal.

"There's a good boy," she said, and hefted him into her arms. He was still cold—he always would be—and when he licked her face, his breath smelled a little like dirt.

The boy was still standing on the stoop, pacing. His face lit up when he saw the zuppy wiggling in Cordelia's arms.

"Cabal!" he cried. The zuppy leapt straight for the boy, nearly knocking him backward on the crumbling steps. The boy accepted several licks to his face and then set Cabal down, where he ran in happy circles around the boy's boots.

"You did it." The boy looked wonderingly up at Cordelia. She was reminded of a flame, as if the boy were lit up from within, once again. She wondered where he had slept the night, whether he had had to make a bed above a heating grate, or in one of the stable yards, where he might nest in the straw with the animals. She had a momentary desire to tell the boy to come inside, to sit by the fire, to talk a while. But of course she couldn't. "You saved him. How did you save him?" the boy asked.

"It was no big deal," Cordelia said, avoiding the

question. She wasn't sure how the boy would react to finding out that the dog running circles around his feet was neither technically a dog nor technically alive. "Here," she said, passing him several glass vials and a pipette filled with blood. "Make sure he takes some three times a day."

The boy made a face. "What is this stuff?"

"Medicine," she said evasively.

The boy shrugged and stuffed the vials and pipette into the pockets of his too-small coat. For a second, they stood there awkwardly, staring at each other.

Be my friend. The words were pressing at the back of Cordelia's throat before she knew that she had thought them. But just then the boy gave an awkward wave. "Well, thanks a lot. See you around."

"Okay. See you."

Cordelia watched as the boy retreated down the overgrown path, with the newly revived zuppy trotting at his heels. The urge to call him back was suddenly overwhelming. But what would she say? She knew how to calm a growrk, and catch a pixie, and cure a hufflebottom of asthma. She knew a thousand things. But she didn't know how to tell the boy that she was lonely.

She started to close the door. "Wait!" the boy called out to her.

She opened the door again, her heart hammering. "Yeah?"

The boy was now standing at the end of the path, near the crooked gate that led onto the street. "I'm Gregory, by the way."

"Cordelia," she said. Then: "Would you like to come in for—?"

But the boy had already disappeared into the smoky light of a new dawn, leaving Cordelia alone.

Cordelia shut the blinds against the daylight, which was starting to seep across the cluttered countertops like the drool of a *Mattahorn salivus*. She very carefully spooned a half tablespoon of powdered chocolate from the inch or so that remained, then heated it on the stove, thinning it with water and adding a dash of milk only at the end. Once, she would have used two tablespoons of chocolate for each cup. Once, she would have used only milk. But that was before Hard Times.

When the chocolate was heated, she divided it into two mugs: hers, a pale blue; her father's, a vivid red. The third mug, a pretty lavender color, had been her mother's, and still sat on the shelf above the stove, where it had always been. It comforted Cordelia to see it there, as if someday her mother might return, shaking rain out of her hair, bubbling over with the excitement of her discovery.

I found it, she would say, before she had even removed her boots. *The missing link. Proof that monsters are as natural to the world as we are.*

Cordelia had just set the mugs on the table when she heard her father's footsteps coming down the hall. He reentered with the dragon. Now unmuzzled, the dragon blinked sleepily at Cordelia. She saw that its wing had been repaired and splinted carefully with pencil-thin pieces of birchwood.

When he noticed the twin mugs on the table, he smiled. "Ah, Cordelia. You're a mind reader. Hot chocolate will be just the thing. Open the oven for me, will you?"

The oven hadn't been used for cooking in years. Instead Cornelius and Cordelia had transformed it into a pen, fitted with blankets and a covering of clean straw. It was warm, and dry, and cozy, and would be perfect for the baby dragon.

Once their newest monster was happily settled in his new home, Cordelia's father took a seat at the table. Cordelia slid into her customary place across from him.

"Was it my imagination, or did I hear the bell ring?" he said, taking a sip of hot chocolate and watching Cordelia carefully over the rim of his cup.

"It was just the wind," Cordelia said quickly. She knew she couldn't tell her father about the zuppy. And she didn't want to tell him about the boy, Gregory. She wanted to keep him her own little secret.

Cornelius set down his mug and reached for Cordelia's hand. "Are you lonely here, Cordelia? With just your old father and a bunch of smelly monsters for company?"

Though she had been thinking exactly that only a few minutes ago, her father's face was filled with such an open worry that she shook her head. "I love it here," she said. "And the monsters don't smell. Not all of them, anyway."

Cornelius smiled feebly. "I fear I've been a terrible father," he said. "Too wrapped up in my work. Too wrapped up in the past—"

"Don't say that," Cordelia said. "You're the greatest father in the world."

An expression passed across Dr. Clay's face that Cordelia couldn't identify—sadness, almost, but deeper than sadness, as if Dr. Clay was staring out at her from the bottom of a well. But when he spoke, he sounded normal. "I want you to know I'm very proud of you."

"Okay." Cordelia fidgeted in her chair. She didn't like when her father got mushy. She didn't like the way he was looking at her, either—as if there was a secondary meaning behind his words, if she could only decode it.

"I'm proud of you, and I love you very much. You have to promise me that if anything ever happens to me—" His voice hitched, and he cleared his throat, spinning his mug between his hands. "If anything ever happens to me, you'll take good care of yourself. And you'll remember what I told you—we all grow up sometime. It's only right."

"Nothing's going to happen," Cordelia said. But even after her father kissed her forehead and bid her good night, she stayed at the table, wondering what could have made her father—her fearless, monster-loving father—so sad.

CHAPTER
4

Cordelia knew something was wrong the moment she woke up. The sun was already sinking, and long violet shadows were striped across the threadbare rugs. Why hadn't her father woken her to help soften the diggles with their weekly milk bath, and give the filch its cold medicine?

She sat up. It was so quiet she could hear the *cluck-cluck-cluck* of the grandfather clock downstairs.

Too quiet.

A feeling of dread overcame her. Her hands and feet felt numb and overlarge, clumsy, as if she were moving in a body that wasn't her own. She went into the hall, listening for the familiar sound of her father's footsteps, for the growls and snarls and slurps of the monsters. The numb feeling spread to her throat, making it hard to breathe. She ran down the stairs and burst into the kitchen.

Empty. The clock kept up its clucking; she saw that it was nearly five o'clock in the evening. The pan in which she had heated hot chocolate was still sitting on the stove.

"Dad?" she called out. Now the panic was gripping her from all directions at once, making her chest vibrate.

She raced down the hall and threw open the doors to the great room. Empty. She dashed into the sunroom, skidding across the polished stone floor, and burst into the parlor. Her knees turned liquid. A whimpering sound worked its way out of her throat.

They were gone. All of them. The succubus and the hufflebottom, the pixies and the filch, the wailers and both growrks—gone.

"Dad? Dad!" Cordelia was screaming now. She moved blindly back into the hall and raced upstairs to her father's bedroom, flinging open the door. The sheets had been pushed violently off his bed, as though he'd woken in a hurry. His window was open.

She couldn't breathe. She couldn't think. She dropped

onto her knees, as though her father might simply be hiding under the bed. Of course, he wasn't there.

She plunged downstairs again, through the kitchen, through the overgrown courtyard—mindless of the fact that she was barefoot, and still in her nightgown. She dashed out the gate onto Cedar Street and turned left onto Pinckney, brushing roughly past a sharp-beaked man wearing a tall hat and a high-collared coat, ignoring his cry of surprise.

Had she been thinking rationally, Cordelia might have realized that it was highly unlikely her father would have simply taken all the monsters with him on a stroll. They were difficult to control, and evidence of *any* quantity of monsters would have caused a panic in the city.

But she wasn't thinking rationally. The word *Dad* kept beating through her brain.

Dad, Dad, Dad. Beneath its constant rhythm, another word kept tempo. *Gone, gone, gone.*

Her footsteps pounded on the slick cobblestones. She barely even noticed it was raining. Left, right, left, right. She cut across Louisburg Square, careened down the byway that ran parallel to Charles Street, scanning the face of every passerby, searching the reflections in every shop window, her feet pounding out the same urgent message. *Dad, Dad, Dad.*

On the north side of the Boston Common, she ran straight into the boy, Gregory, who had come to her with the zuppy.

"'Allo, Cordelia," he said cheerfully, as if they were old friends. He was eating pistachios straight from a pocket. Cordelia noticed he was carrying a very wriggly rucksack and figured the zuppy was inside. "I was just on my way to see you, actually. Cabal's in tip-top shape, never been better. Whatever you gave him must have been—"

He didn't get any further. She flung her arms around his neck and let out a sob into the soft wool of his old coat, which smelled faintly like sour pickles. She couldn't help it. She had no one else.

"What's wrong?" Gregory's voice inched higher. It had been years since anyone had hugged him, and he had a brief, overwhelming impression of a woman with a crown of dark braids, the snug fit of a warm blanket, a sense of warmth and closeness. He wasn't sure whether he was supposed to hug Cordelia back or just stand there. He opted for the latter, since she was squeezing him so tightly he felt like he was in a strait-jacket. "What's happened?"

"They're gone," she sobbed.

"Who's gone?" Gregory pulled away and gripped her shoulders tightly. "What are you talking about?"

"The monsters," she wailed, and a woman wearing a great bustled skirt shot her an alarmed look and hurried rapidly past her. "Every last one of them." Cordelia realized, too late, that she had broken the rules. Her father had forbidden her from speaking of the monsters to anyone else.

But her father was gone.

For a moment, Gregory said nothing, and Cordelia felt a terrible, gnawing anxiety. Would he believe her? Would he think she was crazy? Would he scream, or run away? Cordelia found that she was holding her breath.

After a pause that felt like an hour, Gregory reached up and rubbed the hat back and forth on his head, as if he were trying to heat up his brain. "I think—" he said, squinting at her. "I think you'd better start at the beginning."

CHAPTER
5

All in all, Gregory reacted surprisingly well to the news that not only were there monsters in Boston, but many of them had been, until earlier that day, living in Clay Manor. He kept moving his hat back and forth, back and forth, as if working the idea into his scalp.

Finally he said, "Cabal's not a regular dog, is he?" Cordelia shook her head.

Gregory's hat tilted right. "I knew there was something strange about him when I saw him come up out of that grave." His hat tilted left. "He's still a good dog, though."

"He's a good zuppy," Cordelia corrected. "A zombie puppy," she added, when Gregory stared at her with both eyebrows raised. "Although the name is a little misleading, because it implies . . ." Cordelia shook her head. She didn't have time to explain her mother's research. "Actually, just forget it."

They were still standing on the street—Cordelia in her bare feet and nightgown, Gregory in his patched, small coat and too-large boots. The mist was clinging to Cordelia's skin, and the wind felt like a cold, damp touch.

"All the monsters are gone?" Gregory asked.

Cordelia nodded. "And—and—my dad's missing too." Just saying the words made her feel like she was going to cry again. "Something terrible must have happened. He would never have left on his own." Her father had seemed worried yesterday. Had he anticipated that this would happen? If so, why hadn't he warned her directly? Why hadn't he tried to prevent it?

"Okay. Okay." Gregory scratched his head, leaving a long, smudgy black mark across his forehead in the process. "So . . . so he was forced."

"Maybe he was kidnapped," Cordelia said. She wouldn't think about the other possibility, the even *worse* possibility.

"Grown-up-napped," Gregory said thoughtfully. "What about the monsters?"

"They must have been taken too," Cordelia said. She didn't see how one person could control so many monsters. Maybe it was a *conspiracy*. She'd learned that word from her father only a few months ago. It meant that a group of people was working together to do something awful.

Never believe the people who tell you there's no magic left in the world, he'd said to her. It's a big conspiracy, designed to keep people sewing buttons and buying ribbons and thinking only about pork roast.

"So . . . what now?" Gregory asked. It was already late. The sky was a bruised color, and fog was rolling into the streets off the harbor, like billowing clouds pulled to earth.

"I don't know." Panic threatened to overwhelm her again, rising like a wave from her stomach to her throat, and she took several long, deep breaths. *The* Aeriol complainus *are known for their piercing shrieks, loud enough to pierce an eardrum*, she thought. *The bogey cannot actually fly but only coasts on air currents, scanning for prey*. It helped her to recite from *A Guide to Monsters and Their Habits* when she was very afraid.

The number one rule of tracking monsters: you must never, ever panic.

All at once, she felt as if a lamp had flared to life inside her. Tracking monsters. That was it.

She had no doubt that her father and the monsters were together. And she, Cordelia, knew how to find monsters. She had once surprised a sniffly hufflebottom in its lair. She had once tracked a family of feverish diggles to the bottom of a burrow. She had recognized an injured succubus from the way its shadow fell across a tree stump.

She could find them. She *would* find them.

She would begin at the house, and follow the trail of the missing monsters, wherever it led.

"I have an idea." She seized Gregory's hand, gripping him the way she would have a life preserver in the middle of open ocean, and started walking. She did not think about the fact that she barely knew him. She did not think about what would happen when Gregory abandoned her to search for the monsters on his own, as she was sure that he would. He was here now, and for the moment, that was enough. She didn't even notice the way that people were staring.

At the corner of Spruce and Chestnut, Mrs. McGregor was just leaving her bakery for the day, carrying a basket of day-old pastries, and she startled as Cordelia and Gregory hurried around the corner of Spruce Street. "Cordelia!" she said, and then frowned as she took in Cordelia's nightgown, bare feet, and generally disheveled appearance. "What's wrong with you, child?

Where's your coat? And your shoes?"

"I was in a hurry," Cordelia said quickly. Her toes were purple from the cold.

Mrs. McGregor's face was like the wrinkled surface of her raisin bread. She frowned even more deeply. "I'm going to have a word with your father when I see him. Young girls shouldn't run wild in the streets like stray dogs after a scrap o' meat."

"Her father's—" Gregory started to say, and Cordelia nudged an elbow in his ribs before he could say *missing*.

"Busy," she burst out. "Very, very busy."

Mrs. McGregor shook her head. "Don't think I won't give him a piece of my mind, Cordelia Clay, about what's what. I heard what you did to little Henry Haddock. You should be at St. George's playing with other nice young girls, not keeping company with . . ." Her voice trailed off into a disapproving rumble as she looked Gregory up and down. "Well, with *whatever* that is."

"His name is Gregory," Cordelia said defensively. Only then did she notice the sign prominently placed in the bakery window: *No Beggars. No Foreigners. Absolutely NO Catholics.* Since the start of the Hard Times, identical signs had sprouted on more and more businesses, like some fast-growing and devilish varietal of weed.

"If only your mother were still alive," Mrs. McGregor

said, clucking her tongue.

"My mother loved running wild," Cordelia burst out, with such ferocity that Mrs. McGregor startled again. "She was running wild in the jungle when she"—at the last second, she couldn't say *died*—"disappeared."

"Well, let that be a lesson to you," Mrs. McGregor said. She took one more look at Gregory and sighed. Then, in a softer voice, she said, "Go on, take some sweet buns home for you and your father. If you get any skinnier, I might mistake you for a broomstick and start sweeping with you." She passed Cordelia her basket, piled high with walnut-studded sweet buns.

Cordelia realized she hadn't eaten since a poor supper of nettle soup and seed bread the night before, and she was starving.

"Thank you," she said stiffly.

Mrs. McGregor sniffed. "Go on, then, both of you," she said, but didn't miss the opportunity for a final warning. "Tell your father I'll be along one of these days to have a word."

"What'd you do to Henry Haddock?" Gregory asked, as soon as they left Mrs. McGregor behind.

"Not half as much as he deserved," Cordelia said. Just thinking about it made her insides spark with anger again. Haddock was a bully, the kind of kid who'd liked to pull the wings off moths and butterflies when he was little. He'd moved on to sticking frogs with pins and yanking cats by the tail. Now, apparently, he'd moved on to people.

"What did he do?" Gregory asked.

"Breathe," Cordelia said. She didn't want to think about Henry Haddock, or his blockhead friends, who trotted after him like dogs starved for attention. She usually managed to ignore them when she was unlucky enough to pass them in the street, even though they never ignored her—insulting her clothes for being ratty, her face for being narrow, her father for being poor.

But for the first time, only a week ago, they had ignored her. They were busy taunting a man who'd made a home of old shipping crates not far from the park. He didn't speak English, and thankfully couldn't understand what they said. But Cordelia heard him cry out when they snatched up his duffel bag and shook out his belongings in the mud.

"You want to learn some English? Try this: *we don't want you here*," Henry said.

Cordelia's feet carried her in his direction before she could think about telling them to run. "Stop it!" she said. "Stop!"

Henry finally noticed her. "Cordelia Crazy, right on time. You want to help us clean up some trash? Because you're either trying to stop the mess, or you're the one filling the city with litter—"

Then she drove into him with her shoulder and knocked him to the ground. She got in two good punches, and her only regret was that she hadn't had time for ten.

Luckily, Gregory didn't ask any more questions. He didn't say anything at all, just kept pace with Cordelia as she carved around the corner and cut down Willow Street. She was grateful for the silence. Worry and fear were screaming loud enough inside her head.

But no sooner had they reached the corner of Mt. Vernon Street than a shrill voice stopped Cordelia in her tracks.

"This is a private street, you know. That means you're trespassing."

The high, reedy voice was like the crawl of spiders up a spine. Horrible, and impossible to ignore.

She turned to see Elizabeth Perkins, insufferable snot, horrible snob, and her former best friend, standing just behind the iron gates of Number 122. Her new house was so large it looked like it had digested a few other houses and then burped them out into wings.

"Look," Cordelia said loudly. "The little windup doll knows how to speak." There was no one in all of Boston that Cordelia despised more than Elizabeth and her empty-headed friends from St. George's.

"Very funny." Elizabeth narrowed her eyes. Her hair was curled into ringlets. She wore a fur-trimmed cape fitted with a shiny gold clasp at the neck, a frilly dress, and shoes polished so well they reflected the fog drifting past. "Where are you off to, looking like a street sweep?"

In an instant, Cordelia saw herself through Elizabeth's eyes: the mess of her uncombed red hair, the scattershot of her freckles, the hem of her old nightgown now filthy from the streets. "Where are you off to, looking like a cream puff?"

"Nowhere that you'll ever go," Elizabeth said serenely. "I'm afraid that most theaters have a strict policy against admitting wild animals."

"Then I'm surprised they allow sheep," Cordelia fired back. It was hardly imaginable that the girl at the gates—coiled and steamed and carefully pressed as a linen closet—had once been called Lizzie, Cordelia's best and dearest friend. But of course, they weren't the same girl, not at all. Lizzie had liked to dig in the mud and help tend to the dogs and cats that came to the Clay home seeking treatment, long before the steady accumulation of monsters meant that Lizzie was invited less and less to Cordelia's house, and Cordelia more and more to hers. Still, Lizzie had a passionate interest in Cordelia's stories about monsters, although she thought they were just that—stories.

Then one day, when Cordelia was nine, they'd

decided to go on an adventure to discover any monsters they could find nearby, a ritual of theirs. They had explored the wharves and the woods, the park and the playground. That day they decided to explore the Perkins' garden. By chance, Cordelia had stubbed her toe on a slab of flagstone, and shifted it by a few inches, revealing the mouth of a gently sloping tunnel.

Only by chance, Cordelia and her father had not yet come across a goblin burrow, so Cordelia didn't think twice about following Elizabeth inside to see where it went.

The answer was: to a goblin.

It was one thing to pretend to be on the hunt for monsters. It was another to discover a sixty-five-pound goblin living beneath your potatoes—especially a goblin startled awake by your screaming.

Afterward, Elizabeth changed. It was as if she blamed Cordelia for the discovery of the goblin; as if by ending her friendship with one, she could deny the reality of the other. Cordelia had never forgotten the way Elizabeth had looked after fleeing the burrow—her hair entangled with a scattering of dried leaves, her face dirt-streaked and leeched of its color, her eyes like two puncture wounds. She had never forgotten the way she trembled, or the way she spoke the two words that ended their friendship.

"Get. Out."

That was three years earlier, when Cordelia was eight. She didn't see Elizabeth for a full year. And by the time they began speaking again, it was only to insult each other.

"At least sheep have a *flock*," Elizabeth said. "You've always been more of a *black* sheep, I suppose." She swept her eyes briskly over Gregory, like a broom hurrying up the dirt. "I suppose you've begun collecting strays now?"

"Gregory," Cordelia said, through gritted teeth, "is my friend." The words were out of her mouth before she considered them, and she felt a tiny thrill of excitement. Was Gregory her friend? Probably not. Still, it felt nice to pretend.

"Well, you know what they say. Quality over quantity. And since you've neither"—Elizabeth's teeth were small and sharp—"remember that beggars can't be choosers."

Another surge of anger swept through the whole of Cordelia's body, from toes to head. Before she knew what she was doing—before she could remind herself she should be staying out of trouble—she scooped up a rock and hurled it. Gregory shouted. The rock hit Elizabeth square in the hand, and she jumped backward, shrieking, bringing her fingers to her mouth.

"What's wrong with you?" she shouted, clutching her hand. "Why are you such a *monster*?"

"Come *on*." This time it was Gregory who dragged her down the street.

CHAPTER
6

Cordelia made Gregory wait in the kitchen while she went very slowly through the house, starting with the upstairs. In her father's room, she immediately spotted an unusual trail of green goo she had missed in her earlier panic. It stretched from just beneath the open window to the foot of the bed and back, as if a large slug had oozed its way in from outside and then made a rapid escape. Except she didn't know any slug that would climb a house and try to gain entry. She certainly didn't know any slug that could beat a hasty retreat.

She went to the open window and looked out into

the misty courtyard. The crooked branches of the oak tree outside her father's window swayed in the wind. A sudden gust lifted the curtains, and a loud *bang* made Cordelia jump. But it was only the closet door, slamming shut behind her.

A monster might be responsible for the slime, she supposed—it might have climbed the tree and come in through the window. But then what? She couldn't imagine. And the only monster she could think of that left a similar trail was the *Bilious caterpillarus*, related, according to her mother's theories, to both a variety of twice-molting newt and the common gypsy caterpillar. But those had been extinct for a hundred years now.

She was about to leave her father's room when she heard a faint scratching from inside the closet. She froze. *Scratch, scratch, scratch.* And a soft, whimpering sound.

She picked up the old brass candlestick from her father's nightstand. She crept toward the closet, arm raised, ready to strike . . .

Then seized hold of the door handle, and flung open the door.

Instantly, a ball of white fur rocketed out at her, knocking her off her feet and sending the candlestick clattering across the floor.

"Cabal!" she cried, as Cabal licked her face enthusiastically and drooled all over her. He must have gotten away from Gregory and followed her upstairs. "You scared me, little guy."

Cabal made a noise somewhere between a howl and a bark. Cordelia sat up and returned him to the floor. Only then did she see what he had been doing in the closet: he had made a kind of nest by ripping apart several newspapers and various items of clothing, including her father's favorite work pants.

"Bad zuppy," she said, and even though she supposed it didn't matter, she began to separate the torn paper from the shreds of her father's now-destroyed work pants, as though by collecting them, they might spontaneously repair themselves—and repair, too, what had gone wrong, bring her father and all the monsters back.

She was almost finished arranging the scraps of fabric in a neat pile when she noticed a piece of paper, largely intact, buried among the cloth. It was soft, as though it had been handled often, and for some time.

She unfolded it and saw words written in unfamiliar handwriting. Portions of the letter were blurred by a liquid spill, so only certain phrases were legible. She sniffed. Fungal oil. Her father must have been carrying some in the same pocket.

Hello . . . I should thank . . . making my work easy . . . <u>*Do not underestimate what I can do*</u> *. . . I*

am coming for you . . . and for your monstrous col-
lection . . . soon.

The last word was underlined with such force, the
pen nib had left a hole in the paper. At the bottom of the
note was an ornate signature; Cordelia could make out
only what she thought was a comma, and the initials of
the first and last name, *HP*.

She stood up, dizzy with both fear and excitement.
Here, at last, was a clue: a message from a person
unknown. And now she thought she knew why her
father had been acting so strangely. He had known that
he was a target. He had suspected that any day he might
be compelled by HP—whoever he was—to leave Cordelia. And now the day had come.

Downstairs, Gregory was sitting in front of the stove.
"Look what I found," he said. He had a curious expression on his face, as if he'd swallowed a mouthful of
quince paste when he'd been expecting chocolate, and
now was trying to puzzle out the flavor. He leaned forward to open the oven door.

Cordelia couldn't believe it: Icky, the filch, was huddled in the oven, sniffling piteously. It was no surprise. Filches—amphibious, mud-dwelling monsters very
closely related to monkeys—were notoriously cowardly.
The baby dragon, its wing still splinted, was squirming

inside Icky's panicked grasp, clearly agitated, and let out a burst of flame when Gregory leaned too close. He drew back. A small portion of his eyebrow caught flame and then, when he clapped a hand to his head, was quickly extinguished.

"Why'd he do that?" Gregory said.

"He's a dragon, Gregory," Cordelia said. "He can't help it."

"A dragon," Gregory repeated. Once again, he started nudging his hat back and forth, a gesture Cordelia now recognized as a sign of deep thought.

"I warned you, didn't I?" Cordelia said. She squatted, extending one hand tentatively toward the monsters. "Come on," she cooed. "I'm not going to hurt you." Her throat was so tight she could hardly swallow. They had survived. Somehow, while the others had been taken—while her father had been taken—they had stayed hidden and so they had survived.

It took some further coaxing, and their last meat pie from the pantry, before the dragon poked his head tentatively from the oven and at last ventured out into the kitchen. The filch emerged soon afterward and promptly leapt for Gregory and began anxiously gnawing at his shin. The more Gregory tried to shake him off, the more desperately he wrapped his arms around Gregory's leg, and the more he gnawed.

"He's traumatized," Cordelia explained apologetically.

"So's my shin," Gregory responded. But after that, he didn't complain, and clomped around the kitchen with the filch still clinging to him. Cordelia had never much liked Icky. He was old and bad-tempered, and he farted. But she was so grateful to see that two of the monsters remained, she could have leaned down and kissed him on his puckered nose. The dragon, too, had she not suspected that he might set her hair ablaze.

"Did you find anything upstairs?" Gregory asked.

Cordelia wasn't ready to tell Gregory about the slime she'd found upstairs. She didn't know what it meant, or whether it meant anything. But she showed him the note she had found among the tattered remains of her father's clothing. It took Gregory a long time to work out the message.

"I never went to school," he explained, squinting over the page, until Cordelia showed him that he was holding it upside down.

"I never went to school, either," Cordelia said. "I learned everything I know from books, and from my father. My mother too, before she . . . went away." Cordelia had never gotten used to saying the word *died* out loud. And in truth, she didn't actually *remember* how her mother used to read to her—for hours, sometimes, occasionally from a book of old nursery rhymes, and sometimes simply by reciting from the manuscript she worked on painstakingly every night. But her father had told her that when Cordelia was a baby, she could fall asleep nowhere but in her mother's study. So they had installed her crib next to the desk, where, lulled by the gentle hiss of her mother's pen across fresh pages, and by the murmuring recitation of her words, Cordelia had slept peacefully through the night.

"Never had any books," Gregory said nonchalantly, forgetting even to complain that Icky had gnawed a hole in his trousers. Or maybe he merely hadn't noticed, since his trousers were already so full of holes. "Never had a mother and father, neither. Aha! I know that first letter. *H*. It's a funny-looking shape, isn't it? Looks like two I's got stuck together with a stick. Oh, look! Speaking of I's, there's one right there. Sneaky things. They slink past so quick you hardly notice."

Cordelia was quiet. She tried to imagine what it would be like if she had never had a father or a mother, but she couldn't. She imagined an empty room, stretching in all directions. She suddenly felt like hugging Gregory again. But he was still puzzling out the letters, so she didn't.

"I know that word. *C-O-M-I-N-G*. Like 'the train's coming in five minutes, boy, so scram out of here before

I boot you.' And that word too. *Y-O-U.* 'You can't be in here! You don't belong here! It's people like you dirty-ing up Boston! You should go back to where you came from!' See? I taught myself to read just fine, didn't I? 'I'm coming for you,'" he finished triumphantly. Then, as the meaning behind the message registered, he frowned.

"Let me get this straight," Gregory said at last. "Some guy named HP—"

"Or girl," Cordelia said.

"Okay, some guy or girl named HP—"

"Some Hideous Person," Cordelia suggested.

"Okay, some *Hideous Person* was threatening your dad. And maybe he wanted the . . . monsters for himself." Gregory tripped only a little over the word. "Somehow he sneaks in, convinces your dad to go with him, and gets all the monsters out without making a noise."

Cordelia had to admit it sounded unlikely. Still, her father was gone, and the monsters were too. And the letter was proof someone had come for them. She tried to think whether she knew of anyone who might want to hurt her father or steal the monsters. But she came up blank. No one even *knew* about the monsters—she and her father had been so careful over the years. And how could her father have enemies, when he didn't even have friends?

Still, she could think of no other possible explanation.

"My dad couldn't have had any other choice," she said. "And the Hideous Person might have had help."

Gregory sighed. "There's only one thing to do, then," he said. At last he succeeded in shaking the filch from his pant leg, though unfortunately, Icky scurried off with a large square of fabric from Gregory's cuff. The filch retreated to the corner, where the dragon was keeping Cabal at bay by breathing smoke into his face every time the zuppy got too close.

"I can't go to the police, if that's what you're thinking," Cordelia said.

Gregory made a face. "The police won't do anything but take notes and poke around a bit. No." His eyes were a very clear green, like the color of new grass. "We find HP."

CHAPTER
7

"We?" Cordelia was so surprised to hear Gregory say the word that for a second she couldn't even react to the rest of his suggestion: *We find HP.* As if it were as simple as strolling down to the butcher and asking for a sausage link.

"I'm going to help," he announced, puffing out his chest slightly—which, since he was so narrow, had the effect of making him look like an upside-down exclamation point. "You helped save my dog."

"Zuppy," Cordelia corrected.

"Sure, zuppy. Dead or alive, Cabal's a friend. And you're a friend too."

Cordelia couldn't speak immediately. *Friend*. Funny how a bundle of letters could add up to so much. *Friend* meant she wasn't alone, not entirely. *Friend* meant she had hope.

Even so, the idea of trying to find HP was overwhelming. Where could they possibly begin? Cordelia had never been outside Boston; it was rare that she ever left the *house*, unless her father accompanied her. She had no idea how far the world extended, how long and wide it might be, what it looked like beyond the familiar slanting streets of her hometown.

"They've had a head start," Cordelia said. "They might have gone in any direction."

"Do you have any better ideas?" Gregory swiped his straw-like hair from his eyes. In the corner, Cabal and Icky were fighting over a canister of dung beetles, which the dragon, in his awkward attempts to fly, had knocked off the pantry shelf. Icky poked Cabal in the nose.

Cordelia had to admit that she didn't. Still, she felt almost sick with fear. "We'll have to be very careful. HP—whoever he or she is—managed to steal two bullieheads, two growrks, and a family of pixies without any trouble. He's strong, and clever, and sneaky."

"That's all right," Gregory said. "Careful's what I do best. Besides," he added and grinned, "we got a dragon."

At that moment, the dragon coughed out a long stream of flame. Gregory yelped and jumped backward, knocking over one of the kitchen chairs. As he sprang forward to put out the smoldering wallpaper, and succeeded instead only in breaking Cordelia's favorite mug and a jar full of dried arrowroot, Cordelia's stomach sank all the way to her toes.

"Why," she sighed, "do I get the sense that we're about to do something very, very stupid?"

The filch let out a delighted fart.

Gregory packed a bag with supplies from the pantry while Cordelia went upstairs to change out of her nightgown. She put on a pair of old corduroy pants and carefully transferred the note into a pocket. She layered a large, moth-eaten sweater that had once belonged to her mother over a turtleneck and wrestled on her favorite jacket, which was fitted with seven deep pockets in which she liked to keep various tools of the monster-hunting trade: a spyglass, a sound-amplifier of her father's own invention, and nose plugs (useful when hunting the bogs); a wrench, wires, pincers, and dingle clips; goggles, adjustable harnesses, square nails, and a pair of pliers whose handles had been gnawed practically into uselessness by one of their diggles.

She retrieved her rucksack from her closet, where she had discarded it the night before, and checked it to make sure her lantern, blanket, and collapsible net were still undisturbed. Satisfied that everything was in place, she shoved her feet into her mother's rubber boots, slung the bag over her shoulder, and returned downstairs. In the pantry, she found her father's leather coin purse, tucked away in an empty tin of biscuits. She counted out the total inside: twelve dollars and eighty-five cents. They would have to make do.

In the kitchen, Gregory ticked off pantry items he'd packed. "Salted beef jerky, sardines, seed bread, dung beetles"—he made a face—"tinned peas, a dozen bone cookies, a jar of peanuts, and Mrs. McGregor's sweet buns."

"What about the wormroot and the yak grease?" Cordelia asked, bending down to fix a collar and leash onto Cabal, Icky, and the dragon in turn. The dragon twisted his head and tried to spit flame at her fingers, but only succeeded, this time, in coughing out smoke.

"Got 'em," Gregory said.

"And the fermented fish cakes? Icky—that's the filch—is crazy about them."

"Check," Gregory said.

Standing in the warmth of the kitchen, surrounded by the clutter of familiar objects, Cordelia felt a sharp pang. She had no idea how long it would be before she returned, sat by the warmth of its ancient stove, or walked its warped floorboards.

"Hang on," she said. "There's one last thing I have to do."

CHAPTER
8

Cordelia had been inside her mother's study on only one occasion since her mother had left it for the last time: the day the confirmation of Elizabeth Clay's death had come back to them by wire, a full three years after she had first set sail for the jungles of Brazil.

Her father had delivered the news in the old parlor, as a drift of feathers fell from the overhead chandelier, where two adolescent squelches, the first monsters he had ever kept at home, were encamped to grow their wintertime fur. They had been there since they had sprouted their summertime feathers, the year before.

And although for a long time, Cornelius had pretended he would let them go "any day now," he had recently stopped speaking of their release at all. Then, the week before, he had brought home four baby squinches, abandoned by their mother, rescued from the bottom of an old laundry chute in Chinatown.

Now, one of the baby squinches bounced rhythmically on Cordelia's toes for her attention.

And for the first time in her life, Cordelia felt a sudden well of hatred—for the squelches, mindlessly shedding feathers, happy and unaware. For the baby squinch, the size of a golf ball but quite a bit more rubbery, thunking her toes over and over. For all the monsters, everywhere, and for her mother's stupid desire to protect them, even though they would never protect her back.

"It isn't the monsters' fault, Cordelia," her father had said, as if reading her mind. "Your mother believed in her work. She died doing something that mattered to her. If you have to blame someone, blame me. I should have gone with her—"

"Great idea. Then I could have been an orphan." The baby squinch had gummed onto her bootlaces, and she tried to shake him off. "She went to the jungle for the monsters, didn't she?"

"Cordelia . . ."

"She chose to go. She knew it was dangerous."

Cordelia looked down, blinking back tears. The squinch had latched onto her bootlaces, using its mouth for suction. "Let go of me," she ordered it. But it only clung tighter. "I said *let go*."

And in a sudden fury, blinded by a flash of grief and hatred, she *kicked* it.

For a split second, as the squinch spun through the air, time seemed to slow. Cordelia had time to register the squinch's startled expression, her father's look of horror, and a stabbing guilt that drained away all her anger.

Then the squinch hit the baseboard with a horrible, wet *splat*.

And Cordelia *ran*. She careened into the hall, pinballing off the radiator. And as the thunder of her own guilt, and the sound of her father shouting her name, filled her head with terrible echoes, she threw herself inside her mother's study and bolted the door behind her.

She had killed the squinch.

Her mother was dead.

It wasn't the monsters' fault. It was her fault, for being a monster.

Otherwise her mother would never have left Cordelia to sail to the jungle. She would never have left Cordelia at all.

She heard the drumming of her father's footsteps as he moved from room to room, looking for her. She dropped onto her hands and knees beside the fireplace and folded herself into the hearth, still covered in a silt of old ashes. She had been five years old when the telegram came, and whenever she thought of the word *dead*, it brought with it the taste of ashes.

When her father had finally found her, shivering inside a cold wind that swept down the flue and lifted the grit of old fires all around her, like a snowstorm in reverse, he had merely dropped to his knees and opened his arms. She had fallen into him, sobbing, choking on the taste of all the ash she'd inhaled. He had held her tight, rocking her like a baby, until at last she'd run through her store of tears, and felt as dark and empty as a chimney, swirling with cold ash.

Only then did he say, "You didn't kill the squinch."

In an instant, an ember of joy sparked to life inside her stomach. Cordelia pulled away, swiping at her nose. "I—I didn't?"

Her father stood up and moved to the bookshelves. By then, it was after dawn, and sunlight peeked through a fissure in the curtains, illuminating the spires of books rising toward the ceiling. He withdrew *The Guide to Monsters and Their Habits*, her mother's first book, from the place she had long kept it. He thumbed through the pages until he found what he was looking for. Then, clearing his throat, he read:

"'The squinch at rest resembles a small, furry globe, "plumped up" by a normal circulation of liquid through the flexible tubing. In this state, squinches move primarily by bouncing, often reaching heights of twenty feet or more. At that point, the squinches "shed" water, expelling liquid from the structural tubing that keeps their shape intact, and flattening to the shape of a disk. . . .'

"'In this "disk" shape, they are effectively conserving energy, and are capable of gliding or flying great distances, before landing without any harm to their structure. Starting from an early age, North American squinches are lulled to sleep when they are dropped from a height . . .'"

For a second after he finished reading, Cordelia could only stare at him, speechless. "It was *sleeping*?" she said.

"Thanks to you. I couldn't understand why the little beast wouldn't bed down. I'd forgotten all about your mother's research." He had snapped the book closed, letting up a drift of dust from its pages.

Then, very deliberately, he'd extended it to her.

"I think, Cordelia," he said, "that it is time for you to begin your *real* education."

And Cordelia, holding the book to her chest, felt the echo of her own heart, beating fast against the binding.

"Come," her father had said, in a quiet voice. He

placed a hand on her shoulder. "Let us leave our ghosts in peace."

That day, he had closed the door to her mother's study for the last time, and locked away their memories inside it.

The key was still right where her father had left it—hanging on a faded purple ribbon on the crooked nail on the wall outside the door. It took her several tries to fit the key in the lock. She jumped at every creak and groan of wind. She half expected to hear her father shout and demand to know what she was doing.

She had to remind herself that her father was gone, and that she was leaving, too, to go look for him.

Finally, she got the door open. She slipped inside, holding her breath, as if otherwise the room might hear her coming and startle away.

Inside, it smelled just like she remembered: like ash, and paper, and ink. In the bare moonlight trickling through the curtains, Cordelia could just make out the silhouette of her mother's desk, and the familiar shape of her crib positioned next to it. Seeing it there made a lump grow in her throat. She swallowed quickly and felt her way carefully to the small paraffin lamp that stood on the mantel. She was now tall enough to reach it, and easily got the wick lit before replacing the lamp chimney.

Warm light leapt suddenly across the carpet. Now Cordelia could see another oil lamp, this one standing on the bookshelf, next to the long, curved talon of an extinct breed of cockatrice her mother had mounted behind glass. She lit that one, too.

Now light washed the shadows from her mother's desk, still stacked with the pages of her unfinished manuscript. Cordelia had never looked at it closely. She had been too young before; and of course, for years the study had been strictly off-limits.

But now she approached, leaving faint imprints in the carpet thickened with heavy dust.

The pages of her mother's unfinished manuscript had been brittled by age into the texture of old leaves. There was a stack of nine-year-old correspondence, pinned beneath the sterling silver letter opener engraved with her initials; there was her leather blotter, splotched with ink stains, and a sketch pad filled with diagrams and illustrations she intended for the inserts of her book. In one, her mother had drawn the arterial branches of the whole vast evolutionary tree of life, as it fissured from kingdom to phylum and all the way down to different species, from snapping turtles to squinches. In another, she'd carefully detailed the mandible of both an armadillo and its distant cousin, the growrk, to demonstrate the similarity. In a third, she'd resurrected the long-extinct Giant Hippogriff in the glorious details of her pen strokes, and given it a head that very clearly suggested a relationship to the common dairy cow.

Then there was her manuscript itself: every page drafted and redrafted painstakingly, crosshatched with corrections and amendments. She had been only weeks away from finishing her book when she set sail for South America, hoping to find definitive proof of a prehistoric, shape-shifting monster called the morpheus, and forever prove that the kingdom Animalia and kingdom Prodigia were just two branches on the same evolutionary tree.

Her mother's manuscript was weighted down by what looked to be an oval stone, but bone-colored, and imprinted with a complex pattern of fine veins that coiled up and down its surface. In Cordelia's hand, it seemed to pulse with secret life, and she spent some time peering at it, forcing the pattern on its surface to take on a shape she knew. Finally, she slipped it into her pocket. She didn't know why. But it felt like good luck.

She reached out with a finger and followed the graceful slope of her mother's handwriting across first one page, and then the next. *The question of the origin of monsters is in fact really a question about the nature of categorization. . . . How do we define difference? How do we decide which traits unite, and which divide?*

Words leapt to her imagination—words that opened

up to enfold everything on the planet that had ever grown, crawled, soared, budded, or squirmed—and in them she saw a vast unfolding cartography of life and more life, ever unfurling, like the green palm of a new leaf touched by spring sunlight.

Cordelia turned back to the beginning, and to the Latin phrase her mother had inscribed beneath the title: *Vince malum bono*. Her father would know what it meant.

Cordelia felt the sudden urge to cry. It was so quiet in the house without the monsters, and so still. Like a tomb.

She stepped back from the desk and heard the crinkle of paper beneath her boot. Her mother's wastepaper basket was overflowing, and had loosed several crumpled letters onto the carpet. Her mother, Cordelia thought, must have been sorting mail just before her departure. Curious, she sifted through the envelopes from the trash, and saw that they had come to her from all over the world. From individuals and from universities, from scientific journals, religious publications, and public societies with long and complicated titles, like the American Collective for the Promotion of Humanistic Principles. There were letters from Oxford University in England, from the University of King's College in Halifax, Nova Scotia.

But the content of their messages was largely the same: Elizabeth Clay's work was an abomination. It was unscientific, or satanic. Monsters didn't exist. Or they did, and they must be killed. They were an *aberration* of life, not an expression of it.

She was a nut. She was deluded. She was demonic.

But for some reason, it was the final letter—the one that she had stepped on—that bothered Cordelia the most, perhaps because it was written with such courtesy.

Dear Elizabeth Clay,

Every life has value.
But some have more value than others.

Sincerely,
A Patriot

CHAPTER
9

The church bells were chiming midnight when Cordelia slipped outside to join Gregory in the yard. She found him struggling to keep hold of all three monsters, and so entangled by their leashes it was impossible to say who was pulling whom.

"Ready?" he asked, after Cordelia had helped free him, and taken hold of both Icky and the dragon.

"Ready," she said. But just saying the word made her feel as if she'd swallowed a big fistful of wormroot.

How did she expect to find her father? Where would they even begin?

"So where do we start?" Gregory asked, as though reading her thoughts. "Should we just pick a direction and—Cabal, no! Cabal, stop! Drop it! Drop it!"

Cabal had just made an abrupt lunge for an object halfway across the courtyard. Gregory stumbled forward, and Cordelia hurried to help. By the time she reached him, he had his mouth around something greenish-gray and soggy. She rapped his nose sharply and he yelped, dropping it.

Cordelia reached down and picked up the sodden mass, now half-coated with zuppy drool. Immediately, she recognized the scales of a molting diggle, which Cabal had mistaken for something edible.

That meant the monsters must have passed through the courtyard. Just beyond the gates, she saw a tuft of what looked like werewolf fur, quivering in the chink between paving stones. She stood up, her confidence restored. "This way," she said. "And keep your eyes open."

"What are we looking for?" Gregory asked.

"Signs," she answered. Every creature, her father had taught her, left tracks. Even specters, which had no body, left faint chalky outlines on the surfaces they had touched.

They started off. A heavy yellow fog hung like a curtain in the air and transformed people—and, Cordelia hoped, monsters—into silhouettes. She had never risked venturing outside with a monster, much less three of them. Her father had made it clear, again and again, that it would only put them all in danger.

Things had only gotten worse since the Hard Times: the specter of hunger was scarier than a real specter ever could be, and fear bred cruelty. If people like Henry Haddock thought that only certain *kinds* of people belonged in Boston, what would they think about dragons and zuppies and filches? If newspaper editorials proposed shipping immigrants back across the ocean, where would they propose the monsters be shipped?

And now, Cordelia couldn't shake those ugly words from her head: *Every life has value. But some have more value than others.* She hoped the darkness would give them cover, at least for a little while.

At the corner of Mt. Vernon Street, Cordelia spotted another tuft of bristly gray fur, this time caught in the iron slats of the fence that surrounded Howser Bank & Trust. They hurried on, Cordelia pausing every few seconds to give the filch, who was lagging, a sharp tug. Several blocks later, Gregory gave a cry. There was a large fang embedded in the dirt near Walnut Street, in front of a dressmaker's that had gone out of business. Cordelia thought it might have come from the carbuncle, which had long been suffering from a toothache.

Cabal proved to be enormously helpful. Cordelia's father had once told her that zuppies made great hunters, and Gregory let Cabal off the leash once it was obvious he wasn't going to run away. Cabal kept his nose to the ground, searching for smells, and twice turned up evidence of the monsters that neither Cordelia nor Gregory had noticed.

He unearthed a bit of yellow dungaroo claw from a pile of rubbish at the corner of Joy and Beacon Streets; he found a black-tipped feather of the hufflebottom concealed in a tuft of brown grass in the empty Boston Common, not far from the Frog Pond, sheeted over with thin ice.

"We must be getting closer," Gregory said excitedly.

But on the other side of the Common, the tracks went cold. Cabal sniffed the ground in circles, tail twitching, growing increasingly frustrated. They walked all the way to the harbor before doubling back: there were no signs that the monsters had passed this way, and the wharves, teeming with activity at all hours of the night, were a good place to get caught.

Instead, they went south on Tremont. At the corner of Boylston, Cabal turned up a tuft of fur that *might* have come from a squelch—and might have come from someone's dog. Still, Cordelia pocketed it, and they went on in that direction.

The dragon was so sleepy that Cordelia had to lift him in her arms, and burned a bit of her jacket sleeve when he began to snore. And Icky had obviously had enough. The filch plunked itself down at every occasion, refused to be moved, and hissed when Gregory tried to bribe it with wormroot.

They had reached Chinatown, a part of Boston that Cordelia knew only vaguely. The low-lying tidal flat had been built on top of an old landfill to accommodate the city's expansion, and an influx of immigrants had given the area its nickname.

Cluttered with commercial buildings and old warehouses, it was a home and also a prison: landlords wouldn't rent to immigrants in other neighborhoods, and stores wouldn't serve them. The same year Cordelia was born, the Chinese Exclusion Act had made prejudice the law of the country.

People fear difference, her father had always told her. But that didn't explain why they hated it too.

She had ventured to this side of the city only twice, to visit Mr. Hyung, who fashioned and repaired her father's delicate bridles, or to take tea with the proprietor of Hei La Moon, whose basement Cordelia's father had once exorcised of a ghoul. At night, the wind chased trash through the cavernous streets and carried the scent of rotting fish and seawater from the wharves nearby.

Up ahead, she could see the looming outlines of the old train station, in disuse since the newer station had been built on Utica Street. Here, the streets were rutted with dirt and leaves and piles of things that Cordelia didn't care to identify. The few buildings were narrow and mangy-looking, with broken windows and flaking paint, and had the same sad, abandoned look as starving alley cats. Every so often, Cordelia heard a rustling in the dark—and whether it was the motion of someone unseen, or the wind through dried leaves, she couldn't say.

"It's no use," Gregory panted out. He had long ago taken over Icky's leash; now he strained and tugged, as Icky held on to a gas lamp and let out a howl of rage. "We'll have to stop for the night."

"We can't stop now," Cordelia said, even though her eyes felt grainy with exhaustion and her fingers were numb from the cold. "You said yourself we were getting close."

"That was hours ago," Gregory said. "We don't even know if we're going the right way. Besides," he added, "it'll be light in just a few hours."

He was right, of course. As soon as the sun rose and bullied away all the fog, the streets would be unsafe for travel.

But Cordelia didn't care if he was right. She cared

only that Gregory was ready to give up so soon. She imagined time like a train: every hour that passed whipped her father farther and farther out of sight.

"Fine." Cordelia wrenched Icky's leash away from Gregory. "Give up, if you want to. But I'm going on. I don't need you, anyway." She turned around and began stalking off toward the train station, too angry to care that she had no idea whether she was going in the right direction. If she stopped moving, even for a minute, she, too, might be tempted to give up.

"Cordelia!" Gregory shouted. She didn't turn around. Her heart was pounding. Icky whined and tried to resist, but Cordelia was too angry to care about him, either, and yanked him sharply forward. Half of her was hoping that Gregory would leave her alone. The other half was praying he wouldn't. "Cordelia, wait!"

She heard his footsteps pounding after her. Then he had caught up.

"Listen to me." He got in front of her, so she had no choice but to stop. Cabal, sensing a disagreement, began to run around their feet, barking agitatedly. "I told you I would help and I meant it. But we have to be smart. Your father could be anywhere. You said so yourself. We don't even know if he's still in Massachusetts. We don't even know if he's still in *America*."

"You're just making up excuses," Cordelia fired back,

letting the anger grow in her stomach, coaxing it higher like a flame to warm her. Cabal barked even louder and began pawing at her rubber boots. She nudged him aside with a foot; he immediately started barking again. "You're just scared."

"I'm not *scared*," Gregory said. Two splotchy bits of color had risen in his cheeks. Cabal's barking had reached a frenzied pitch. "But I'm not crazy, either."

Cordelia pushed him. She didn't mean to push him hard, but she did. Gregory stumbled backward and landed on his butt with a loud squelch in a pile of mulchy leaves. His hat tumbled off his head.

Cordelia froze. She had the sudden urge to laugh, but the look on Gregory's face made her heart shrivel up to the size of an ice cube. He looked as if he was trying to make flames materialize from his eyeballs.

Slowly, Gregory got to his feet, still glaring. Without saying a word, he reached down, snatched up his hat, and jammed it on his head, ignoring the fact that it was now coated with mud.

Then he turned and strode off.

Now it was Cordelia's turn to call after him. "Gregory!" The farther he got, the more afraid she became. "Come on, Gregory. I'm sorry. I didn't mean it."

She took a step forward, but Cabal clamped down on her ankle. Cordelia yelped. A low growl worked its way out of the zuppy's throat.

Cordelia frowned. "What is your problem?" She reached down to push Cabal away and caught sight of something small and shiny, glinting in the crevice between two paving stones. A brass button, engraved with a miniature of a wolf howling at the moon.

Cordelia's breath whooshed out of her lungs. She hooked one finger in the crevice, pushing the button up and into her palm. Cabal had gone silent. She realized now what he'd been trying to show her.

Her hand was shaking. The button felt warm in her palm. "Gregory!" she cried out.

"What?" he said sharply, whirling around. When he saw her face, his expression softened. "What is it?" he asked, coming closer.

"This is my father's button," she said, showing him. "It must have fallen off his jacket. It was loose—I was supposed to fix it. I forgot." She felt the sudden urge to cry. What if she never saw her father's jacket again? What if she never saw him stuff his pipe, and sit back by the stove, eyes closed, plucking at his ancient fiddle?

Cyrex familiaris, she recited to herself. The common garden gnome. Lives in burrows underground and makes its diet on the roots of plants. "He must have come this way," she said. "Don't you see? We're still on the right path."

Gregory stared down at the shiny button in her palm. He said nothing. For a second, Cordelia was afraid he would turn around again and keep walking, leaving her alone in the dark.

Instead he said, "We can camp in the station. I've done it hundreds of times. We'll pick up the trail as soon as it's safe to travel again."

He spoke in a funny voice, as if he were all grown up. Cordelia was so grateful she could have hugged him. Instead she just nodded, tucked the button into her pocket, and followed Gregory as he took up the filch's leash.

The rail station crouched ahead of them like a vast and ancient monster, silhouetted by the moon. Gregory steered them toward a side entrance, fortunately unlocked. Inside, it was completely dark, and filled with a faint howling, as if the wind were whipping down unseen tunnels. But it was dry, at least. Cordelia removed the lantern from her bag and coaxed the wick to light. Still, it cast only a dim circle of light on the sprawling stone floor, trod to smoothness by many generations of feet. Even Cabal was being uncharacteristically quiet, padding silently behind her, his eyes glowing like two points of flame.

"Smell that?" Gregory whispered. Cordelia realized she'd been holding her breath. "Coal and boot polish.

Smells like change, doesn't it? Like saying goodbye."

"Do you really spend the night here?" Cordelia asked. "All by yourself?"

"Of course not," Gregory said scornfully. "I always have Cabal with me, don't I? But I don't mind being alone," he went on thoughtfully. "It's other people that get you in trouble. Can't ever trust what they're saying."

"Not everyone is a liar," Cordelia said, a little offended.

"Oh, half the time they don't mean to be," Gregory said breezily. "Like Mrs. Gooding at the Gooding Home. She took me in back in New York, where I'm from. Said she'd found me a home in Boston with a good family to take care of me like I was one of their own. The Wellingtons, their name was. I was going to go to school, and learn to read and write and do arhythmic." (*Arithmetic*, Cordelia assumed he meant.) "And I bet she believed it, too. I bet she thought all the other orphans packed onto those northbound trains were heading to Wellingtons of their own."

Cordelia had heard of orphan trains. But it had never occurred to her that Gregory might have traveled on one himself. For some reason it was her mother who came to mind, belched from the belly of a vast steamship into a wilderness of strange growth and animal cries. Her mother, alone, on the hunt for a different kind of orphan: a fragment of a solitary, shape-shifting specimen, looking to be named, looking for a place it belonged.

"The Wellingtons never came for you?" Cordelia asked.

Gregory laughed. But it was a funny kind of laugh, closer to Cabal's bark. "Oh, they came," he said. "But it wasn't a child they were after. At least, it wasn't a child to care for. What they wanted was a whipping boy. Had me sleeping with the dogs in the horse stables, and I'll tell you they treated those hounds better than me by a mile. At least they got fed on the regular. I had to *earn* my bread and water." He said it matter-of-factly, which somehow made it worse. "Even the horses felt sorry for me. I took Mr. Wellington's whip more than they did."

Cordelia felt a hard squeeze of sorrow and regret. "How did you escape?" she asked.

"Snuck off with the other stiffs when the meat wagon came for old Mrs. Wellington," he said. "I figured what was one body more or less for the counting?"

"I'm sorry, Gregory," was all Cordelia could think of to say.

He only shrugged. "That's old history. I look out for myself now. Well, Cabal and I look out for each other. Isn't that right, boy?" Cabal yipped twice, as if in agreement, and butted Gregory's ankles. "I can trust Cabal, see? He doesn't even *know* any words."

A little way down the hall, they spotted an old waiting room. Gregory leaned a shoulder into the door to open it. Milky moonlight filtered in from a shattered window set high in the wall, illuminating rows of old chairs with ripped-up seat cushions and rusted metal legs. Yellowed newspapers and dried leaves crackled under their feet. Cordelia could see her breath when she exhaled.

Gregory made a careful pile of newspapers, twigs, and leaves in the center of the room, bundling the whole teetering structure together with bits of twine he fished from his pocket. The matchbook in his pocket had gotten damp, and for a terrible moment it seemed that they would have to sleep without a fire. Then the dragon sneezed loudly, expelling several bursts of flame in a row. All of a sudden, a fire was crackling merrily in front of them.

Instantly, Cordelia felt a hundred times better. The light from the fire chased shadows into the corners and cast the room in cheerful brightness. Soon, she was able to unbutton her jacket.

Gregory and Cordelia ate dried jerky for dinner, and two stale sweet buns each. Gregory fed Cabal three drops of blood from the pipette, and Icky licked a half-dozen dung beetles straight from Cordelia's palm. Afterward, Cordelia fed the dragon a handful of peanuts and some dried wormroot and checked to make sure that his splint was still secure.

Sitting next to the fire, in the big room with its walls covered with moving shadows, made Cordelia feel like she was at the very center of a glass lantern. "I'm sorry for pushing you," she blurted out.

Gregory swallowed a big mouthful of jerky. "That's all right." He wiped his mouth with the back of his hand. "I'm sorry for what I said. I don't think you're crazy. If I had a father, I would go looking for him too."

Cordelia thought of her father's button, nestled in her pocket, and the strange note signed by HP. She thought of her home in Beacon Hill, and all the empty rooms where the monsters should have been. She thought of what it would be like to have never had a father at all. She thought of the orphan train, packed with hundreds of frightened children. She thought of those silky words, like the cold, quivering eggs of a lionfish, dropped right inside her eardrum: *Every life has value. But some have more value than others.* She imagined it was someone like Mr. Wellington who had written them.

People like that were the *real* monsters. For people like that, every ugliness that showed in the mirror was just pointing to a danger lurking over their shoulder.

"What if we don't find him?" she whispered. "What if we can't get the monsters back?"

Gregory reached out and squeezed her hand. "Don't worry, Cordelia," he said. "Everything's going to be okay." She was glad he said it, even though she wasn't sure if she believed him.

Gregory lay down on the floor and Icky promptly curled up next to him, though Gregory several times tried to move him off. The dragon slept as close to the fire as he could, every so often exhaling a spark that would intermingle with the other flames and keep the fire burning for hours. Cordelia used her jacket for a pillow and stretched out across the chairs, pulling Cabal up beside her. Even the zuppy felt a little warmer than usual, though his skin was still cool to the touch.

She thought she would have trouble sleeping in a strange place, with a jacket for a pillow, after a poor dinner of sweet buns and jerky. She closed her eyes and saw flames, and then dozens of dragons, beating the air to shreds under their great wings. Then she felt a great wind and was blown backward, into a place of darkness and dreams.

CHAPTER
10

Cordelia woke up with her teeth chattering and ice coating her eyelashes. Cabal was still next to her, his fur clotted with snow. She sat up, pulling on her jacket with trembling fingers.

It was just after dawn. The room was filled with long shadows the color of ash. Sometime in the middle of the night, it had begun to storm. Snow had flowed in through the broken window, extinguishing their fire. Gregory was still sleeping, but his lips were blue and he was shaking underneath his coat, which he was using as a blanket.

The dragon wasn't moving.

Cordelia searched the room for the driest twigs and leaves she could find. She piled it all together, as she'd seen Gregory do the night before. His matchbook was still poking out of his pocket. There were two matches left, and neither one felt dry. She put both match heads together and struck them as one, a trick she'd learned from her father. A small flame sputtered to life. She cupped it carefully with one hand and dropped the matches into the collection of dried twigs and leaves.

For a second, nothing happened. Then the kindling caught, and flames soared upward, and Cordelia could breathe again. She pulled the dragon into her lap, rubbing her hands against his knobby spine, kneading his thick skin, willing him to wake.

Eventually, after what seemed like forever, he opened one eye, and then the other.

After another minute he yawned, revealing a mottled pink tongue.

Cordelia exhaled. She blew gently on the fire, stoking it a little higher, and saw the dragon squirm happily in the warmth.

She was just debating whether it would be safe to try to sleep for a few more hours when she heard footsteps from the hall. Her heart stopped.

"Gregory," Cordelia whispered, as she smothered the

fire with her jacket and stamped out the embers that still glowed. "Gregory, wake up." She took his shoulders and gave him a shake, but he only moaned and swatted her off. The footsteps were getting louder. Someone was heading straight for them.

She seized her bag and fished out the jar of dung beetles, which had the most awful smell, somewhere between dirty sock, spoiled milk, and rotten cabbage. She opened the jar and shoved it under Gregory's nose.

He woke with a start, choking and gagging. "What the—?"

She clamped a hand over his mouth. "Shhh." She gestured to the door with her chin. Outside in the hall, they could hear muffled conversation. Gregory's eyes went wide. Cordelia withdrew her hand.

"First things first, we got to make a clean sweep o' the place," a man was saying in a rolling accent. "Start at the top, head straight to the bottom. There been hobos and crooks makin' a home in these halls for too long. Crafty as rats after dark, they is."

There was a pause. Cordelia thought she heard a snarling sound. Then the man spoke up again.

"Well, you're exactly right, o' course you are. Round 'em up and throw 'em in prison, or ship 'em straight back to where they came from. Turnin' the station into a muck pit, that's what they is."

There were another few seconds of silence, and then the man laughed—a dry, rattling sound, like leaves blown against glass.

"Now, now, don't get upset. There might be one or two juicy morsels for you in it. I'll make sure you get your feed, boy, never you worry. Who's to miss a hand or arm or foot from these filthy little night crawlers? That's one more hand they can't be thievin' with, I say."

Slowly, careful not to make any noise, Cordelia inched across the room and raised herself onto her knees, so that she could peek through the dirty window that overlooked the hall.

A man so old and skinny he looked like a walking cadaver was stomping down the hall, pausing every few feet to kick open doors and make a sweep with his lantern.

With him was the largest, meanest-looking dog Cordelia had ever seen. Its fangs were long, protruding, and webbed with spittle. It kept its nose to the ground, sniffing and snuffling, loud with a wet and excited hunger that made her shudder.

Cordelia backed quickly away from the door, as if the dog might smell her sooner if she remained where she was. She knew it was only a matter of seconds before they were found. There was no chance of escaping through the hall. She looked frantically around the room and saw, immediately, that there was nowhere to conceal them. Then her eyes landed on the broken window, high in the wall, which was still admitting swirling flakes of snow.

The window. With any luck, they'd be able to reach it.

She pointed to the window. Gregory nodded to show he understood. Cordelia shoved the jar of dung beetles back into her bag and put on her jacket. She managed to ease the dragon into one of her larger pockets, ignoring his hiss of pain and simply hoping that his wing wouldn't get further damaged, then swept Cabal up into her arms. He was stiff with fear; it was like carrying a block of ice. Gregory eased Icky onto his back, and Icky looped his long arms around Gregory's neck. Gregory wore the rucksack in reverse, across his stomach.

"Patience, Crunch, patience, m'boy," the man was saying. Cordelia assumed Crunch was the name of the dog—it didn't take much imagination to figure out where he'd gotten the nickname, and she shivered, thinking of the bones in her hand snapping in the dog's jaw. If only the dragon were full-grown.

Gregory wiggled a chair underneath the window. Cordelia set Cabal down and maneuvered onto the chair. If she stretched on her tiptoes, her fingers just grazed the icy windowsill. She would need help. Gregory stepped up next to her, and the chair shifted under their weight. Cordelia's heart stopped. Had they been heard? But the man was still blabbering on. "What's that yer got, Crunch? Picked up a trail? Lead on, lead on, m'boy. Maybe we'll catch a big one."

"You go first," Gregory whispered. He webbed his fingers together and gave Cordelia a boost. She hooked both arms around the windowsill and heaved. For a second, her legs flailed uselessly in the air, and the dragon squirmed in her pocket, and her feet scrabbled against the wall, and Cordelia felt a desperate rush of terror. Then Gregory took hold of one of her feet and pushed, and she managed to swing a leg up and out, so she was straddling the windowsill.

"Cabal," she whispered, perched half in and half out the window. Gregory jumped lightly off the chair, scooped up Cabal, and passed him to Cordelia. It was only a short six feet to the street, which was piled high with new snow. Cordelia launched the zuppy out the window. Icky was next. He was evidently afraid of heights. He whined and clutched Cordelia's chest and hair.

"Sorry, boy," Cordelia said. Down he went. He belly flopped with a *whoompf*, leaving a filch-shaped imprint in the snow when he managed to right himself.

The footsteps were right outside the door. "Somethin' special, is it?" the man was crooning. "Somethin' large and meaty for you?"

"Hurry," she whispered to Gregory. He stood up on the chair, pinwheeling his arms for balance. He stretched a hand up to Cordelia. She wrapped a hand around his wrist. She pulled at the same time that Gregory jumped. The chair toppled and clattered to the ground. For one terrible second, time seemed to freeze, with Gregory's wrist slipping, inch by inch, from her hand, his feet dangling in midair, and the knowledge, heavy and horrible, of what was waiting for them just outside the door.

Then the door burst open and time sped forward.

"Get 'em, Crunch!" the man roared, his mouth wide to reveal blackened teeth, his eyes wide and wild. "Get those filthy, thievin' rats! Slurp 'em up like stew! Crunch 'em like cookies!"

The dog, big as a horse, was halfway across the room in two bounds. Gregory was still twisting in the air like a fish caught on a line, eyes wide, face white and terrified, his fingers just grazing the windowsill.

Cordelia was gripping Gregory so hard she worried that his wrist would snap. Just before the dog lunged, Gregory got his arm over the windowsill. Cordelia leaned back and he rocketed upward as the dog's jaw closed on the space where Gregory's foot had been only a second earlier.

Cordelia lost her balance. Suddenly she was falling,

tumbling backward. She landed in the snow, and the air was driven out of her. She saw a massive bird above her, tumbling through the snow, blotting out the early morning sky. Then she realized it wasn't a bird, but Gregory, who had leapt out of the window after her, coat flapping behind him. He landed next to her and hauled her to her feet. She gasped in a breath. From inside the station came sounds of furious barking, and the man cursing and shouting.

As the snow spiraled through the air and light seeped back into the streets, Gregory and Cordelia took up their monsters and ran.

CHAPTER
11

At last, when they had left the old rail station behind and crossed over the Fort Point Channel into South Boston, Cordelia and Gregory stopped to catch their breath, hands on their knees, gulping in deep lungfuls of thin air. Cordelia's thighs ached from the effort of slogging through the snow. All around them, the streets were concealed underneath a thick layer of powder, as though the world had been frosted overnight. Cordelia's and Gregory's footsteps—and Cabal's, plunging alongside them—were the only markings in the otherwise pristine surface of white.

"What are we going to do?" Gregory asked, jogging Icky a little higher on his back. He toed a bit of snow with his old leather boot. "Fat chance of tracking the monsters through this fluff."

With a sinking feeling, Cordelia realized that the snow had completely buried the track they'd been pursuing. If any further evidence of her father and the monsters existed, it was lost to them now, concealed under four inches of new powder. The wind whipped snow down the empty street.

"I don't know," she admitted. "We've lost the trail."

"We're lost, period," Gregory pointed out.

So they picked a direction at random and started walking. With each minute, the anxiety in Cordelia's stomach grew. The sun had risen behind the gray veil of the sky; the city was coming awake. At least the storm was keeping everyone indoors, dawdling in their heated rooms. But although it was possible to keep to the side streets and alleyways, she knew they could not travel for long without being seen.

The neighborhood grew dingier with every passing block. They skirted a House of Corrections, where all the grimy windows were encased in iron bars. In the distance, a steamer bellied up to the Commonwealth dock. A crowd of new arrivals, exhausted, filthy, and thin from the journey, shuffled down the gangplank toward the inspection checkpoint, which had no windows at all. A newsboy was pacing the corner, huffing on his hands to keep warm. Cordelia and Gregory veered in the opposite direction.

Age-darkened textile factories blackened the sky with smoke. Foul-smelling fumes rose from the chimneys, and Cordelia heard the rattle and cough of distant machinery. She had the sense of eyes watching her from every smoke-clotted window.

They entered a narrow street where the buildings were so close together they squeezed the daylight to a fine, narrow shaft. Cordelia felt a chill move up her neck that had nothing to do with the cold.

"Cordelia?" Gregory said, in a low voice. "You ever feel like you're being watched?" She opened her mouth to say yes. But before she could answer, there was a shout behind them.

"There they are, Crunch! The filthy runners. The scummy filches! *Get them!*"

Cordelia's heart stopped. It was the man from the station. He had followed them all this way.

"Run!" Gregory shouted, and sprinted down the street with Icky, terrified, clinging tightly to his shoulders. Cordelia grabbed Cabal by the scruff of his neck and careened after him, her heart jigging in her throat. Behind her, Crunch was baying furiously, hungry, eager;

she heard the continued roar of his owner's voice—"Get 'em! Get 'em, boy!"—like the noise of a distant ocean.

Gregory had already turned the corner at the end of the street. Cordelia was falling behind. It was her stupid boots—too big for her feet, they risked slipping off at every step. Her lungs and thighs were burning. She skidded around the corner just in time to see Gregory dart down an alleyway.

"Come on, Cordelia!" His voice floated back to her.

She risked a single glance behind her and her heart seized up. Crunch was only twenty—no, fifteen—no, ten—feet behind her, spattering black saliva, his dark gums drawn back to reveal razor-sharp teeth. Even the growrks hadn't looked so terrible.

Cordelia's father had always taught her that no creature was all bad, even the most fearsome-looking ones. *Remember, Cordelia*, he would say, *fear is the only true monster.*

But her father had never seen Crunch. She hurtled around the corner and instantly knew it was a mistake. The alleyway dead-ended at a high brick wall less than forty feet ahead of her. The buildings on either side of her were plastered with flyers and old advertisements, the paper whispering quietly, as if expressing condolences. *I'm sorry,* they seemed to be saying.

Gregory had reached the end of the alleyway already

and was trying unsuccessfully to scale the wall. Cordelia wanted to scream his name, but the word was frozen in her throat. There was nowhere to go. She kept running, even though she knew it was useless.

They were trapped.

Crunch slid around the corner, snarling, and snapped at the air just three feet behind Cordelia's heels. She could feel the hot blast of his breath. Gregory, she saw, was now trying to wrestle open the door to a shuttered Print Works. The wood splintered and groaned, and she felt a surge of hope. If she could just make it—just a dozen more feet—if they could just get inside, behind that heavy door—

She slipped. One second she was upright, and the next second she felt her foot fold in the big rubber boot and she was toppling forward. She reached out to steady herself on a wall but managed only to tear away a paper flyer. Then she was plunging face forward into the snow, and Cabal went spinning out of her grip, tumbling a deep channel through the snow before coming to rest near Gregory's feet.

Cordelia tasted blood and realized she must have bitten the inside of her cheek.

Everything hurt. Gregory was shouting to her, but her brain felt fuzzy and she couldn't make out what he was saying. She tried to push herself onto her hands and knees, but a sudden clamping pain went all the way from her foot to her knee, and she sprawled back into the snow. She twisted around to look and felt a white-hot spark of terror.

Crunch had her by the foot. Even through the thick rubber, she could feel the sharp points of his teeth, and Cordelia knew that if it weren't for her boot, he would have sunk his jaw straight through her tendons.

Panic fueled her, cleared her mind. Now she knew what Gregory had been yelling so frantically: *Look out! Look out!*

Gregory was shouting, "Get off her! Leave her alone, you big brute!"

She managed to flip herself onto her back and was blasted by the stench of the dog's breath, like the butcher's shop in mid-July. She didn't want to think about what he'd been eating. She aimed a kick at Crunch's nose with her free foot. But the angle was wrong, and she barely made contact. He kept gnawing at her boot, wrestling it off with his mouth. She felt it slipping . . . slipping . . .

A large white blur soared over her head. Cabal. The loyal zuppy launched himself on Crunch's back, claws out, howling with outrage. But Crunch shook him off easily, as if he were no larger than a fly. Cabal landed a few feet away, somersaulting through the snow, until he thunked nose-first against the wall. He stood up, dazed, and collapsed again.

"Cabal!" Cordelia tried to reach for him but Crunch yanked her, hard, and she thudded onto her back as pain ripped through her. Her boot slipped off, taking her sock with it, so Cordelia's bare toes were left wiggling in the air. Crunch tossed the boot away, grinning raggedly, his mouth dripping dark slobber on the snow. Cordelia's heart stopped: it was over.

Crunch lunged. Instinctively, Cordelia closed her eyes. She would be gobbled up like a dog biscuit. Crunch would chew her from her ankles to her eyeballs.

"Leave . . . her . . . *alone!*"

She heard a loud *thwack*, followed by a whimper. When she felt no thick fangs sinking into her thigh— when she heard no bones snap—she opened her eyes. Crunch had drawn back, shaking snow from his whiskers. As she watched, a second snowball whizzed past her shoulders and whacked Crunch directly between the eyes.

"Hurry, Cordelia!" Gregory bent down and straightened up in one fluid motion, and let loose another volley of snow, his arm moving so fast it was a blur.

Cordelia grabbed her boot, from which her sock was still dangling limply, and scooped up the still-dazed Cabal. Floundering through the heavy powder, snowballs still whipping past her face, she dashed toward the door to the old print works, which Gregory had managed to open. She hurtled in through the darkness of the doorway. Icky was perched on a piece of old machinery, gnashing his teeth, chittering agitatedly. Gregory plunged in after her.

They slammed the door and Cordelia collapsed against it. A second later, she felt the wood shudder, as though punched from outside by a giant fist. She could hear Crunch snarling on the other side of the door. There was a pause, and then the frame rattled again and nearly sent Cordelia sprawling.

Crunch was trying to break through the door.

"A little help, Gregory?" she shrieked, as the door flexed behind her again and wood splintered and showered her with sawdust.

"Give me a second." Gregory had disappeared into the dark. There was a tremendous creaking and the groan of something heavy on the floorboards, and a moment later he reappeared, pushing one of the vast metal printing presses, his face beaded with sweat. With Cordelia's help, he shoved the iron machine against the door. Almost instantly, the wood stopped rattling. Cordelia could finally breathe. They could still hear Crunch growling and snarling outside, but she knew there was no way he could make it past the door now.

"This way," Gregory whispered, taking the hand that wasn't holding her boot. They threaded through the old print shop, past a network of rusted machinery, hunched like slumbering beasts in the dark. A bit of light filtered in through cracks in the ceiling, illuminating old tools encased in cobwebs and paper trampled to pulp on the ground. Everything was covered with a thick layer of dust, so their footsteps were muffled.

At the back of the shop was a creaky spiral staircase that wound up into a narrow, musty attic. There, Gregory located a small trapdoor in the ceiling. Balancing on a trunk, and using a broken broom handle for leverage, he managed to pry the door open, revealing a drop-down ladder, a soft white square of pale sky, and the brick peak of a nearby chimney. Snow drifted gently through the opening and landed on Cordelia's cheeks like individual kisses. She suddenly felt so happy, she wanted to shout.

Icky, a natural climber, was up the ladder first. Gregory followed him, holding tight to a whimpering Cabal. Cordelia pulled on her sock, now soaking wet, and wiggled her foot into her boot. She tucked the dragon deeper into her pocket before making the climb to the roof.

Now, a vast portion of Boston was spread out in front of them, dazzling inside a fine white blanket. Cordelia could see the entirety of South Boston, bracketed by two harbors, and the narrow Fort Point Channel that separated their spit of land from Back Bay. Horses trudged carriages sluggishly through the snowy streets. Smoke threaded the air from hundreds of chimneys. The snow was at last letting up, and long fingers of sunlight broke through the clouds in the east.

Gregory let out a long crow of satisfaction. "Yahooo!" His voice bounced from roof to chimney and back. He started trudging toward the edge of the roof, which closely abutted its neighbor. They could make it across the whole of Boston without once touching the ground.

When Cordelia removed the dragon from her pocket, her fingers brushed against the flyer she had accidentally ripped from the wall. She must have unconsciously stuffed it in her pocket. Now, smoothing out the page, she saw the words emblazoned in red across the top of the page. Suddenly, she felt as if she'd opened her mouth and swallowed a snowball.

COME SEE SERGEI'S

NEW AND IMPROVED

WORLD-FAMOUS MONSTER CIRCUS,

FEATURING THE WORLD'S MOST HORRIFIC

AND HORRIFYING MONSTERS!!

AFFORDABLE FAMILY FUN!

UNION SQUARE PARK, NEW YORK CITY, 8 P.M.

EVERY DAY BUT SUNDAY

NOT SUITABLE FOR CHILDREN UNDER AGE SEVEN

(PLEASE DO NOT FEED OR TICKLE THE MONSTERS.)

NO PUBLIC TOILETS

"Gregory, look." Cordelia read the advertisement aloud, placing particular emphasis on the words *Monster Circus*. Gregory's eyes grew wide.

"Do you think . . . ?" he asked, in a hushed voice.

Cordelia read the words over and over, as if her father's face might come floating out of them. She had never heard of anyone else keeping any monsters, much less enough monsters to make up a *circus*. Could the circus have stolen them from her father, eager for a new moneymaking attraction?

It was the best lead they had. The only lead they had. She took a deep breath. "It can't be a coincidence," she said. "The trail led us here."

Gregory let out a long whistle. "Well, then," he said, pivoting his hat to the right, "I guess we're going to New York."

CHAPTER
12

ABSOLUTELY NO ANIMALS ALLOWED. The sign, written in very large red letters, was posted just outside the vast glass doors of the new South Station.

Gregory and Cordelia were tucked away across the street in the shadowed alcove of an abandoned warehouse, watching the flood of men and women entering the train station, and debating what to do. Technically, neither Icky nor the dragon was a pet—but she didn't think it likely that the train station would make an exception for monsters. And then there was Cabal, who was both a monster *and* a pet. If she and Gregory waltzed into the crowded train station with a filch, a zuppy, and a dragon, they were likely to cause mass confusion, if not panic—even if the dragon was only a baby, the filch too cranky and old to do any harm, and the zuppy more likely to lick a person to death than to bite.

"The dragon can stay in your jacket pocket, just so long as he doesn't breathe too hard," Gregory said.

"But that still leaves Cabal and Icky to deal with," Cordelia said.

Gregory tried, unsuccessfully, to coax Icky into the rucksack. It was no use. Icky was too big, and he squirmed too much. The whole effect was of a leather satchel that had grown furry limbs and come alive, which was, Cordelia expected, just as likely to gain unwanted attention as a regular filch.

Cordelia chewed on her lower lip. Across the street, merchants were hawking clothing and trinkets in front of the station doors. Carriages clattered loudly up and down the street, the noise of the horses' hooves like the constant chatter of gigantic teeth. Women in vast skirts, and men in tall hats and long overcoats, swept through the glass doors.

Everyone seemed busy and preoccupied and Important. Their faces all seemed to blend together, as if Cordelia were actually watching one image endlessly repeated. . . .

An idea blinked in her brain. Of course. They must *blend in*.

If they looked just like everybody else, then no one would single them out for trouble. It was like her father always said—people were afraid of monsters only because they were afraid of *difference*.

"Stay here," she commanded Gregory. She darted out into the street before he could stop her and quickly zigzagged around the maze of carriages and horses, crossing over to the wooden stalls arrayed with bits of fabric, hats and buttons, leather gloves, and cheap pocket watches. It didn't take her long to pick out what she wanted: a pair of dusty spectacles, a floppy brown hat, a cheap woolen shawl, and a soft green scarf. She dug in her pocket for the leather purse she had taken from the biscuit tin and paid with a dollar.

"You picked a funny time to go shopping," Gregory said, when she made it back across the street.

"Don't be a blister," she said, unfurling the scarf. "None of it is for *me*. Don't you see? We'll disguise the monsters so they'll *blend in*." She reached for Cabal, and—with several expert twists—cocooned him in the scarf, so that only his eyes and the very tip of his nose were showing. "Congratulations," she said, passing the wriggling bundle to Gregory. "You're a big brother now."

Gregory made a face. "He makes a pretty ugly baby."

"Shhh. He'll hear you." Cordelia kneeled so she was eye level with the filch. As though sensing her intentions, Icky scooted away, but Cordelia was too quick. She threw the old woolen shawl over his shoulders and knotted it quickly at the throat. Before the filch could resist, she had jammed the hat over his head and rammed the spectacles onto his small, sloped nose. She stood up again, admiring her work. From a distance, Icky might easily pass for a very small, very old person—especially since the shawl constrained his movements, and he could only hobble along.

"What's he supposed to be?" Gregory asked, squinting.

"That's your grandfather," Cordelia said, feeling pleased with herself. "So you might as well show him some respect. Now come on. Let's go."

Cordelia moved confidently into the street and Gregory, carrying Cabal, trailed behind her. Icky limped forward, gnashing his teeth, doing a very convincing impression of someone's ill-tempered relative. Cordelia felt a small thrill: they waltzed by a patrolman and passed easily into the train station. No one spared them even a glance, and Cordelia had to scold Gregory only once for tucking Cabal under his arm like a football instead of carrying him the correct way.

Inside the station, Cordelia paused, overwhelmed. The air vibrated with voices and footsteps. The vast space was teeming with people: women in long skirts and laborers crowded the platforms, where enormous trains sat steaming and blazing like mythic monsters. Wandering families, tented in threadbare clothing, sat among the heaps of paltry belongings, waiting for the chance to sneak onto one of the freight trains. Policemen prodded vagrants awake with their billy clubs and chased off hungry orphans hanging big-eyed near the vendors hawking day-old pastries for twice what they were worth. Many rail lines had gone out of service due to Hard Times, and half the ticket windows were shuttered or papered over with newspapers pointing blame for the Hard Times on everything from greedy factory owners to foreign plots.

If Cordelia squinted, she saw not individuals but dizzying patterns of color breaking apart and rearranging themselves. It occurred to her, standing there, just how vast the world was, and just how many people it contained. She wished herself momentarily back in her house, with its familiar curves and corners, its worn green carpet and burbling faucets.

"There's a train for New York at half past eleven," Gregory said. He was staring up at an enormous board and proudly indicated the departure, written in big wooden letters. He seemed oblivious to the noise and the rush all around them. Then Cordelia remembered that he had already made the journey from Boston to

New York, but in reverse.

"We need tickets," Gregory said. "Have you got any money?"

"Enough," Cordelia said. She hoped. Gregory pointed out the long line of people in front of the ticket booth. Cordelia gripped Icky's hand and tugged him forward, speaking out loud in a high-pitched voice. "This way, Grandpa. Almost there now . . ."

"Two tickets for New York City, please," Gregory said, as soon as they reached the ticket booth.

The man behind the smudgy glass window had a face that reminded Cordelia of the species *Salientia groticus*, or venomous toad. "Round-trip or one-way?"

Gregory looked at Cordelia and shrugged. Her stomach squeezed up. She had no idea how long it would be before they could return to Boston. "One way," she said, fingering the coins left in her purse. The words sounded very final.

The man scowled, which only furthered the impression of a toad that had soaked too long in the water. "What about 'im?" he said, jerking his chin toward Icky.

Cordelia's stomach sank. She hadn't considered that she'd be forced to pay Icky's way. "Please," she said softly. "We don't have very much money."

"He's old," Gregory piped up. "He might even croak before he gets to New York."

Icky gnashed his teeth in Gregory's direction. Luckily,

the man behind the ticket counter didn't notice.

"Three people, three fares," he said. "That's nine dollars." Cordelia paid, feeling sick to her stomach, and received three printed tickets in exchange. They had only two dollars left, and a handful of change.

But she forgot to be anxious when she saw the train: a large, gleaming bullet of metal, fitted with shiny brass rails and tasseled curtains, snorting billows of dark smoke like a full-grown dragon. The gears and the wheels, the smoke and steel, the bell that was even now ringing, and the conductor calling for passengers to board—it all spoke of adventure.

Magic, the train seemed to say. There is still magic in the world.

Inside, the corridors were very narrow and thickly carpeted, so that it felt like walking across a surface of pudding. Cordelia and Gregory found an empty compartment fitted with two small cushioned benches, and curtains to draw across the doors so they would not be visible from the hall. As the train chugged away from the station, Gregory unrolled Cabal from his scarf so the zuppy could stretch his legs. Icky had grown fond of his disguise, it seemed, and was happily gnawing on a corner of his shawl, every so often adjusting his glasses on his nose with one long, crooked finger. Cordelia extracted the dragon from her pocket and let him hop onto her lap.

"But as soon as the conductor comes along, back in the pocket you go." The dragon bared his tiny fangs. "No arguments," she said, and rubbed his knobby spine with a thumb.

Cordelia leaned back as the train picked up speed, rolling them past a blur of streets and buildings, until the individual shapes became a mere wash of gray. At last they were on their way.

But Gregory wouldn't settle down. He paced. He crossed and uncrossed his legs. He picked at the sleeves of his coat. Every few minutes, he got up and moved to the doors, twitching apart the curtains to peer into the hall.

"Will you stop jumping around like a grasshopper?" Cordelia said finally. "It's making me nervous."

"I can't help it." Gregory closed the curtains again. "I keep thinking . . . I don't know. It's stupid." He sat down, then almost immediately stood, then sat again.

"What's stupid?"

He leaned forward, his eyes ticking nervously from left to right, as if he expected someone might be hiding behind the cushions of the benches, ready to jump out at them. "I keep feeling as if we're being followed," he whispered. "My stomach is all knotted up."

Cordelia had had that feeling too—of being observed and watched from afar. But she shook her head. "You're probably just hungry," she said.

"Maybe," Gregory said. He looked unconvinced, but at least he stopped fidgeting, and he accepted the jerky and the seed bread that Cordelia gave him from her rucksack.

Outside the train, the buildings melted away and became brown hills, spotted with snow. They saw blue skies, and clouds like puffs of white smoke. Cordelia pressed her nose to the glass, which misted under her breath. She imagined, for an instant, that she saw her mother's face drawn in the curves of a nearby cloud.

Your mother is everywhere now, her father had once told her. She's with the magic. She's in the ground and the air and the trees, and in every creature, seen and unseen. He'd meant it to be comforting, not understanding that Cordelia didn't want her mom to be everywhere. She wanted her to be one place: with Cordelia.

Don't worry, Mom, she thought up toward the clouds and the sky. I'll find Dad. I'll get our monsters back. Everything will go back to the way it was.

She drew a heart in the condensation from her breath and watched it evaporate to nothing.

CHAPTER
13

The Limited train to New York was one of the fastest in the country and would arrive at Grand Central Station in exactly six and a half hours. Cordelia soon fell asleep to a view of the rich patchwork of snow-dotted fields outside her window, and awoke with a start to discover that the sun was already setting behind interwoven threads of a reeking industrial smoke: they had reached the outlying sprawl of bone-boiling factories and tanneries just north of New York City. Gray buildings, gray smoke piping from gray tin chimneys, gray horses—even gray people moving, hunched, along the tracks. Cordelia's stomach tightened.

"Gregory." She reached out and toed him. He had fallen asleep with his head tilted back against the leather seat and his mouth open. He came awake with a start. "We're here," she said. "New York." She added, "Wipe your chin. You've been drooling worse than a *Mattahorn salivus*."

Gregory blinked sleepily. "A what?" he said, yawning.

"Never mind," she said. "Just do it." He dragged a hand across his chin and adjusted his hat, which had begun to gravitate backward.

The train came to a halt just north of the city, and its furnaces were extinguished. A team of horses rigged to the front carriage would tow the train into the underground tunnels that fed into Grand Central Station. Cordelia was almost relieved when they descended into a darkness that swallowed up the view.

Soon, the tunnel belched them out at the platform, and once again, the train lurched to a stop. This time, everyone disembarked, and there was a sudden chaos of shouting and pushing, a blur of luggage loaded and unloaded. Cordelia had a hard time getting ahold of Cabal, who had gotten used to their little compartment and dodged her neatly when she tried to come at him with the scarf. Finally, she and Gregory teamed up to snatch the zuppy, and with a few twists and turns of the fabric, Cordelia had once again turned him into something resembling a furry, squirmy little baby. Cabal, however, refused to play along this time and managed to extract both front paws. Cordelia could only hope that no one would notice that their baby brother had very sharp claws.

Wrestling the dragon back into her jacket proved even harder. He swiped at her and even let out a burst of flame, singeing the lining of her pocket.

"Bad dragon," she whispered fiercely, once she had him tucked away again. A bit of smoke puffed up from her pocket in response.

As they joined the crowd of passengers shuffling out of their compartments, unloading luggage and flowing onto the platform, Icky toddled along happily, baring his nubby teeth at anyone who stared at him too closely. They merged with the vast river of people coursing along the platform into the waiting room. There, Cordelia realized they might have gone undetected even if they had been accompanied by a full-grown dragon and a whole menagerie of monsters. Everyone in New York City, it seemed, was too busy to take notice of anyone else.

The air was sooty and filthy and swelteringly hot, despite the winter chill that seeped in from the platforms. It reeked of machine oil and human sweat. But the energy was thrilling. Cordelia could practically feel it, humming in the air all around them. She quickened her pace as they approached the doors that let out onto the street. Her father was here. The monsters were here.

She, Cordelia, would rescue them.

Suddenly Gregory whipped around with a little cry. "What is it?" Cordelia said.

He shook his head, frowning. "That feeling again," he said. "Like a ghost licked my neck. We're being followed, Cordelia."

Cordelia turned around and scanned the teeming crowd. She saw no one. That is, she saw a vast number of people—a big-bosomed woman screeching at a porter, a mother trying to herd along her four children, men in greatcoats crowding the entrance to a beer saloon— but no one who looked familiar, or seemed to have any interest in Cordelia and Gregory.

"Stop it," she said sternly, turning back to Gregory. "It's all in your head. You'll only drive yourself bonkers."

"What if Crunch is still after us?"

"Crunch is back in Boston, picking splinters out of his snout." She didn't want to admit that even thinking about the dog made a zip of fear go up her back.

Gregory didn't look convinced, but at least he shut up about being followed.

Outside, their breath condensed in little clouds on

the cold air. But at least it wasn't snowing. Though it had been years since Gregory had lived in New York City, he still remembered they had to go south to reach Union Square, and the numbered streets made it easy to know their direction. Soon, Cordelia was warm enough to unbutton her coat.

She felt a spike of nervousness. New York City was even larger than she had imagined. Her father had told her stories of his infrequent trips to the city: of the towering mansions on Fifth Avenue, with dozens and dozens of rooms patterned with marble, and electric lights that burned through the night; of the bridges like vast metal insects that spanned the snaking East River; of the museums and theaters, and the crowds of sheep that grazed like earthbound clouds in Central Park; of the pickpockets and vandals, the criminals and con artists.

But his stories could never have prepared her for the sheer *scale* of the city, and its great avenues lined with towering buildings, dazzling hotels where white-gloved attendants carted masses of luggage through revolving doors, cabs and carriages, buggies and broughams, whole boulevards filled with nothing but shops. Every street sizzled with light and electricity, holding the night at bay. High street poles threw cones of electric light down onto the sidewalks, and theaters threw it up into the sky. The whole city, it seemed, was under construction: rickety towers of scaffolding encased half-finished buildings that flowed ever northward. Private homes loomed behind massive iron gates, and all of their doors—positioned high above the street, at the top of sweeping stone staircases—reminded Cordelia of upturned noses.

And yet . . . even here Cordelia heard the whispers of Hard Times. She heard it in the shushing of the stray newspapers tumbling the streets, shouting headlines of injustice. She heard it in the mournful cry of the peddlers and the newsies, in the angry signs plastered on darkened storefronts. *No vagrants. No immigrants. No Jews.* It was a bright city, and a hard one, scaffolded in steel and stone and greed.

One thing was clear: it was no place for monsters.

As they got closer to Union Square, flyers identical to the one Cordelia was keeping in her pocket sprouted on the streetlamps and scabbed the store windows, until at last they were moving through a forest of paper, words emblazoned across every surface. There were flyers posted on top of flyers, so that the words overlapped, creating new nonsensical phrases: *COME SEE NO CHILDREN. AFFORDABLE FAMILY MONSTERS. WORLD-FAMOUS TOILETS.*

Cordelia's pulse picked up. She could hear tinny notes of circus music, and the swell of excited conversation—like the sound of distant waves, breaking against the wharves. Soon, she caught a glimpse of a purple silk tent in the distance, puffed above a fringe of dark trees like a hugely swollen grape.

"What is it?" Gregory said. He was trying to hold Cabal back from a bloat of garbage piled in the gutter, and the rats that had nested inside it.

"What do you think? The *circus*." Cordelia grabbed hold of Gregory's arm and steered him across the street, where the view was even better. "There. See?"

But Gregory didn't answer. He had stopped, rigid, like a hound dog that had just caught wind of a squirrel.

"Do you . . . do you smell that?" he said in a hushed voice.

Cordelia took a deep breath and nearly fell to her knees. The smell was heaven. It was better than heaven. It was . . .

"Popcorn," she breathed.

Unconsciously, they began to speed walk, and then to jog, and then to run. They cut into the park, following the footpaths through the barren trees and scrubby patches of grass. Icky squeaked in protest and did his best to keep up, tripping every few feet over his shawl and landing in a pile of furry limbs and fabric.

Now Cordelia could make out a voice shouting to the crowd, "Step right up, step right up! For the amazing and the awe-inspiring! The marvelous and the manic!

The wondrous and the one-of-a-kind!"

Then the footpath whipped them through the trees and emptied them out in front of the circus, and Cordelia lost her breath.

An enormous crowd had assembled in the square. Cordelia had the impression of looking at an ever-shifting ocean of fabric and color. She had never seen so many people in her whole life. Shoeless beggars shouldered up next to women in fur-trimmed coats and diamond earrings; kids hung on the streetlamps and swarmed the frozen fountain, craning for a better view. Jugglers and magicians moved through the square, causing the crowd to ripple and part, again like waves; there were fire-breathers and sword-swallowers, men with tattooed faces, and tall women on stilts waving colorful banners. The tent loomed over all of them, like some kind of enormous violet mushroom, dwarfing the crowd in its shadow.

But the thing that struck Cordelia speechless, and made her heart rocket into her throat and her tongue stick to the roof of her mouth, was the monster.

In front of the gaping mouth of the entrance, a very small man with an oversize head was standing on several overturned milk crates, and gesturing grandly with a brass-topped cane to the very angry-looking growrk crouched in the cage beside him.

Her growrk.

One of them, at least.

"Ladies and gentlemen, boys and girls, step right up and don't be scared . . ." The barker's voice rolled out over the crowd, but Cordelia's heartbeat was throbbing so hard in her ears, she could barely make out what he said.

"It's him," she said, elbowing Gregory.

"Who?" His eyes lit up. "Your father? Where?"

"No. Him." She pointed to the cage. "The growrk!"

"The *what*?" Gregory stretched onto his tiptoes, as a woman in a huge, bustled skirt shuffled to the left, blocking their view.

She gripped Gregory's arm. "Gregory, *that's our growrk.*"

He squinched up his nose. "How can you be sure?"

"What do you mean? I can tell. I *recognize* him. See those spots on his nose? I remember those spots." In truth, Cordelia didn't recognize the growrk—she had never paid any attention to whether the adolescent growrk had spots on his nose or not. But she was sure she was right. "We have to get into the circus. We have to rescue the growrk, and the rest of the monsters, and find my father."

Even now, as she spoke, two enormous tattooed men emerged to wheel the cage back into the tent.

"Expertly done, don't you think?" trilled the woman in front of Cordelia. "They look so *real*. It gives me goose bumps!"

"The circus is all about deception, m'dear," said the skinny man next to her. Cordelia didn't have time to puzzle over what they meant.

Just then, the carnival barker crowed that the circus was open for business, and the crowd surged forward.

"Ladies and gentlemen, boys and girls, step right up, step right up!" The carnival barker didn't so much speak as open his mouth and let a thunderous stream of words pour out of it. Cordelia wondered how he didn't faint from lack of oxygen. "This is a show you just can't miss, a spectacle of epic proportions, a pageant of wonderful and weird . . ."

"Come on," Cordelia said to Gregory. She at last judged it safe to put Cabal on a leash; he was squirming so badly, Gregory could barely keep hold of him, and everyone was too busy shouting and jostling to get into the circus to pay him any mind. In her pocket, she could feel the dragon furiously batting his wings, mimicking the rhythm of the music floating out of the tent.

They pushed forward toward the entrance. It was slow going. She was blocked at every turn by a new kaleidoscope of people, a knot-like formation of elbows, arms, and backsides. Gregory trailed her and Icky struggled to keep up, holding up his long shawl like a skirt to keep it from getting trampled. Cabal darted back and forth, scooching under legs and around wagon wheels, yipping with excitement, as though urging them forward.

Slowly, the crowd poured into the tent, thinning, like a wide river being filtered into the mouth of a narrow bottle. As they drew closer to the small man on his milk crates, Cordelia noticed canvas banners strung up on either side of the entrance, painted with the images of various attractions the audience could expect inside: trapeze artists and elephants, clowns and jugglers, and—her heart leapt—a giant feathered bird that must surely be her baku; a shaggy beast with a ferocious scowl and multiple eyes that looked just like Tomkins, their Atlantic Firr; and a wrinkled dungaroo she would have known anywhere as Alexander I. Or perhaps Alexander II. They were twins, after all.

All the monsters were imagined in vivid detail, roaring or gnashing their teeth, while a painted audience cowered in terror. An absurd bit of artistic liberty: the baku were notorious cowards, and the dungaroo twins were as sweet as twin kittens. But Cordelia supposed it was how they justified the cages.

The square was nearly empty by now. Cordelia and Gregory were among the last dozen people jostling to get up to the entrance and take their place in the tent.

Cordelia was so focused on the painted images on the banners, and the idea that her father might be near, that she sped right past the man on the milk crates without even pausing.

"Not so fast."

Suddenly Cordelia received a hard blow to her chest. She was thrown backward and landed on the ground, directly in the remains of a trampled tea cake.

"Hey." Gregory helped Cordelia to her feet and glared up at the man. "What'd you do that for?"

The man on the milk crates aimed his cane at Cordelia in an accusatory fashion. She rubbed her chest, which was still smarting, and backed up a few inches, in case he decided to whack her again.

"That'll be one dollar and thirty cents, please," he said, in a prim voice. He jerked his chin at Icky. "Plus fifty cents for grandpa." When he was speaking at a normal volume, he sounded very different. He rapped his cane against the uppermost milk crate, across which was written: PRICE OF ADMISSION: 65¢). 50¢ ADMISSION FOR SENIORS OVER 65 AND CHILDREN UNDER 3.

Cordelia swallowed. That would leave them with barely any money to return to Boston.

"Before I go gray and the elephants lose their tusks," the man added, tapping a highly polished shoe. When he smiled, Cordelia saw his teeth were yellow and very crooked. "The show is about to start, dearie. Are you in, or are you out?"

"In," Cordelia said firmly. She reached into her pocket, carefully avoiding the dragon, and felt for her little leather purse. It wasn't there. She reached into a second pocket, thinking she must have put it elsewhere. Nothing but the spyglass and a pair of pliers.

The man tapped his shoe faster and faster. "Well?"

"Give me a minute," Cordelia said. She was unloading pockets desperately now, wiggling and tugging, patting and poking. She turned out all her tools, and the funny stone she'd found in her mother's library and forgotten about. No purse. She must have looked like her skin was crawling with fire ants.

"What's the matter?" Gregory whispered.

"My purse," she whispered back, casting a nervous glance up at the small man. He was glaring harder and harder at them every second. Even his mustache curdled into a look of disapproval. "I can't find it."

"You must have it," Gregory said. "I saw you put it in your pocket."

The man's foot was now tapping so rapidly, it was practically a blur. His face was the color of an eggplant. "You're wasting my time, girlie. And if there's anything I hate in the world—besides balloons and broccoli—it's wasting time!"

"You hate balloons?" Gregory said, frowning.

"Be quiet, Gregory," Cordelia said. "Please, sir. Just one more second . . ." She shoved her hand into the first pocket again, ignoring the nip of the dragon's teeth, thinking she must have simply failed to feel the coin purse. Her fingers went to the very bottom of her pocket.

And through it.

Her heart sank all the way to her shoes. She stood there, wiggling her soot-covered fingers in the empty air. The dragon had burned a hole straight through her pocket, and her little purse, with her remaining money, was now lost somewhere in the vast city of New York.

"Gone," she whispered.

"What?" Gregory cast a nervous glance at the small man on the milk crates. "What—what do you mean?"

"The money." Cordelia's voice was hoarse. The pavement underneath her feet was turning slowly. "I lost it."

The man leaned down, so his unpleasant face floated directly above Cordelia's, like a moon—so close she could smell the wax on his mustache, and the sickly sweet cologne clinging to his clothing. "If you don't have the money, young lady," he said softly, "kindly do me a favor and GET OUT OF MY WAY!"

"Please," Gregory jumped in. "We've come all the way from Boston. . . . We've *got* to get into that circus."

"No money, no ticket," the man sniped. "It's as

simple as that." He pivoted neatly and rapped his cane twice against the milk crates, summoning the two tattooed giants who had earlier taken charge of the growrk. "Tomaseo! Alonzo! It's showtime, please. If you would be so kind as to take over the box office . . . ?"

The two oversize men, with arms as thick as tree trunks and coils of veins in their tattooed necks, came stomping toward their master obediently. They hooked him under the arms and lifted him cleanly off the milk crates, setting him gently on the ground. Standing, he was even shorter than Cordelia. She attempted to plead with him one last time.

"You don't understand," she said, following as he trotted toward the entrance of the tent. "It's really very important. It's urgent. If you could just make an exception—"

He spun around and shoved the point of his cane directly into the soft cavity of her chest. "No exceptions! Can't you read?" And once again, he whacked his cane against one of the milk crates, across which more words were scrawled: *NO REFUNDS, COMPLAINTS, BACKTALK, OR BALLYHOO! AND ABSOLUTELY NO EXCEPTIONS!*

"But—"

"No buts!" he screeched. *Whack.* The cane went down to another line of text, these words painted so minutely that Cordelia had to lean in to read them.

No buts, either.

A great tide of frustration welled up in Cordelia's chest as the man once again turned his back on her.

"Please!" she cried out. She was desperate—desperate and angry. Her monsters were here. Her *father* was here. "Five minutes—just give us *five minutes*—"

"Enough!" The man's eyes glittered dangerously. "I have been very fair, and very kind." Cordelia opened her mouth to protest; he had been neither of those things. "But you've abused my patience long enough. Tomaseo? Alonzo? See that these two troublemakers stay far away from my circus—or I will call the police and have them thrown into jail for trespassing. Good day to you both."

And with a short bow, the man disappeared into the darkness of the tent, swishing the fabric closed behind him.

CHAPTER
14

Cordelia heard the roar of applause within the tent, and the tinny rise and fall of horn music. The circus had begun, and she and Gregory were left outside, among the pastry peddlers and candy sellers, among the trampled hay and the discarded waste of the crowd.

The square was empty now, except for the cart-pushers and market stalls and a dozen raggedy children, barefoot and filthy-faced, who swarmed the streetlamps, straining for a glimpse of the action inside the tent, and trying to pocket food from the stalls when no one was looking.

"We need to get into that tent," Cordelia said. But no sooner had she taken two steps toward the entrance than the oversize men, Tomaseo and Alonzo, reached for identical leather whips hooked to their belts. Cabal let out a squeak of fear and Icky ducked behind Gregory's leg.

"It's no use, Cordelia," Gregory said, raising his voice so he could easily be heard by the two giants. At the same time, he gave her a wink. "We'll never get into the circus without a ticket. We might as well give up."

Cordelia, catching on, heaved a sigh. "You're right," she said loudly. "I guess we'll just head home."

They turned around with exaggerated care and began to move off in the direction of the train station. Cordelia, feeling the eyes of the two giants on the back of her neck, was careful to hang her head and look disappointed. Gregory walked with as much dignity as he could muster, considering the fact that he had a filch clinging to his lower leg.

At the first opportunity, however, they hid behind a fruit stand.

"We'll have to circle around," Gregory said, prying Icky from his leg with difficulty. "Maybe there's a way to sneak into the tent through the back."

Cordelia stretched onto her tiptoes, ignoring the rows of pears glistening like jewels on their cloth beds, candied apples shining with caramel drizzle, the smell of fresh-brewed cider, and the terrible whining of her stomach. She spotted a narrow path through the maze of carts and food stalls. If they were careful, they could circle around the tent and stay completely out of sight of the beastly men guarding its entrance. And maybe Gregory was right. Maybe there was another way in.

Cordelia turned to him. But before she could open her mouth, a loud scream made her jump.

"Thief! Scandal! Villainy! Murder!"

An old woman with a nose like a fishhook and a very large wart trembling in the middle of her forehead stepped out from behind the towering stacks of candied apples, wielding her broom like a sword.

"Get away from my apples, you miserable little monsters!" *Swoosh*. She struck out with her broom. Cordelia ducked to avoid getting a face full of bristles. "Keep your sticky paws where they belong!" *Swoosh*. She aimed another blow in Cordelia's direction. Cordelia rolled aside as the broom thudded to the ground not an inch from her stomach, releasing a cloud of dirt.

"This way, Cordelia!" Gregory hooked a hand in her collar and dragged her forward as the old woman continued hopping and waving her broom, shrieking insults in their direction.

Cordelia and Gregory ducked under the enormous body of a glossy Clydesdale and snuck around a vendor roasting chestnuts over an open flame. Safely distanced from the old woman and her stiff-bristled broom, they slowed to a trot, scanning the purple tent for entrances or gaps in the stitching where the panels were bound together. They might, Cordelia thought, sneak *under* the tent—it was lashed to a stake in the ground every few feet, leaving plenty of loose fabric between tethers—if it weren't for the guards stationed at every entrance, all of them equally as large as Tomaseo and Alonzo. Perhaps, Cordelia thought, they came from the same family of giants?

On the west side of Union Square, the street had been closed down to accommodate an overflow of props, wagons, trunks, and performers' trailers. Gregory and Cordelia ignored the temporary fence that had been erected around it, and vaulted easily into the jumble of old costume racks, rusted washbasins, and empty cages.

Almost immediately, they heard the shrill of a woman's voice and ducked behind a painted wagon. A dozen feet away, a bearded lady was combing and braiding her hair, singing absentmindedly, and missing nearly every note. A man roughly Cordelia's height was standing in a barrel full of water, wearing nothing but a child's bathing suit, washing himself, seemingly oblivious to the cold. Two acrobats dressed in spandex costumes were practicing their routine. A sword-swallower was massaging his jaw muscles, a sword staked next to him in the dirt.

And just behind *him*, a vertical sweep of light pushing between tent panels marked an unguarded entrance to the circus.

"What do we do now?" Gregory whispered. "You think we can get past them?"

Cordelia shook her head. "*We* can't," she said. "*I* can. You're going to cause a distraction." Her stomach gave a nervous lurch. But they had come this far. She had to be brave.

"Uh-uh, no way." Gregory shook his head so emphatically, his hat nearly slipped off his head. He righted it quickly. "I'm not letting you go in there alone."

"Please, Gregory," Cordelia said. She didn't want to confess that she also didn't want to venture into the tent alone. "It's the only way."

Left and right went the hat while Gregory debated. "Fine," he said at last. "If you say so. You want me to dance a jig? Start a riot? Juggle sausage links?"

"Easier," she said. "All you have to do is light a fire." Cordelia cracked a smile for the first time in what felt like ages, reached into her pocket, and passed Gregory the dragon. Gregory took Icky, too, but insisted that Cabal stay with Cordelia "for protection," and even though the zuppy's attacks resulted only in enthusiastic and aggressive face-licking, Cordelia didn't protest.

With a quick look in either direction, Gregory eased into the open and Cordelia quickly lost sight of him. She stayed where she was, concealed behind the painted wagon, and waited. Every so often, she heard an appreciative roar from the crowd. She wondered whether her growrks were being forced to turn somersaults, whether her pixies were dressed up in costumes to make them look like fairies—an absurd idea, and one she knew the pixies would detest, since they despised their fairy cousins and made a point of cannibalizing them whenever they could.

She thought of wild living things kept in cages, and the ugly letter her mother had received. She thought of Henry Haddock, and the man whose belongings he'd shaken into the mud. And for a second she wished she could simply will herself back home, and shut the doors forever on the world and its fears and cruelty.

But she couldn't. Her father needed her. The monsters needed her—to save them all from the *real* monsters.

Even though the wind had picked up, carrying with it the promise of snow, Cordelia was sweating. Her thighs had begun to cramp. She felt like she'd been crouching forever. She shifted a little, trying to give her legs some relief, scanning the market for signs that Gregory was carrying out the plan. So far, nothing.

"Come on, Gregory," she muttered. If he didn't hurry, she would lose her chance.

Then she spotted it: a fine thread of smoke unspooling a short distance away between the trees. At first it was no wider than a finger. Then it was a black branch, growing quickly to the sky, and suddenly there was an eruption of shouting, the drumming of footsteps, and overlapping cries of "Fire, fire!" Cordelia said a quick prayer that Gregory had successfully escaped—otherwise, he'd be trampled by the crowd.

"Ready, Cabal?" she whispered. Cabal was rigid, tense, ready to run. All the performers rushed to give aid. The man toweling off in the bathing suit began hauling the barrel full of his old bathwater in the direction of the flames. The bearded lady trotted over to help him. The acrobats shouted competing advice, until the sword-swallower threatened to skewer them both if they didn't stop squawking.

The tent was left momentarily unguarded.

"Now!" Cordelia said. Instantly, she was up and running, staying as low as she could, while Cabal darted beside her, kicking up miniature clouds of dirt. Her heart was pounding so loudly she couldn't hear anything, not the continued sounds of shouting, not the crackle of fire. At any second, she expected to feel a thick hand on her back. She expected the terrible tattooed men to appear before her, for someone to shout and command her to stop.

She was almost there. She was so frightened she could hardly breathe. Any second now she would be caught, she would be thrown into a cage beside the growrk.

But then she was at the tent, and no one had cried out, and no one had stopped her.

Cordelia risked one glance behind her. Gregory had done his job to perfection. A hastily collected pile of straw and old newspaper was burning cheerily, and a crowd had gathered to try and put it out. Now the sword-swallower was trying to extinguish the flames with an old blanket but had only succeeded in stoking them higher. The bearded lady had somehow managed to overturn the barrel of water onto both acrobats.

No one was looking in Cordelia's direction at all.

Quickly, with no further hesitation, she lifted the tent flap and slipped into the circus.

CHAPTER
15

Almost immediately, Cordelia saw her mistake: the performers' entrance fed straight into the wings, where only a single sweep of curtains divided her from the stage, and a trio of clowns stood awaiting their cue.

The first thing Cordelia noticed, as she stood blinking, waiting for her eyes to adjust, was the sawdust. It coated everything and hung in the air like a veil, shimmering in the darkness. It muffled the sound of her footsteps and coated the inside of her nostrils and gummed the back of her throat.

Cabal sniffled beside her. His pale nose quivered, as it did when he was about to sneeze. Cordelia whispered, "Don't even think about it."

Cabal swallowed.

The music was louder inside the tent, and she could hear a booming voice, which she recognized as belonging to the awful short man with the mustache. Slowly, shapes began to assert themselves in the gloom: crates upon crates stuffed with straw, overturned stools and discarded costumes, old trunks and ladders. She even saw a hot-air balloon, deflated, lying among a tangle of ropes, like a vast squid that had been lashed to the ground.

She began picking her way through the labyrinth of junk. Cordelia felt like she was on a ship, moving through vast swells of gray: furniture, half-built set pieces, and stacks of plywood loomed on either side of her. She saw no cages, though—that meant the monsters must be kept somewhere else. At least the sawdust made it easy to move quietly. . . .

The sawdust!

Now that she was paying attention, she could make out the shuffling tracks of performers, footsteps big and small.

And paws. Though the tracks were confused and blurry, she could definitely make out various animal—or monster?—tracks leading off to the left. She followed them, scanning the ground, listening, always, for signs of disturbance—a voice, a footstep, a sniffle or snort, as her father had taught her to do.

She came around an old set piece designed to look like a pirate ship and saw them: crouched in the half-gloom, massed in their cages, miserable and silent. Monsters. Dozens and dozens of monsters.

Tears welled up in her eyes and she didn't bother to wipe them away. In the low light, she could just make out the jointed flippers of the hufflebottom and the scaly spine of the bulliehead.

She had found them.

There was no sign of her father, but she quickly put that worry aside. She would free the monsters—she wasn't sure how yet, but she would—and worry about her father afterward.

"Don't worry," Cordelia whispered, drawing close to the hufflebottom's cage. "I'm here."

To her surprise, the hufflebottom drew back even farther into the liquid pool of shadows on the far side of the cage. She could just make out the gleam of her dark eyes and the curve of her noble beak.

"It's me, Cordelia," she said, threading her fingers through the cage bars. The hufflebottom adored Cordelia and liked to playfully nip at her fingertips. In fact,

Cordelia had not cut her own fingernails in ages. The hufflebottom happily did it for her. But today the hufflebottom remained still, silent, and watchful, and did not approach. Cordelia felt a momentary pull of anxiety. Could this be a different hufflebottom?

No. The coincidence was too extreme. Huddled silently in their cages were diggles and squinches, and hufflebottoms and goblins: monsters rare and dangerous and difficult to procure.

Perhaps—and the thought made fury well up inside her—the monsters had been mistreated. Traumatized. Perhaps that was why they were so frightened and seemed not to recognize her.

Cordelia withdrew her hand from the cage. "I'm going to get you out of here," she said. Each cage was encircled by a rusty chain and padlock; she jiggled one and found it sturdy. No hope of snapping it, then.

From the stage, the ringmaster's reedy voice floated back to her. "Ladies and gentlemen, boys and girls, children of all ages . . . now for a finale that will leave your ears spinning and your eyes ringing!"

The crowd roared with applause as the band swelled and the drums pounded out a frenzied rhythm.

Cordelia's palms began to sweat. Still standing in front of the hufflebottom's cage, she crouched down so she was eye level with the padlock. It looked as if it took a standard key; it was likely that a single key opened all the cages. But she didn't see a keyring anywhere.

She turned out her pockets, sorting through her tools to see if any might be useful. The old metal spyglass had come partially apart in her pocket, revealing innards of glinting copper coil.

She ripped off a wire and bent it in half, so it formed a narrow metal pin. Carefully, she inserted the wire into the old lock and began pushing and twisting. One time, she and her father had tracked a pair of highly contagious ghouls to the locked basement of a hat factory. She had watched him pick a lock with her mother's hairpin.

Then, as now, it took only a moment of wiggling before she heard the lock release with a small, satisfying *click*. She let the chain thud down into the sawdust and slowly swung open the cage door, wincing as it whined on its hinges. But the music and clapping were so loud, no one could possibly hear.

"All right, girl." Cordelia stretched a hand toward the hufflebottom, who was still trembling in the far corner of her cage. "Come to me. You're all right. It's going to be all right."

The hufflebottom didn't move. Cordelia swallowed a sigh.

"Stay here," she instructed Cabal. Then she stepped into the cage and inched forward toward the terrified monster, still keeping one hand outstretched. "What's the matter with you?" she whispered, when the hufflebottom drew back even farther, until it was pressed against the bars of the cage. "It's *me*."

She finally got a hand around the hufflebottom's collar. Cordelia heaved, and the hufflebottom slid forward a few inches, scrabbling desperately for purchase with her heavy hind legs and letting out a panicked whimper that Cordelia had never heard before.

"Why," Cordelia panted, "are—you—making—this—so—*difficult*?" She grabbed a dorsal flipper, hoping for a better grip. . . .

And it snapped off in her hand.

Cordelia reeled backward, horrified. But the hufflebottom didn't even seem to notice. She just sat there, blinking at Cordelia with her big brown eyes.

Brown eyes . . .

Cordelia felt her chest go hollow, as if she'd once again been whacked with the ringmaster's cane. Hufflebottoms had gold eyes—everybody knew that. She peered more closely at the broken flipper. Now that she was paying attention, she saw small seams of glue, where the scales had been attached to a kind of flexible fabric. She saw stitching where small rents in the wing had appeared and been mended.

A fake. An *illusion*.

She moved once again to the hufflebottom-that-wasn't and ran a hand over its remaining dorsal flipper, her fingers easily detecting the leather harness where it was attached. *Snap*. It came right off. Cordelia saw now that its "beak" was actually a curved wooden horn, painted to resemble the real thing, affixed to the animal's face by a nearly invisible wire. She extracted a pair of clippers from her pocket and snipped the wire.

The false beak tumbled into her hands, revealing the perfectly ordinary face of a perfectly ordinary sheep. Just as quickly, the rest of the illusion was revealed: the heavy casts molded around its legs, to give the impression of huge hindquarters. The garish dye, which turned its fleece a golden color.

Cordelia stumbled backward out of the cage, practically dizzy with disappointment. The sheep opened its mouth and let out a single, plaintive bleat, as though in apology. She stumbled down the long line of cages, as the music swelled and crested and the audience shrieked with pleasure. To her, it sounded like a prolonged scream.

Fakes. Fakes. Every one of them—fakes. Lions decked out with horns and long snake tails made from rubber hose, so that they resembled griffins. Deer fitted with shaggy fur coats so they could pass as elusive slints. An enormous iguana wearing paper wings. A dog dyed white, fitted with false fangs, meant to be a zuppy. Again, it was the eyes that gave it away. They weren't red, like Cabal's, and they certainly didn't glow.

They were fakes, frauds, cardboard cutouts. She'd been wrong about the monsters. Her only real clue had proved pointless. And they'd wasted time.

She was so consumed with disappointment, she didn't hear the approaching footsteps until they were only a few yards away. Someone—no, *two* someones—were moving through the backstage area and headed directly toward her.

"I'll skin her alive! I'll feed her to the lions! I'll poke her eyes out with a pencil! This is the second time she's missed her cue in a week . . ."

She recognized at once the voice of the ringmaster, who had greeted them so unpleasantly and refused them entrance into the circus. For a second, she was paralyzed with fear. She couldn't see him—yet—but from the sound of his voice, he was just on the far side of a tumbled-down series of wooden crates.

"I'm sure she was distracted, sir—there was some kind of disturbance outside—Richie and the others were helping—"

"I don't care if there was a purple elephant dancing a jig on top of a poker stick! I'll have them all fired . . . I'll have the twins use them for shotput practice . . . I'll stuff them into cannons and shoot them into space!"

Cabal caught hold of Cordelia's pant leg and pulled. Cordelia unfroze. Quickly, she hurried back up the line of cages, calculating, estimating. Could she hide? She glanced behind her and saw the dark silhouette of the ringmaster's top hat bobbing between the crates.

She made a sudden, desperate decision. Grabbing Cabal by the scruff of his neck, she climbed into the fake hufflebottom's cage, which was still hanging open, and backed with him into the shadows. The sheep, now rid of its disguise, blinked lazily at her. Cordelia squeezed herself into the darkest corner of the cage, holding Cabal in her lap, making herself as small as possible. She prayed that the lights would stay off long enough for her to make an escape.

"Missing the finale . . . outrageous . . . what am I paying them for, I ask you?"

"Well . . . sir . . . to be fair . . . you *aren't* paying them. . . . It's been weeks since you paid any of us. . . ."

"And why should I? You should be grateful I don't ask *you* to pay *me*! A useless, layabout lot . . . absolutely sickening . . . you should all be ashamed . . ."

Cordelia held her breath. The voices were closer, closer . . . nearly on top of her now. And then she saw them: the ringmaster stumping along with a walking stick, and a willowy blond woman beside him, wearing thick glasses and carrying a tall sheaf of papers. They were less than a dozen feet away and had only to look to the right to see Cordelia, huddled in the darkness next to the sheep that had once been a hufflebottom. *Keep walking,* Cordelia thought.

Please keep walking.

It was as if her silent pleas had the opposite effect: the ringmaster stopped directly in front of the cage in which she was hidden. Cordelia's heart froze. She remembered that the padlock and chain were now coiled in the sawdust. Had he seen them? Cabal quivered in her arms and she squeezed him tightly.

"Now look what's happened. My boot's come untied. Go ahead, girl. Make yourself useful."

"Useful, sir?"

"You don't expect me to tie my own laces, do you? Are you a stage manager or a slug?"

The woman mumbled an apology and kneeled down to tie the ringmaster's shoelaces, pinning her papers to her chest by tucking them under her chin. Soon they were moving off again. Cordelia exhaled. The ringmaster's continued complaints, and the stage manager's stuttered responses, drifted back to her. Once they were a little farther, she and Cabal would make a run for it. . . .

Cabal was still trembling like a leaf in her arms. She gave him another reassuring squeeze, but he only shook harder, as if he were the victim of his own personal earthquake.

Too late, she realized that he wasn't shaking from fear.

He was holding back a sneeze.

Before she could clamp a hand over his nose, the shaking became a full-body convulsion, and Cabal let out the longest, loudest sneeze she had ever heard. Like a cork exploding from a bottle, he shot backward, hit the cage bars, and landed on his nose with a small whimper. The sheep let out a surprised bleating sound.

All the lights came on at once.

Cordelia sprang to her feet and plucked Cabal up and tucked him under her jacket. Panic made her bold. She burst from the cage, no longer worried about keeping quiet . . .

And fell.

She lost her hold on Cabal. Her arms pinwheeled through the air. The wind was knocked out of her as she went sprawling. Rolling over onto her back, gasping for air, she caught a glimpse of a pair of highly polished boots and the brass-topped cane that had tripped her. The ringmaster's face floated above her like a bloated red sun.

"Not so fast, girlie," he said. He smiled, showing all his teeth.

CHAPTER
16

Sometime between the moment the ringmaster directed his henchmen to rope her into an extremely uncomfortable chair, and the moment he directed them to drag her—now trussed up like some enormous Christmas roast—into the very center of the ring, Cordelia decided she *hated* the circus.

The performance was now long over, and the audience gone. There would be no one to hear her scream. Her only hope was Gregory. Maybe, just maybe, he'd gotten away. . . .

But almost as soon as the idea sparked to life, the ringmaster snuffed it out.

"And now for the final act." He rubbed his hands together, addressing an invisible crowd. "The *extremely* final act. For this, we will require *two* volunteers. . . ."

Hearing a muffled shout, Cordelia turned—at least, she turned as much as she could, given that her hands had been lashed to her small wooden chair. She let out a small cry as one of the massive tattooed men dumped a dazed Gregory onto the chair next to her. A large purple bruise, the exact shape of a giant fist, was visible on his forehead.

"Did they hurt you?" Cordelia whispered.

"I'm all right." He tried to touch his forehead. One of the giants—Cordelia thought it was the one called Tomaseo, but it was difficult to tell, since even their faces were covered with tattoos—wrenched his arms behind his back and restrained him. "He's got a wicked left hook."

Before Cordelia could whisper a word of comfort, the ringmaster trumpeted, "Ladies and gentlemen, step right up, step right up, and don't be shy." This he addressed to the circus performers, many of them still in their stage makeup, and sweating paint under the bright lights. "Believe me, you won't want to miss it."

At the ringmaster's bidding, the performers shuffled a little closer. Cordelia knew they must be afraid of him. She read fear in the stoop of an acrobat's shoulders, and the nervous twitch of a contortionist's fingers; in the fiddling of the bearded lady with her beard and in the frantic jumping of the sword-swallower's Adam's apple.

Still, she wondered whether they weren't also simply eager to enjoy a show of their own—relieved, at last, to be on the audience side of the performance.

Sweat tickled her lower back. She could hardly breathe. It was as if her chest were full of sawdust. She felt like one of the squelches, nesting among the flames of the old chandelier, or like the lionfish, finning around and around a bathtub.

Thinking of the monsters she had sworn to get back, she felt the stirrings of unease. Were the monsters happy? Or did they, too, feel trapped, imprisoned by Cordelia and her father for their comfort?

"Sergei, sir. We snatched another one." Another tattooed giant came stomping across the ring, trying to keep his grip on a large, wriggling bundle Cordelia recognized as Icky. "Careful. He tried to chew my hand off."

"Violent, is he? Here. Hand him over, we'll show him how we treat troublemakers at Sergei's World-Famous—ahhhh!"

Sergei had just succeeded in disentangling Icky from his disguise. Immediately, Icky bit down on one of the ringmaster's fingers. Sergei let out a wicked howl and drew back, clutching his hand. Cordelia felt a surge of affection for the old filch—she couldn't believe she had ever despised him, just because he rarely bathed and his breath smelled like an old swamp.

Icky lunged for the ringmaster again, but the giant reached down and conked him over the head. Gregory shouted and Cordelia cried out. Icky tottered in a circle, then sat down hard, shaking his head. The giant raised a fist, as though to strike again.

"Wait!" the ringmaster shouted. "Wait." Still cradling his hand, he took a careful step forward. His eyes gleamed in a way that reminded Cordelia of a particularly nasty cat contemplating a large plate of sardines. "I don't believe it," he murmured. He crouched in front of Icky, so they were practically nose-to-nose. Cordelia wished Icky would take a bite out of the ringmaster's mustache, but Icky was still dazed.

After a moment, the ringmaster straightened up.

"Alonzo," he said, "You have, for once in your miserable, thickheaded life, done something wonderful."

"I have, sir?" The giant scratched his head, which was quite bald, with one sausage-like finger.

Sergei seemed to be swelling, as if an invisible pump was filling him with air. His chest practically doubled in size. "Do you know what that is?" He pointed a finger at Icky.

There was a short pause. "A boy, sir?" Alonzo ventured at last. "An ugly, hairy, smelly boy?"

Sergei clapped the giant on the elbow, which was the

only portion of the man's body he could reach. "That, you pin-brained lug, is a *filch*." His eyes fell on Cordelia and his lips narrowed to a thin smile. "A monster," he said for effect.

The performers began to murmur.

"It's a clever trick, sir." A scowling clown plucked Icky up from the ground and held him at arm's length. "I'm guessing invisible wire and putty. Papier-mâché and mechanical bits. The best work I've ever seen."

"It's not a trick," the ringmaster said quietly. His eyes gleamed coldly, like knife blades. "These monsters are real. Of flesh and blood, bone and feather. *Real*."

There was a short pause. Then somebody coughed.

"There's no such thing as monsters," one of the acrobats squeaked. "That's just an old story."

"It's no story," another one said. "It's a *plot*. A foreign scourge . . ."

"What if there are more of them?" the bearded lady shrilled. "What if it's some sort of invasion . . . ?"

"It's not natural, I'll tell you that. It's not right. We don't truck with that kind of thing here in New York City. . . ."

"We should turn them over to the police. . . ."

"We should turn them over to the president. . . ."

The clamor of angry voices only whipped Cordelia's thoughts into uselessness. She wanted to explain, to defend, to tell the performers that monsters were as natural as anything else that grew or walked or swam or slithered. To remind them that nothing existed that didn't belong, that the monsters posed no threat, any more than the giants did to the paying audience that came to ogle them. She wanted to point out that monsters were monsters only because we'd deemed them too strange, too ugly, and too different to be called something else.

But she couldn't work the words out from behind the weight of her panic.

The stage manager let out a sudden, piercing shriek. "The boy's got something in his jacket. It's . . . squirming, sir."

Gregory struggled and kicked as once again, Tomaseo leaned over him. There was a shriek. Tomaseo drew back, cursing, as a cloud of smoke drifted up to the ceiling: he was holding the dragon upside down, by his claws, and his fingers were raw and red.

"The little blister burned me," he said. But no one paid any attention to his complaint. They were staring, wide-eyed, at the dragon in his meaty hand. Cordelia saw wonder in their eyes, and fear.

Her stomach sank. She felt the strong pull of hopelessness. Her monsters had been taken. Her father was still missing. It was all her fault.

She had failed.

"Impossible," Sergei whispered. His eyes were so

large, Cordelia was sure they would come loose from his head and roll away. The way he licked his lips, as if the dragon were a large piece of chocolate cake, made her insides shiver. "A dragon . . . a real dragon . . ." His eyes were shining and his mustache quivered. "I've been waiting my whole life for this. Oh, yes. Ever since I was a boy I've dreamed . . . and now the time has come. I'll be rich. Rich beyond the wildest imagining!"

He reached for the dragon and then, thinking better of it, dropped his hand, leaving the monster to flutter and writhe in the giant's hand, letting out occasional streams of pale fire, screeching and flapping both wings. Even though the dragon was obviously healing, Cordelia felt nothing but regret. Who cared whether the dragon had two perfect wings, if he spent the rest of his life in chains?

Sergei looked once more to Cordelia. Now, alongside the expression of calculated greed, she saw also a gleam of fear. "How is it," he said softly, "that two miserable little termites have possession of three real monsters? Where did you find them? How did you steal them?"

"We didn't steal them," Cordelia said. "They belong to us."

"Stupid girl," Sergei spat. He leveled his cane at her. She jerked her head back a few inches to avoid getting poked in the nose. He spoke quietly, so no one else would hear. "Monsters belong to no one. Tell me the truth."

"I *am* telling you the truth," she said. "We found them. They're ours." She wished she could grab the awful man's cane and conk him over the head with it, or reach into her pocket for the pliers and pluck out his eyebrow hairs one by one. But her hands were tied too tightly.

"Correction," he said smoothly. "They *were* yours. They're mine now." He lowered his cane. "Tomaseo! Alonzo! Find a cage for the newest members of our monster collection. And take care not to bruise them, or I'll have you both shipped back to the colony where you belong. Wait!" Before the giants could move, he held up a slender hand. "On second thought, let's deal first with our . . . *uninvited* guests. Have Frederick bring out the lions." With this last pronouncement, he smiled thinly at Cordelia and Gregory, his eyes gleaming with malice.

"What—what are you going to do to us?" Cordelia stammered.

"My dear, I'm not a monster. Forgive the expression," he added casually, as Icky screeched. "*I'm* not going to do anything. I'm merely going to turn the lions loose for exercise. I should warn you, however, that they're very hungry—and they've grown particularly fond of the taste of naughty children."

Gregory struggled against his ropes. "Let us go! You can't do this to us!"

"Oh, but I'm afraid we can." Sergei's eyes winked

cruelly. "It's right in the Rules and Regulations, Article Seven. 'Anyone found in violation shall be subject to trial by lion.'"

"Trial by lion?" Gregory repeated. "But—but—"

"'Article Eight'!" Sergei interjected, before Gregory could say any more. "'Anyone who objects to trial by lion shall be subject to trial by piranha, and anyone who objects to trial by piranha will be subject to trial by boa constrictor, and anyone—'"

"We get the point," Cordelia said. She didn't want to hear any more.

"You heard the girl," he said, with a satisfied smirk. "Bring out the lions. Let the trial begin!"

The stage lights came up all at once. Embedded all along the periphery of the ring, so bright they were practically blinding, they turned everything beyond the stage area—the seats, the backstage, the curtain rigging and masses of equipment—to a dark blur. Cabal began barking furiously.

Cordelia squinted. There. A shadow passed in front of the lights. She blinked, desperately trying to clear her vision. Two shadows.

Cabal's barking reached a fever pitch.

The shadows came farther into the light and became solid. Cordelia's heart stopped. Lions.

There were two of them, lean with hunger, but still much larger than she had expected—about double the size of a full-grown growrk. Their necks were bowed under the weight of metal collars, but still their eyes roved hungrily over the group and landed on Cordelia and Gregory. A man stumbled along behind them—the lion tamer, Cordelia assumed—his feet nearly lifting off the ground as he struggled to restrain them.

"Frederick has a way with the lions," Sergei said, gesturing casually to the man, who was sweating and straining, tugging on leather lead lines to keep the lions from lunging. "He's been with me since the very beginning and has suffered only one accident. Isn't that right, Frederick?"

"Actually, it was five accidents, sir," Frederick panted out. He held up a hand and Cordelia gasped. He was missing all his fingers.

Sergei waved dismissively. "Who needs ten fingers, anyway? Brutus, one of our most successful acrobats, has no arms at all!" He leaned closer, so Cordelia was forced to endure the warm stink of his breath. "Don't be afraid, little dear. The lions are cuddly as kittens with good old Frederick. Of course, they've never been especially fond of strangers. . . ."

Sweat trickled down Cordelia's forehead and pooled in her eyes. She blinked rapidly. She was desperately trying to remember something, *anything*, that might help her. There was a special variety of gremlin known as the leonines, or lion breed, because of their tawny facial hair and sharp, curved teeth. Though typically quite aggressive, they were hopelessly soft about violin music and would curl up and weep over a single melody, even one very badly played. But no. That would be of no help. Leonines weren't related to actual lions. Besides, she didn't have a violin and couldn't play so much as a scale even if she did.

"You can't do this!" Gregory cried. He was trembling so badly, his chair rattled. "You'll never get away with it!"

Sergei ignored him. "How refreshing," he said, clasping his hands behind his back and rocking back and forth on his heels, "to be a spectator for once. We do get so terribly sick of performing. Shall we take our places in the audience, my friends? I believe the show is about to begin."

Beyond the stage lights, Cordelia spotted another shadow growing, massing, resolving into a shape. She squinted. Could it possibly be *another* lion? The lights made it so hard to tell.

Sergei was still prattling away. "Let's take a seat in the front row, shall we? On second thought, perhaps the third row is better. Cleaner, perhaps, should any body parts attempt to make a quick getaway . . ."

It was not a lion. Whatever was moving—whatever was coming—was much, much bigger than a lion. An elephant? But no . . . it was even bigger than that.

Sergei, whose eyes were glued to Cordelia and Gregory as if he were going to be the one to eat them, hadn't yet noticed. "It's a shame, in a way, that the rest of the audience has already gone. It would have made for a brilliant encore. Ah, well . . ."

The blond stage manager coughed. Her face was very white. "Um, Mr. Sergei, sir . . . I—I think you ought to have a look at this."

"Not now," he snapped, without so much as glancing in her direction. Now the Thing was swelling upward and outward, casting an enormous shadow that was rapidly eating up the ground. "Go on, Frederick. Unchain the lions. Let's get on with it."

"Sir, I *really* think—"

It was too late. Frederick the lion tamer turned the lions loose, just as the shadow solidified and became more than a shadow.

Became, instead, a balloon.

A giant, purple, hot-air balloon—the same one that Cordelia had noticed earlier, deflated and bunched limply on the ground—was now hugely swollen with air, bobbing and bumping through the tent, seemingly unmanned. *Crash.* It collided with the footlights, and there was a faint explosion of glass. Suddenly everyone was screaming. The air smelled like smoke.

Kicking up sawdust, crashing through set pieces, the balloon came, like some single-eyed cyclops let loose.

Everything was chaos. Everyone was screaming, running, toppling chairs and circus equipment, while the frenzied lions lunged and snarled, and the balloon continued to thunder forward, roaring hot air, thumping on the ground and lifting off again, rebounding from the tent ceiling before dropping. One of the lions knocked Sergei off his feet. Tomaseo, in his fear and shock, released the dragon, who went screeching, flapping through the air, his broken wing hindering his flight, barely dodging the balloon as it came crashing toward them. Loose papers spun through the air like snow stirred up by the wind.

Cordelia and Gregory were still tied to their chairs. "Help!" Cordelia shrieked. "Somebody, help!"

No one paid them any attention. And suddenly one of the lions was in front of Cordelia, grinning, revealing the long slick of its pink tongue. She kicked out and struck its nose. It drew back, but only for an instant.

"Cordelia!" Gregory screamed, as the lion opened its enormous mouth and moved as if to swallow her.

But at that moment she felt a blast of heat against her wrists, and in an instant, her hands were free. The soft rush of leathery wings beat against her back, and she realized that the dragon had been the one to save her. He had burned away the ropes—just in time.

Before she knew what she was doing, she reached out and shoved her thumbs against the lion's nose. His eyes went wide; his body seized; and then he sneezed. The force of it toppled her backward in her chair. She landed on her back with a loud *oof.*

"Not so fast." Before the lion could lunge again, Gregory, free now of his bindings, sprang up and grabbed hold of the lion's tail. Cordelia fumbled to untie the ropes around her ankles. The dragon swooped through the air above them. He was flying lopsided, struggling even to stay aloft, exhausted and still hindered by the splint.

"Watch out!" she shrieked, as the lion, pinned in place, roared and made a go at the dragon circling his head. The dragon dodged, but clumsily, and came crashing to the ground. Cordelia scrambled to her feet and dove for him. She managed to scoop him into her arms and rolled to safety just as the lion shook Gregory off and pounced.

She coughed out a mouthful of sawdust. Her eyes were blurry with grit. The dragon panted against her chest, his small tongue lolling from his mouth. His damaged wing was trembling. Where was Gregory? Where was the lion?

She blinked the dust from her eyes and her vision cleared. She screamed.

The hot-air balloon was coming down—directly on her head.

CHAPTER
17

Cordelia could do nothing but squeeze her eyes shut and wait to be squashed into splinters. She felt a tremendous pressure, a blast of wind and air, as if a giant were bringing down its fist. She heard Gregory calling her name and felt the dragon beating his wings against her like a second heartbeat.

And then: nothing.

The expected impact never came.

She opened her eyes. The balloon had stopped with its basket hovering barely two inches above her nose. Cordelia was almost afraid to move—afraid that if she did, the balloon would collapse on top of her and she'd be flattened like a pancake.

Gregory's face appeared in the narrow gap between the ground and the hovering basket. Behind him, she could still see the threshing of feet and paws.

"Give me your hand!" He had to shout to be heard over the chaos.

Keeping the dragon pressed to her chest with one arm, she reached out with the other and grabbed hold of Gregory's outstretched hand. He pulled, and she slid out from underneath the basket. As soon as she did, like magic, a rope ladder appeared over its side. Gregory and Cordelia exchanged a look.

She hesitated for only a second. It was their best—their only—chance of getting out of the circus alive. "Follow me!" she cried. She began climbing one-handed, and Gregory, who had Icky riding his back like a furry backpack, started up after her.

Cordelia had nearly reached the lip of the basket when she heard barking and froze.

She twisted around. "Cabal!" she called down to Gregory. To her horror, she saw that the balloon was moving again, lifting off the ground inch by inch. "We forgot Cabal!"

Cordelia scanned the crowd, her eyes jumping over the screaming stage manager, who was perched on a chair; and the bearded lady, who had gone into a clean faint; and Sergei, who was defending himself from one of the lions, using an overturned chair as a shield. The other lion had turned on his trainer and was chasing the poor fingerless Frederick around in circles, nipping at his coattails. Cabal was cowering at the edge of the ring, barking furiously and dodging Alonzo's attempts to retrieve him.

The balloon was picking up speed. They were hurtling toward the exit: a small bright triangle beyond which she could see blue sky and sunshine.

"Hit the brakes!" Gregory yelled, leaning heavily against the ladder, as though he might stop the balloon from going forward. "Stop!"

"There are no brakes!" Cordelia pried the dragon from her chest. "I'll be back for you," she whispered, and heaved him over the lip of the basket, trusting that he would be safe.

Then she jumped.

She soared over Gregory's head, hit the ground, and rolled to her feet. She sprinted for Cabal, leapfrogging over a toppled chair, zigzagging through the panicked performers, ignoring Gregory's frantic shouts.

Cabal saw her coming and let out another volley of barking. Alonzo spun around, his face contorted with fury. He staggered toward Cordelia with a roar. Before he could grab her, she dove, sliding on her stomach through the gap between his legs. Cabal was in her arms, wiggling, licking her face. She vaulted to her feet just as Alonzo reached for her again. She felt a sharp tug and nearly lost her balance; but then there was a ripping sound, and as she catapulted forward, several tools clattered into the dust. Alonzo had ripped out one of the pockets of her jacket.

She didn't care. She was running, holding Cabal to her chest, breathless. The hot-air balloon was nearly six feet off the ground now, moving higher and faster with every passing second. Soon it would barrel through the tent exit and go floating to the sky, taking Gregory with it. And she, Cordelia, would be lost.

"Hurry!" Gregory was still clinging to the rope ladder. "Run!"

At the same time, Sergei spotted her. "Stop her!" he howled from where he sat, cowering behind his chair and dodging the lion's attacks. "Somebody stop that girl!"

Cordelia didn't have to look behind her to know that Alonzo the giant was after her.

His footsteps thundered behind her, sending vibrations through the soles of her feet. She tasted sweat and sawdust. A dozen feet away, her rucksack was lying forlornly on the ground, but she had no time to grab it.

The balloon had reached the exit.

"No!" Cordelia didn't realize she had screamed until the word echoed back to her, foreign-sounding.

Then: a small miracle. For a second, the balloon stuck, caught between the tent folds like a blueberry between the tines of a fork. The momentary delay gave Cordelia just enough time to catch up.

"Jump, Cordelia!" Gregory was hanging off the bottom of the ladder, straining, reaching for her hand. She jumped, extending an arm to him.

Their fingertips barely touched; and then she was falling again.

"Try again!" Gregory's eyes were wide and panicked. He was hanging practically upside down. "Try harder!"

But this time, their fingertips didn't meet at all. The balloon was bullying its way through the narrow exit—squeezing, squeaking, forcing the opening even wider. Now it was like an eggplant being crammed into a mouth: the mouth widened, stretched, screamed.

Cordelia dropped again. Gregory lurched toward her, arms outstretched.

"Cordelia!" he screamed, as the tent gave a groan and a shudder.

Just as Cordelia had given up hope, Icky scrambled down Gregory's back and shoulders. Like an acrobat, the filch hooked his knees around Gregory's neck and stretched his long arms out to reach her.

"Now!" Gregory shouted.

"Now!" Sergei screamed.

Wheeeee, went the balloon through the narrow opening.

Cordelia jumped—

Gregory lunged—

The tent spat the balloon into open air—

And just as the balloon went soaring, soaring, soaring away, Cordelia felt Icky's hands close easily around her wrist, and she was pulled along with it, leaving the circus tent far behind.

CHAPTER
18

With Icky's help, Cordelia caught hold of the bottom rung of the ladder. With her other hand, she passed Cabal up to Gregory, who was still hanging upside down, his hat long gone, his hair a curtain over his face.

Then, hand over hand, Cordelia climbed, even as the rope ladder swayed through the open air, whipping past slate roofs and stone towers. Higher and higher the balloon climbed. Wind stung Cordelia's cheeks and made tears spring up in her eyes.

"Go on," Gregory shouted, when she had reached his

level. He had righted himself. Icky was still clinging to his back and Cabal was tucked inside his jacket, so Cordelia could only make out his eyes and the tufted white hair on his ears. Gregory reached out, put a hand on Cordelia's back, and pushed. "You go first."

She didn't argue. Just looking down at the network of gray pavement flowing like rivers below her was enough to make her dizzy. The balloon swerved left around a church spire and Cordelia felt her stomach launch into her throat. She turned her attention upward, to the swollen purple balloon, and the solid basket suspended underneath it. Not too far now . . .

Both Cordelia and the balloon continued to climb. The dragon appeared on the lip of the basket, flapping his wings, squawking encouragingly, and then just as quickly withdrew. Her arms were shaking. She didn't want to think about what would happen if she slipped— the fall through open air, the long, hard tumble, the *splat*. Almost there . . .

At the end of the ladder she hauled herself into the basket headfirst, breathless and grateful. Gregory was right behind her and landed on Cordelia's back. Cordelia groaned. Gregory grunted. Icky squeaked. And Cabal began barking.

"Very graceful," said a girl's voice. A *familiar* girl's voice.

Cordelia wriggled out from underneath Gregory. For a second, when she looked up, she didn't believe it; she blinked rapidly several times, thinking she must have hit her head. A girl with fat banana curls and a white dress the exact shape of a wedding cake was standing, arms crossed, beneath the small blue flame that kept the balloon aloft.

Still, the girl didn't disappear, no matter how much Cordelia rubbed her eyes and wished for her to.

Which meant that she was really stuck in a hot-air balloon with Elizabeth Perkins, the girl she hated most in the world.

Cordelia had a sudden urge to launch herself out of the basket.

Gregory was the one to speak first. "What are *you* doing here?"

Elizabeth tossed her irritatingly perfect hair. "Is that your way of saying thank you?"

"Thank you for what?" Cordelia said. "You nearly squashed me."

"I saved you, you mean." Elizabeth turned her icy blue eyes to Cordelia. Once, Cordelia had envied Elizabeth's eyes. That was long ago, when they'd been friends. Now Cordelia thought Elizabeth's eyes were the color of mold on cheese. "If it wasn't for me, a lion would be picking you out of his teeth by now."

She was right, of course; but Cordelia would never admit it.

"I told you," Gregory said, turning to Cordelia. "I *told* you someone was following us. Didn't I?"

"Don't flatter yourself." Elizabeth rolled her eyes. "I wasn't following you."

"Oh yeah?" Cordelia said, crossing her arms. "Then how'd you end up at a circus all the way in New York?"

For a split second, Elizabeth hesitated, and in that brief moment, she looked just like the old Elizabeth: the Elizabeth who was afraid of lightning, who loved to play hide-and-seek but always forgot to check the cupboards next to the stove, who had once made matching friendship bracelets out of bits of an unraveled sock. Then the moment passed, and she looked as pinched and unpleasant as ever.

"It's my birthday," she said, with another hair toss. Cordelia wondered how she didn't have a constant crick in her neck. "Daddy said I could have anything I wanted. I wanted to go to the circus in New York." She shrugged. "When I got bored, I decided to . . . *explore* backstage. Good thing I did, too, or you'd be mincemeat. You owe me now, Cordelia. Remember that."

"I don't owe you anything," Cordelia said, when Elizabeth smirked. Elizabeth could have taught a master class in smirking.

Elizabeth ignored her. "So," she said, "where are we heading?"

"We?" Gregory nearly choked on the word.

"*We* are not heading anywhere," Cordelia said sternly. "*You're* going home." She peeked over the edge of the basket and instantly regretted it. They were skimming the rooftops now, the shadow of the balloon leaping over shingle and shale. Cordelia spotted several children gaping at them from an attic window. Up ahead, a bright copper clock tower gleamed in the moonlight. Cordelia quickly turned away from the dizzying view. "How do you land this thing?"

"I'm not telling you," Elizabeth said.

"Don't be a priss," Cordelia said, which was like telling Icky not to fart, but still. "Go on and bring us down. Then you can go running back to *Daddy*."

Elizabeth's eyes flashed. "You listen to me. I'm the captain of this balloon—"

"Balloons don't *have* captains," Cordelia scoffed.

"*This* balloon has a captain, so you better be nice to me, or I'll make you wish that lion had sunk his teeth into you instead."

"Oh, really? Are you going to bat me to death with your eyelashes?"

"Cordelia," Gregory said warningly.

The balloon was rocking a little, picking up speed,

and she struggled to keep her footing. "Or maybe your *daddy* will give me a time-out."

"Cordelia," Gregory said, a little louder.

"Shut up." Elizabeth was staggering too, as the balloon rocked back and forth in the wind. "You don't know anything. You're nothing but an ugly, smelly, *stupid*—"

"CORDELIA!" Gregory roared.

She whipped around to face him. "What do you—?" The words evaporated in her throat and turned to a squeak. The clock tower loomed only a few feet in front of them.

They were heading directly for a collision.

"Get down!" Elizabeth shoved Cordelia, hard.

Cordelia rolled to the left, taking Gregory down with her. The basket tilted wildly under their combined weight. Icky and Cabal tumbled after them. The ropes groaned as the basket tipped. Suddenly she couldn't see. Cabal had landed on top of her, his soft belly splayed across her eyes. Cordelia pushed him off. Elizabeth was standing, pale-faced, gripping the thick ropes that connected the balloon to the basket.

"What are you doing?" Cordelia shrieked. Icky screeched in fear. As the basket once again tilted, Cabal came tumbling down toward Cordelia, landing in a heap at her feet.

"What's—it—look—like?" Elizabeth huffed out. She was leaning all the way back, her slick leather shoes slipping a little on the floor of the basket, as the balloon shuddered and bucked at the end of the line like a dog resisting its lead. "I'm steering."

She was right: slowly, slowly, they began to change direction. The balloon swelled with the wind. They turned a circle in the sky like a humongous ship carving through the frothy clouds. And suddenly Cordelia understood: Elizabeth had used Cordelia and Gregory's weight to help change the balloon's course at the last minute.

Finally the basket stopped bucking like a wild horse. Cordelia felt safe enough to stand. Elizabeth let go of the rope. It snapped into place, tight and taut as a pulled bowstring.

The clock tower was safely behind them; they had left New York City behind, and all around them was nothing but deep navy sky, and wispy clouds touched by moonlight.

Elizabeth had saved them. Again.

Gregory stood up, coughing. "Icky puff hif foot in my mouv," he said, sticking out his tongue and revealing patches of filch fur.

Elizabeth's eyes landed on the filch and she recoiled, as though she were seeing him for the first time. "What *is* that thing?" she said, wrinkling her nose. "It smells like a dirty dishcloth."

Icky, no doubt thinking he had been complimented, chattered delightedly. Cordelia sucked in a deep breath. She thought of the horrified faces of the circus performers.

Fortunately, before she could speak a word, the dragon settled the problem for her. With a sudden, furious flapping, he rose off the floor of the basket and settled on Elizabeth's shoulder. She shrieked and stumbled backward.

"Get your lizard off me!" she cried, trying to swat the dragon down. The dragon, thinking it was a game, let out a delighted caw and dug his claws more firmly into the fabric of her dress.

Cordelia couldn't repress a smile. "It isn't a lizard," she said. "It's a dragon."

Immediately, Elizabeth went totally still. Her face lost all color. With her ringlet curls and white dress, she looked like a porcelain doll come to life. "A—a what?"

"A dragon," Cordelia said matter-of-factly. "A member of the northern ridged species, and a baby. Probably two or three months old."

Elizabeth was trembling like a brittle leaf in the wind. Her eyes settled on Icky and Cabal. "What are—what are those?"

"That's a filch." Cordelia pointed. "He's all right, just a little temperamental. And he snores, especially when his allergies kick up. And that"—she pointed to Cabal—"is a zuppy."

"A zombie puppy," Gregory said, with a certain degree of pride. "That means he's not exactly alive. And he has to eat blood."

"Blood," Elizabeth repeated dully. The dragon was happily chewing on the ends of her curls.

"Only for the first few weeks," Cordelia said. "Zuppies have very sensitive stomachs when they're newly turned."

Elizabeth was still motionless. It was as though she had been frozen in place. Only her eyes moved, rolling back and forth with a kind of suppressed panic. Taking pity on her, Cordelia moved forward and detached the dragon from her shoulder. Elizabeth gasped, as though she'd been released from underwater, and backed up as far as she could go without hurling herself into the air.

"Tell me," she said, still panting. "Tell me everything."

There was no point in trying to conceal the truth. "There are more of them," Cordelia said. "Not just dragons and filches and zuppies, but hufflebottoms and squelches, slints and cockatrices. My father cares for injured monsters. That's what he does." When

Elizabeth's lips curled into a sneer, she added defensively, "*Someone* has to help them."

"But now all the monsters are gone," Gregory finished. "Someone stole them, and dad-napped Cordelia's father."

Elizabeth looked to Cordelia as if for confirmation. Cordelia swallowed down the sudden pressure of grief and reached into her pocket for the note she'd retrieved from her father's closet.

"I found this in his room," she said.

Elizabeth accepted the note wordlessly, and seemed to take a very long time to get to the end of the fragment. As she read, she seemed to go very green. In fact, she turned the exact shade of a particularly pickled pickle.

But finally, she looked up.

"Let me get this straight," Elizabeth said, speaking very slowly, as if each word had a physical shape she had to work her way around. "You're telling me that all those horrible creatures—the slints, the hufflesquelches . . ."

"Hufflebottoms," Gregory corrected her.

Elizabeth ignored him. "You're telling me they're all . . . lost? You're telling me they might be *anywhere*?"

"They're not horrible," Cordelia snapped. "And they're not *lost*. They were taken by a man—"

"Or a woman," Gregory interjected.

"Or a woman," Cordelia agreed. "With the initials

of HP. It says so right in the note."

"And it's our job to find 'em," Gregory said cheerfully.

Elizabeth's eyes took on a cloudy look that Cordelia couldn't decipher. Then she tossed her hair over her shoulder and gave an exaggerated sigh. "It's lucky for you I've no imminent plans," she said. "Now you're *really* going to need me."

"Need you?" Cordelia repeated. "We don't need you. We don't even *want* you."

Elizabeth smiled thinly, the way a cat smiles at the mouse between its paws. "Well, then, I suppose you don't *want* to know what HP stands for."

CHAPTER
19

"You know HP?" Gregory blurted out.

"She's bluffing, Gregory," Cordelia said. "She only wants us to *think* she knows something we don't."

"I wouldn't need to bluff for that," Elizabeth snapped. "Since what you know isn't enough to fill a thimble. You don't even have the right *initials*."

Cordelia stared. Elizabeth rolled her eyes so hard, Cordelia was surprised they didn't turn backward.

"Look again," she said, returning the note to Cordelia. "That isn't an *H*. It's an *N*. See? It's obvious if you compare it to the *H* in 'Hello.' They look completely different."

She was right: the difference was obvious.

"It's an *N*," Elizabeth went on. "And see here? This bit of ink before it?"

"The comma?" Cordelia asked, when Elizabeth pointed.

"It isn't a comma." Even though Elizabeth didn't add an *obviously*, Cordelia read it in her facial expression. "Who signs initials directly after a 'Sincerely' or 'Best Wishes for a Successful Abduction' or 'In Anticipation of Revenge'? Initials go *below* the closing salutation."

"I know how to write a letter, thanks," Cordelia said, before Eizabeth could start explaining how to count to ten.

"Just not how to read one," Elizabeth fired back. "That squiggle? It's the lower half of an *S. S-N-P*. See? You had the wrong initials all this time."

"*S-N-P*," Gregory repeated slowly, puckering his mouth around each new letter.

"Okay, fine." Cordelia stuffed the note back in her jacket pocket. "We had the wrong initials, and now we have the right ones. But right or wrong, initials don't get us very far."

Gregory still had a funny look on his face, like he was chewing on something he didn't quite like the flavor of. "Why do I know those initials?"

Elizabeth looked at him pityingly. "Probably because you've seen them on about a thousand signs around

Boston," she said. And then, turning back to Cordelia, "SNP stands for the Society for National Protection. They're the ones," she added, when Cordelia only stared, "who chased the goblin out from our cellar and tried to kill it."

Cordelia felt a yank of nausea that had nothing to do with the motion of the basket—although the basket didn't help. "To . . . kill it?"

"Well, what did you think they would do? Ask it for a Bundt cake?" Elizabeth snapped. "After *you* found that—*thing*—living under our garden, we had the SNP camped outside our house for days."

"That's right." Gregory's expression cleared up. "They had signs all over the stations, too, and wormy volunteers rooting out the strays and vagrants and don't-belongers."

"They even accused us of *breeding* her," Elizabeth said, with an exaggerated shudder. "As if we'd grown her like a potato plant. The neighbors threatened to burn the house down. Why do you think we had to move from the old house?"

"I'm sorry," Cordelia said. "I never knew—"

"You never asked," Elizabeth fired back.

"Maybe because you stopped speaking to me."

"Oh, sorry. Maybe it was because I was dealing *with the goblin living under my house*—"

"You could have asked for help—"

"You could have offered it—"

"How about both of you pin it," Gregory interjected, before Cordelia could respond. "We've got bigger fish to fry." Then, turning to Elizabeth, "You said you know where to find these SNP lugs?"

"Their headquarters is in Worcester," Elizabeth said, with a little sniff of distaste.

"Worcester, as in *Massachusetts*?" Cordelia burst out. That was only an hour outside of Boston. "You mean we came all the way to New York for nothing?"

"At least we know who HP is now," Gregory said, and then he frowned. "Who SNP is, I mean. Seriously Nasty People."

It was as good a theory as any—and the only one they had. Still, Cordelia hated to admit it. "Bring us down," she said exasperatedly. "We can talk about it once we're on the ground."

That wiped the smirk from Elizabeth's face. "Yeah . . . um, about that . . ."

Cordelia stared at her. "You do know how to bring us down, right, *Captain*?"

Elizabeth at least had the grace to look guilty. "Not exactly."

"You said you knew how to drive this thing!" Cordelia cried.

"I didn't say I knew how to *land*."

"We've got another problem," Gregory said. He was peering over the edge of the basket. "There's no more land to land *on*."

Elizabeth and Cordelia rushed to join him. Cordelia's heart sank.

Gregory was right. While they'd been arguing, the basket had left the city behind. Beneath them was a smooth stretch of black water.

They were heading directly into open ocean.

There was nothing to do but wait until morning and hope they had not gone too far astray.

And hope, too, it didn't begin to storm.

Cordelia hadn't anticipated how cold it would be this high up. She, Gregory, Icky, and Cabal huddled together in the center of the basket, while Elizabeth sat several feet away, staring distastefully at both monsters and swatting at the dragon whenever he happened to swoop near her. The wind rocked the basket gently back and forth and caused the flame beneath the swollen balloon to sputter and spit. Cordelia didn't want to think about what would happen if the flame went out. They'd go plummeting to earth and splatter, like grapes hurled from the air by a giant.

They shared a dinner of hard seed bread and jerky, which Cordelia had thankfully transferred from her rucksack into her jacket pockets on the train. The jerky was as knotty as a tree branch and just as difficult to chew. Elizabeth managed only a few bites.

"That's disgusting," she said.

"Go hungry, then," Cordelia said.

After that, Elizabeth ate without complaining. And although she made a face when the dragon—who had inexplicably taken a liking to her—curled up next to her feet, she didn't pull away.

"He won't light me on fire in his sleep, will he?" Elizabeth asked. When the dragon snored, small bits of steam issued from his nose.

"That depends," Cordelia said. "Are you flammable?"

Gregory nudged her and whispered, "Be nice."

"Impossible," she whispered back.

Gregory lay down. Cordelia was sure she would never sleep, suspended in the air with no idea where they were going or how they would get down. She couldn't stop thinking about what Elizabeth had said about the Society for National Protection. Had they really intended to *kill* the old goblin? What possible danger could it have been to them? Goblins and people had coexisted peacefully for millennia, and for many centuries had even intermarried without a problem. And the goblin they'd found beneath Elizabeth's garden was so old, she was missing her teeth. All three sets of them.

But she curled up beside Gregory anyway. They had no blanket, but once the filch had settled down at their feet and Cabal had folded himself next to their heads, Cordelia began to warm up.

Elizabeth was lying on the other side of the basket, shivering so much her teeth chattered together.

"She'll freeze," Gregory whispered.

"So much the better," Cordelia whispered back.

"Cordelia," he scolded her. "You don't mean it."

Cordelia swallowed a sigh.

"Lie next to us, Elizabeth," she said, attempting to be pleasant and succeeding only in sounding gruff. "We'll keep each other warm."

"I'm fine," Elizabeth said.

"Don't be an idiot," Cordelia said. "It's colder than Cabal outside."

"I said I'm *fine*."

But after another minute, Elizabeth inched closer to Cordelia. Another minute passed, and she came closer again. Another minute, another inch—until by the time Cordelia drifted off to sleep, Elizabeth was lying directly beside her, and Cordelia was breathing in the smell of her hair.

CHAPTER
20

Cordelia woke just after 7:30, when the sky was like a dark gray smudge of charcoal, and the sun rising looked like a fire burning over the horizon. Elizabeth looked out over the edge of the basket, the wind lifting her hair behind her and the dragon perched on her left shoulder. In that moment, she looked so much like the girl Cordelia remembered—like her old best friend, the girl who jumped in puddles and hunted the streams for salamanders—that Cordelia was almost afraid to move and disturb the picture.

Then Gregory stirred and muttered something in his

sleep, Elizabeth turned around, and the dragon lifted off from her shoulder and began circling through the air.

"Come look," Elizabeth said. There was a strange expression on her face—as if she had accidentally swallowed a fly.

"Good morning to you too," Cordelia grumbled, wiping sleep from her eyes with a fist. But she stood up, stamping the cold from her feet, and joined Elizabeth at the side of the basket.

"What is—?" she started to ask, and then she saw, and the words dried up in her throat.

They were skimming over a dark stretch of sea, approaching a coast studded with rocks, where whitecaps were breaking on the shore. Tall ships rose and fell on the swells. Dark pines were interspersed with stubbly beaches, all of them dusted with snow. Beyond them, Cordelia could see crowded spires, touched with gold in the morning light, glittering like enormous icicles pointing in the wrong direction.

They'd made it back to land.

"It's beautiful," she breathed. Elizabeth only nodded. For a while, they stood in silence.

"I'm sorry," Cordelia said. "About the goblin. I wish I'd never found that stupid tunnel."

Elizabeth knitted her hands together. "It's all right,"

she said finally. "It wasn't your fault." But Cordelia wondered whether she really believed that.

They drew closer to the shoreline, descending through a veil of mist, passing so low over the water that Cordelia could see individual waves breaking around the wharves. So low that Cordelia could see longshoremen gaping at them from the docks.

Too low.

Cordelia turned and saw that the flame keeping the balloon aloft was barely sputtering.

No sooner had she taken a step toward the flame than the balloon dropped. Cordelia screamed. Elizabeth toppled backward, landing on Cabal's tail. The bottom of the basket hit the water with a *splat* and a *whoosh*, and Cordelia thought for one panicked second that they would be thrown over into the hungry waves.

Then, just as quickly, the balloon rose again, and the basket rolled back in the other direction. Cabal landed on top of Cordelia, and she pried him off her chest.

She staggered to her feet as the flame once again sputtered and the balloon dropped, rocketing her stomach into her throat. She lurched toward the flame and grabbed the small canister of gas below it.

Empty.

"Cordelia!" Gregory yelled. The balloon skipped over the waves, skimming the surface of the ocean, careening straight for an outcropping of toothy rocks biting up from the shoreline. "Hold on to the—"

Before he could finish his sentence, the balloon plummeted again and he went sprawling to the bottom, on top of the filch. Water sloshed over the sides of the basket, drenching them all. Up and down they went, like a gigantic yo-yo, hurtling toward the shore.

Elizabeth clung to a support rope, her face green, her eyes wide and terrified. The dragon circled overhead, shrieking in distress.

The dragon.

The idea came to Cordelia vividly, all at once: dragons made flames.

She jumped and just missed the dragon's leathery wing tips. Down she went, crashing to her knees as the basket once again touched the surface of the ocean, releasing a fine spray of freezing water. She tried again, and this time managed to grab hold of the dragon. He wriggled in her hands, shrieking, batting his wings against her wrists.

"Come on," she said. She held the dragon to the dying flame and gave him a little shake, as if the dragon were a bottle and the fire was stuck at the very bottom of him. The dragon coughed and two small lines of steam uncoiled from his nostrils. "Come on!" she said again. This time, the dragon did nothing but blink at her.

"Hold on, Cordelia!" Gregory shouted. "We're gonna crash!"

She risked a glance over her shoulder and saw that they were speeding toward a gigantic rock face; any second, they would hit. She was filled with a white-hot panic.

"Please," she whispered to the dragon, "make fire for us."

"*Now*, Cordelia!" Gregory screamed.

Her mind was spitting up random bits of information, churning out memories: how chupacabras have blunt teeth and strong jaws and how specters can glow in the dark and how dragons loved to be tickled on their chins. . . .

And she remembered the time their old dragon, Digbert, had nearly burned down the living room after a particularly lengthy tickle session.

That was it.

As they bumped out of the water and hopscotched toward the giant elbow of rock, Cordelia eased one finger under the dragon's chin and begin to tickle. The dragon shivered. The dragon snorted.

And then the dragon opened his mouth and released a long, vibrant stream of fire.

The balloon soared upward. They were so close to the rock that Cordelia could have stretched out a hand to touch it; she saw their shadow skate across its pitted surface. Then they were above it. They passed safely inland, skimming over trees threaded with mist. Elizabeth and Gregory whooped for joy. Cordelia kept tickling, and the dragon kept exhaling long, satisfied streams of flame.

But they weren't yet out of danger. Cordelia knew they would need a place to land safely, and soon. Dragons couldn't make flames forever, especially not baby dragons—and already she could tell that her dragon was tiring.

As they came over the ridge of trees, a dazzling vista of stone buildings, white-carpeted lawns, churches, and snowy streets unfolded beneath them. Cordelia could see students in university robes huffing through the cold, tracking footprints in the covering of new snow. At one corner of a great quadrangle was a large bell tower, which was just chiming the hour. Eight o'clock.

"We have to find a way to land!" Cordelia called out over the steady roar of the wind.

"I don't think we have much choice," Gregory said.

He was right. They were sinking. They drifted over the complex of redbrick walls like a cloud scudding on the wind; and inch by inch, foot by foot, as the dragon gasped for air and Cordelia's fingers cramped, they dropped.

Cordelia was hoping they might land on the university's central quadrangle—the lawn, at this time of year, blanketed under a heavy layer of snow—where at least the impact would be softened. But no. They were hovering over the quadrangle—she saw a man she took for a professor gasp and stagger backward—and then they were beyond it, heading directly for the bell tower. The bells were still ringing. The noise was deafening; even the air vibrated with it. Cordelia could feel the sound in her nails, in her teeth.

Gregory yelled something, but she couldn't make out what it was. Elizabeth tried to steer, but it was too late. Gregory threw himself to the floor and covered his head, as though it would protect him from the impact of a thousand tons of brass. The bells kept ringing, ringing—vast, large as metal horses, tossing and bucking, and Cordelia imagined being trampled beneath them, mashed into a pulp.

The basket jerked to a sudden stop, barely an inch from the bells' sweeping path. "What—what happened?" Gregory uncovered his head. At that moment, the bells stopped ringing. In the resulting silence, Cordelia could feel her jaw buzzing.

"We've stopped." Cordelia edged carefully to the side of the basket and peered over the rim. They were suspended a hundred feet above the ground; below them, two professors, dressed in maroon robes and matching caps, were shouting and pointing. "Just in time too."

She looked up. The balloon had snagged on the bell tower, hooked by its fabric to the steeple, like a hat pinned onto a hat rack.

"Any idea how we're going to get down?" Gregory said.

A dozen feet below the basket was a small stone ledge abutting a set of narrow glass windows. Cordelia guessed they could enter the tower that way; there must be a staircase that gave the ringer access to the bells. It was worth a shot, anyway. Better than hanging in the air like a rotten fruit, just waiting to drop.

When Elizabeth and Gregory lowered the rope ladder, it just skimmed the top of the ledge. Clutching Icky tightly to her chest, Cordelia took a deep breath and climbed over the side of the basket, ignoring the outraged shouting of the two robed men down below. The ladder twisted violently in the wind, and her stomach plummeted.

But she made it safely down the ladder and onto the narrow ledge and moved into a crouch, trying very hard not to think of the sheer drop only an inch or so to her left. The first window was painted shut, but after a few minutes of digging with her pincers—which, luckily, were still in her pocket—she managed to pry it open.

She shimmied through the window legs first and deposited Icky on the floor, then gestured for Elizabeth and Gregory to follow her with Cabal and the dragon.

Cordelia's instincts were correct: she had landed in a small, circular room, which gave access, via a rickety ladder, to the bells up above. A set of rough stone stairs, spotted with dampness, wound down toward the courtyard. Cordelia caught sight of a dirty brass plaque winking dully on the far side of the room and crossed over to investigate. She had to wipe the plaque clean with the bottom of her shirt before she could make out what it said.

The University of King's College at Halifax, founded 1789.

Cordelia's heart sank. She knew the University of King's College, and Halifax—both from the stacks of correspondence she had turned up in her mother's study.

Halifax was in Nova Scotia.

Nova Scotia, *Canada*.

CHAPTER
21

"Where are we?" Elizabeth said. She had just slid through the window and was doing her best to slap the dirt from her dress—a hopeless cause, given that it was now ripped, stained, and even singed in one place. Gregory dropped to the floor beside her, holding Cabal in one arm, and the dragon swooped into the room behind him. Despite the splint, the dragon was flying almost perfectly now. "What *is* this place?"

Cordelia was too upset to speak. Instead she stepped aside so that Elizabeth could read the plaque for herself.

As she did, her face shed its color, then turned bright red, then finally settled on a swampy kind of green.

"I was sure we were headed in the right direction," she whispered.

"Well, you were *wrong*." Cordelia crossed her arms. "Thanks to you, we've taken a scenic tour to *a totally different country*."

"Thanks to *me*, you're not working your way out of a lion's digestive tract right now."

"Cordelia. Elizabeth." Gregory was still standing by the window, looking out over the quadrangle. He spoke now in a voice so full of repressed excitement that Cordelia fell immediately silent.

"What is it?" Elizabeth snapped.

He didn't budge. "Come look," he said, still in that strange voice.

Cordelia went to join him at the window. After a second, Elizabeth followed.

"I could be wrong," Gregory said. The corners of his lips twitched, and Cordelia could tell he was trying not to smile. "But do those letters say what I think they say?"

Through the dirt-streaked panes, Cordelia could make out a large banner strung across one of the red-brick buildings on the other side of the quadrangle.

**MONSTERS AMONG US: WHEN FEAR WALKS,
8:30 A.M.–10:30 A.M.,
SATURDAY, JANUARY THE 11TH,
A LECTURE AND BOOK SIGNING BY
SAMUEL NATTER, PROFESSOR.
ALL STUDENTS WELCOME.**

SNP.

Cordelia read the words again to make sure she hadn't mistaken any of them—and then again, and again. It was Saturday, just after eight o'clock. Was it possible—was it even remotely possible—that they had flown all the way to Canada only to stumble across the SNP they'd been tracking? The chances were one in a million.

"It's a coincidence," Elizabeth pronounced finally, as if in confirmation of Cordelia's doubts. "It has to be."

"Or it's our lucky break," Gregory said. "It says 'monsters' right there on the sign, doesn't it?"

"So—what? This Professor Natter just dipped down to Boston, abducted a whole house full of monsters, and invited them all to a book signing?" Elizabeth shook her head. Her perfect curls had knotted into a dense, electric tangle, as if even they were losing patience. "I told you. I *know* where to find Cordelia's monsters."

"Oh, sure. Just like you *knew* we were going the right way," Cordelia couldn't help but fire back.

Elizabeth's eyes flashed yellow. Cordelia blinked, and they returned to normal.

A trick of the light.

"That's fine," Elizabeth said, in a voice deepened by fury. "You don't have to believe me. It doesn't matter anyway. If the society got their hands on your little *friends*, it's already too late." When Elizabeth thinned her mouth into a smile, Cordelia thought she looked rather monstrous herself. She had half a mind to seize Elizabeth's tongue from behind her rows of teeth and tie it up in a knot so it could do no more trouble. . . .

Then a shock passed through her. Elizabeth had rows of teeth.

Three of them, stacked one behind the other. Very small—imperceptible except when you were standing close—the extra rows were just beginning to emerge.

She was so startled, she lost several seconds of Elizabeth's speech. ". . . want to waste your time, then be my guest." Finally, Elizabeth caught Cordelia staring. "What?" she said. "What is it?"

Cordelia swallowed. "Nothing," she croaked out. "You—you had something in your teeth."

Immediately, Elizabeth clamped her mouth shut. A muscle twitched in her jaw.

This time, Cordelia was *sure* her eyes turned a fiery kind of yellow. Just for a second.

A long second.

Jaundicing of the eyes was a temporary emotional response. The real change, the discoloration of the iris, the reshaping of the pupil, the double-lidding of the eyelid . . .

Well, all that would come in when all the teething was complete.

Probably around her thirteenth birthday.

According to the relevant entry in *A Guide to Monsters and Their Habits*, thirteen was standard for most goblins.

Cordelia felt curiously calm. In control, even. Elizabeth Perkins, who squealed at puddles, had goblin in her family. Cordelia would have to tell her. But not now. Not yet.

Maybe she'd wait until they were separated by an iron gate, or a wall, or a bank vault.

Elizabeth was going to kill her.

"My father says that 'coincidence' is just a trail that no one knows how to fit together," Cordelia said. "He says there's no such thing as coincidence." If she closed her eyes, she could see in the darkness the wild of Blue Hills Park take shape around her. She could see her father's lantern bobbing between the trees, like an overgrown firefly. She could feel the riot of unseen creatures everywhere—tiny crabs scuttling in the mud, tadpoles finning in the shallows of the marshes, bats coasting on the shadows. *Everything means something, Cordelia,* he always said. *Even trails are just threads, and every one of them is woven together.*

Cordelia opened her eyes. Gregory and Elizabeth were both silent, watching her. "Maybe the society stole the monsters, or maybe they didn't. Maybe the professor did, or maybe he didn't. But we're thousands of miles from Worcester right now, and only a lob of spit from Samuel Natter."

Cordelia turned again to the window. She thought the wind carried the smell of ink and paper, of bound books, of ugly letters.

Of manuscripts unfinished, and ideas left incomplete.

All life comes from the same place, and all of it is equally deserving.

"Besides," Cordelia said. "I, for one, would like to hear what our dear professor has to say about monsters."

They would need to be cautious. If Professor Natter *had* stolen the Clays' monsters, it wasn't, as Elizabeth had pointed out, for the purpose of inviting them as guest speakers. It might be dangerous to confront him directly, and insanity to confront him with three monsters in tow. Cabal, Icky, and the dragon must stay behind, safely concealed, and the tower was as good a place as any.

Gregory coaxed the filch into a corner by feeding him yak jerky, and Cordelia delicately wrapped the dragon's wings in a heavy tarp so that he wouldn't fly away, and set him in another corner. Cabal proved nearly impossible to abandon, however. He whined and yipped so piteously when Cordelia tried to leave him, she was sure someone would hear and come investigate. Then Elizabeth had the idea to leave one of Gregory's shoes behind, so that Cabal would know they were returning. Since it was ridiculous to wear one shoe, Gregory left both, despite the cold.

"Oh, I'm used to it," he said cheerfully, when Cordelia pointed out that he would freeze. "I went a whole winter once with nothing on my feet but a pair of pillowcases. Loaves of bread, too, when I could find 'em. A nice rye loaf'll keep your toes good and toasty."

Cordelia thought of the ragged crowd they'd seen filing down the gangplank toward the immigration checkpoint, back in Boston, and wondered whether all of them had shoes to last the winter.

"You're amazing, Gregory," she said. "You might be the most amazing person I've ever met."

Gregory waved her off. "Nah," he said. "Nothing to it. All you have to do is just take out the middle bit."

At last they were able to make their escape, leaving Cabal happily gnawing on the holey leather.

But as Cordelia, Gregory, and Elizabeth neared the door at the bottom of the staircase, a buzz of conversation reached them from outside.

"Forget the balloon. It's nothing but a student prank," one man was saying. "We should be grateful, actually. Last year they turned out a hundred geese in the dining hall. . . ."

"The dining hall is not a historical monument," another man sniped back. "The tower predates the university by a *hundred years*. The undercroft alone has more history in its tunnels than the entire department can bore out of its students. . . ."

Someone else piped up, "We should organize a committee to vote on a procedure to select the academic office that will organize a vote on whether to open an investigation—"

"Hang on. We'll need a committee to organize a committee—"

"And a vote to determine the procedure for finding one—"

"We'll grow ear hair before they can agree on a fart," Gregory whispered. "And we can't get past them."

"We can get under them, though," Cordelia whispered back. "The woman mentioned tunnels. . . ."

It didn't take them long to find the small trapdoor in the floor. It opened to reveal a set of dirt stairs, leading steeply down into the dark.

The very, very dark.

Cordelia had always hated tracking monsters underground. And not just because of all the slime.

But Gregory scampered quickly ahead of her. He disappeared from view like a stone dropped down a well.

Cordelia crouched down by the opening. Cold air rose out of the hole, clammy as a dog's breath, and she shivered. "Gregory?" she called. "Are you okay?" When he didn't answer, she felt a rising panic. "Gregory? Can you hear me?"

"Sorry," he called up at last. "I had a spider in my throat. At least, I had a *spiderweb*. Didn't taste any legs go down." A moment later, his head popped out of the opening. "Well, aren't you coming?"

Cordelia glanced over at Elizabeth. She looked as if she was about to be sick. Of course, some of the greenish hue was only to be expected. Like the jaundice of her eyes, it was one of the signs of a developing goblin.

A sign that showed especially in times of terror or distress.

"I hate spiders," Elizabeth said, without looking at Cordelia. Cordelia saw that she was shaking.

Cordelia straightened up. She knew spiders weren't

the reason Elizabeth was so afraid: the last time they'd entered a tunnel together, it had taken Elizabeth across the threshold of a totally new reality—and, Cordelia felt, dumped them right at the calloused feet of a family secret. Even now, she didn't know how much Elizabeth understood, or whether she understood anything.

But for Elizabeth, tunnels led not from place to place. They led from *before* to *after*.

"You can wait here, if you want," Cordelia said. "That way you won't mess up your party dress."

Elizabeth's party dress was, by now, hopelessly ruined, and carrying clots of Icky's fur like burrs among the folds. But Cordelia wanted to give her an excuse to stay behind.

Elizabeth looked at Cordelia for a long beat. This time, her eyes didn't change color. Her pupils stayed the same as they always were.

But even so, Cordelia saw someone totally new inside of them.

"I hate this dress," Elizabeth said finally. "It looks like a cream puff."

But the stranger in her eyes smiled. And the smile, Cordelia remembered. Actually, she didn't *have* to remember, because she had never forgotten.

Smiles are like that.

Elizabeth cut in front of Cordelia and beat her down

the stairs. After only a few steps, the light simply ran out. Exhausted by the pressing darkness, it retreated back toward the surface.

Cordelia edged down the last few stairs at Gregory's instruction. But touching ground was no relief. She could have been upside down or sideways or floating in an ocean of nothing: she couldn't see Gregory, or even the white of Elizabeth's dress. She couldn't even see her own feet. She couldn't even see her own *hands*.

She took a step forward, and Elizabeth yelped.

"That was my *toe*," she said.

"Believe me, I wasn't aiming," Cordelia replied. Only a whiplash of hair to the face suggested that Elizabeth was still in front of her.

"This way," Gregory said unnecessarily: there was only one way to go. "I went ahead a little. It gets easier to see a little ways on."

Cordelia took another step, and Elizabeth yelped again.

"That was my *heel*," she said. "Will you watch where you're going?"

"I'd love to," Cordelia snapped back.

"Oh, for heaven's sake," Elizabeth said, and seized Cordelia's hand. "Stop being dramatic. It's not even *that* dark."

It wasn't, of course, for Elizabeth. Goblins saw

perfectly well underground. Better, in some ways, than on the surface. Some goblins found all the color too distracting.

The tunnel narrowed, so that Cordelia could feel dirt walls bumping her shoulders. Every so often she heard claws, the patter of feet, and a dry slithering that might have been made by a snake. She had been down in plenty of tunnels with her father, and every time, she had the feeling that she was walking inside the packed-dirt chambers of a living heart—a breathing, chambered, slumbering monster the size of the whole world.

She'd rather hunt a monster into a mud pit, or down a chimney, or on a roof. She'd rather hunt a monster anywhere but underground.

She was glad that she had an excuse to hold Elizabeth's hand.

After what seemed like an eternity, the tunnel began to slope upward, and the darkness lessened. Shafts of sunlight, fine as tendrils of blond hair, appeared ahead of them: they had found the end of the tunnel, and another trapdoor.

"Let's hope it isn't locked," Elizabeth said.

"Move aside," Cordelia said, and shoved in front of Gregory. She'd helped her father pick plenty of locks before; under the assault of winter storms, injured or sick monsters often shimmied down the chimneys of abandoned houses, or burrowed up into the shelter of old warehouses.

The stairs that led to the trapdoor were no more than a dirt ramp beveled into angles. She scrambled to the top, then pushed hard against the underside of the trapdoor. For one terrifying second, it didn't move.

She leaned in with a shoulder. A fine spray of dirt landed on Cordelia's neck and in her hair, and the door shifted, and groaned, and began to open upward, like a jaw moving in reverse. The light became a blinding stream. More dust rained down on them; Elizabeth coughed, Gregory sneezed, and with a grunt and a final shove, Cordelia pushed the trapdoor open all the way and hauled herself into the light.

Someone screamed.

Hundreds of people murmured, and then fell silent.

Cordelia had emerged onto a large stage at the front of an enormous lecture hall. Every single seat was full, and a thousand faces turned to gape in her direction.

She froze. Her mind seized like an engine around some massive interference. Then, with a hiss and a shudder, it ground completely to a halt. The reel of her thoughts jumped its track and went skittering into nonsense.

She couldn't even think of shouting a warning to Gregory and Elizabeth. She couldn't *think* of thinking it.

She felt like every single person in the room was staring not with eyes, but fingers, pinning her in place. Their weight would crush her. . . .

Then Gregory and Elizabeth popped out of the tunnel beside her, and the accusation of all those eyes shifted momentarily. They were coated in a fine layer of dust and silt, and, when they looked around, resembled two overgrown gophers scenting trouble far too late.

The silence seemed to stretch on forever.

Finally, Elizabeth cleared her throat.

"I *told* you this wasn't the way to the skating rink," she said, addressing the words to Cordelia, but loudly enough that everyone would hear them. "We should have gone left at the first trapdoor."

Someone coughed.

And finally, Cordelia's mind wheezed to life again, and sputtered out an urgent message: they had to get out of there, fast.

She turned to the sea of unsmiling, silent faces.

"Sorry for the interruption," she squeaked. Even so, her voice echoed through the vast hall, and she winced. "We made a wrong turn."

"There are no wrong turns. . . ."

The voice boomed out so suddenly that Cordelia cried out in surprise. She whipped right and then left, scanning the wings—no one. Her heart tried to beat a fast exit through her chest but only ended up pounding against her ribs.

"Only destinations undiscovered . . ."

The voice was bouncing off the wings, rolling back to her from every tier of seats. It came from everywhere and nowhere. She thought of the touch of an invisible specter, like a mist that touched you right on the back of your neck.

"Of course, you are probably too young for evolutionary sociology. . . ."

Then a floorboard creaked behind her.

Slowly, with a dread that turned her body to stone, she turned.

Professor Samuel Natter was older than she'd expected, and taller. He was also missing half his face. A knot of scar tissue where his cheek and jaw should have been twisted his mouth into a sideways grin.

"On the other hand," he said, "you are old enough for a complete education in *monsters*."

CHAPTER
22

"Sorry about the marshmallows," Professor Natter said, half an hour later, as he carefully polished his spectacles with a green handkerchief and leaned back in his desk chair. "Hot chocolate without marshmallows always seems like an essay that ends midsentence."

Cordelia, Gregory, and Elizabeth were now installed in Professor Natter's office, lined up in the row of mismatched chairs that faced his desk, enjoying the warmth of a cheerful fire.

"What's wrong with that?" Gregory said. He had

a ring of chocolate around his mouth that doubled his expression of perplexity. "Leave 'em wanting more, that's what I say."

Professor Natter smiled. "So," he said. "Now that you're warmed and fed"—he gestured to the tray of sandwiches and muffins he'd brought in from the dining hall, or rather, what was left of them in crumbs—"I think it's time for you to give me something." He replaced his glasses and peered sharply at each of them in turn. "What on earth are you doing here? What in the name of a griffin were you doing in a *balloon*? No stories, now," he added, when Elizabeth opened her mouth. "I want the truth."

There was an awkward pause. Cordelia stared down at the mug of hot chocolate steaming in her lap. "We— we wanted to hear your lecture."

"Nonsense." Professor Natter leaned back in his chair, folding his hands across his stomach. "Don't take me for a fool, child. Half my students don't want to hear my lectures. They only come because they have to." When Cordelia opened her mouth to protest, he raised a hand. "Now, now. No more lies. State your business. You got fed. I get facts."

It was quite clear to Cordelia already that Professor Natter *couldn't* be responsible for the theft of the monsters. Despite his appearance—the scars that deformed his face, eyebrows that reminded her of the aggressive

Northern Burr caterpillars, a particularly nasty and biting variety—he had rapidly proven that he was no threat. He had shepherded them upstairs to his office, fending off the enraged dean who had tried to intercept them, and even commanded one of his students to scare up new boots for Gregory from the dormitory Lost and Found.

"And some warm socks," Professor Natter barked. "The boy's have more holes than your last thesis. And while you're at it," he'd thundered, before the boy could slip out, "a decent coat, a winter sweater, and a hat that doesn't slip around his head like a wet fish." The student had returned with a mismatched pair of wool socks and two nearly identical boots that were only three and four sizes too large, respectively. The sweater's arms had to be rolled several times before even Gregory's knuckles showed. He swam inside the jacket.

But the hat fit him perfectly. He hadn't adjusted it even an inch when he put it on for the first time, covering his dense cap of black curls.

The professor was, simply, far too nice to be the SNP they wanted.

But he knew something about monsters. So Cordelia swallowed. "Your lecture . . . ," she began.

"Yes?" His eyebrows jumped all the way up his forehead.

She looked down at her lap. "We didn't come to hear

you speak," she blurted finally. "But we do want to know about monsters. We want to know about the monsters among us, and how you know they still exist. . . ."

"Are you a monster hunter?" Gregory asked hopefully. "Is that where the scars come from? Did a werewolf bite you?"

"Gregory," Elizabeth whispered fiercely. "Sorry," she said to the professor, over the rim of her cup. "He was raised by a well-intentioned canine. He *is* house-trained, though."

"You can tell us, honest," Gregory said, ignoring her. "Even if you got chewed by something kind of stupid. Like a hufflebottom. Or a squelch! Wait. Squelches don't have teeth, do they? Cordelia told me that. She's seen every kind of monster there is, even werew—"

Cordelia elbowed him sharply into silence.

Professor Natter didn't look any longer at Cordelia than he did at Gregory and Elizabeth. But she could tell that he looked *harder*.

Finally, he smiled. But it was a sad smile, resigned, like someone welcoming home a familiar pain. "I did lose my face to a monster," he said. "But it wasn't a werewolf, or a diggle, or a squinch."

"Squelch," Gregory corrected him.

"Nothing so romantic, I'm afraid," the professor said. "I lost my cheek to a bullet. I'm not from here.

I moved to Nova Scotia not long after the war. Thirty years ago, now."

Gregory looked almost disappointed. "But you said there was a monster . . . ?"

"There was." Professor Natter's smile was gone. "The war was born from an evil that made certain people *people*, and others property. The war was fought by kids—kids barely old enough to pop their own pimples—who believed they were dying for their country, but died instead to preserve the right of rich people to stay rich and powerful people to stay powerful. They died for the most monstrous thing in the world—the right to be a monster, and call it being human instead. And die they did."

When he spoke, Cordelia felt as if his words were making shapes—pictures she didn't want to see but somehow understood. Ropes that drew her down into the past and tightened around her throat.

"That is what my lecture was about. That is what my book is about." Now Professor Natter seemed to deflate, and Cordelia was struck by how thin he was, by how old his hands looked on his chair. "The Union won that war, but we won nothing but the right to give our evil different faces, different accents, different names. It's only gotten worse since the depression hit . . ."

Finally, Cordelia understood. "You're talking about

people," she said. "You're talking about what they do to each other." Her stomach felt like a hole. Once again, they were back where they'd started. "You don't know anything about real monsters."

"On the contrary," he said matter-of-factly. "I am an expert in real monsters. What do you think monsters *are*? They are predators that prey on other lives unnecessarily. Not for survival. For fun. For the pleasure of it. That is what a monster *is*. Oh no," he said, "I know more about monsters than anyone."

"So," Gregory said slowly, "you've *never* fought a werewolf?"

"I've never even seen one," the professor said, and his eyes sparked with humor again. "The monsters from stories—the ones with teeth and tentacles and glowing eyes—aren't really monsters. They're myths. They gave us something to be afraid of, so we could believe the real danger was somewhere else. But the danger is never in the woods. It's always inside the wilderness that lives right here." He tapped his heart with a finger. "No. Not werewolves," he said. "But I've seen men who can transform into beasts. I know plenty of people who feed on other people's pain, on their fear. On blood, even."

In the silence, Cordelia felt a terrible hopelessness. She found suddenly that she was on the verge of crying. Maybe Elizabeth was right. Maybe the SNP was the

Society for National Protection, made of people who wanted to clean the cities of anything or anyone unfamiliar or strange. If so, it *was* too late. Too late to save the hufflebottom and the squelches, too late to save her father.

What was the point of saving the monsters only so they could be hunted and despised? What was the point of trying to protect their lives from a world so full of monsters, it demanded that monsters exist only to have someone else to blame?

Her mother had been right and wrong at the same time. *Monsters belong in our family tree*, she had written, in the introduction to her manuscript. But she should have said: *We belonged in theirs*.

"I'm sorry," Professor Natter said. "You didn't come to talk about old fables."

"They're not fables," Cordelia blurted out. "And they're not myths. Monsters—werewolves and pixies and goblins—they're all real. They exist." The words burst out as if someone had punched them out from her chest, and left her breathless and a little dizzy. Professor Natter was staring at her intently, his bushy eyebrows linked firmly together above his nose in a conference of concern. Still, she didn't stop. "There are over one thousand species of monsters that we know of. There used to be ten thousand, before they were hunted or uprooted or fished out of the ocean on hooks. The really big dragons went extinct with the dinosaurs, but even a medium-size North American black-ridge is plenty big when it's breathing fire in your face." Once again, she blinked away tears. An image came to her of her mother, vanished into a vivid mass of jungle leaves that absorbed her with only the faintest hiss. A lost cause. A hopeless battle. A fool's errand.

"I know—I know you probably think I'm crazy," Cordelia said, a little more quietly, swallowing down a stubborn mass of grief. "I know you probably won't believe me—"

"Believe you?" Professor Natter interjected, before Cordelia could finish. And he actually laughed. "Of course I *believe* you."

Cordelia searched his face for a trick and couldn't find one. "You—you do?"

"Why shouldn't I? Just because something is fantastical doesn't mean it isn't true. Most true things are fantastical. The world's existence is itself extremely improbable.

"And yet, here we are, with hot chocolate and regret for missing marshmallows and, in my case, a stack of undergraduate papers that entirely misunderstand the modern political relevance in the great French fairy story 'La Belle et la Bête.'" He smiled, and this time the story reached all the way to his eyes and warmed them to the color of caramel. "And this morning, three children flew right to our doorstop—or rather, our bell tower—in a hot-air balloon. Magic, it turns out, is the most commonplace thing in the world. And do you want to hear the most magical thing of all?"

He leaned forward and laced his fingers together on his desk. Cordelia saw that he was missing his left thumb and wondered whether that, too, had been chewed away by a bullet.

"I saw terrible things during the war. I have seen terrible things since. But I saw wonderful things, too. Acts of bravery and sacrifice, selfless compassion, senseless generosity. I saw them on the battlefield, and I have seen them since."

Cordelia was holding her breath. Even the dust motes turning in the sun seemed to have momentarily stilled their revolution.

"You see, child, when I said that monsters walk among us, I meant of course that they walk *inside* of us. They are born in the human heart, when it is starved of what it needs. A starved heart is a terrible thing. It learns to scream. It learns to bite. It grows fingers to point blame at something for its own hunger. Still, it starves."

Cordelia felt the touch of understanding, like the

ripple of a wave that hadn't broken on the surface yet. She thought of all the monsters she and her father had tracked over the years—cancer-riddled or bleeding, weak from starvation or fever, agonized by invisible wounds. Once, it had taken them twelve hours to subdue a vastly emaciated dungaroo. Every time Cornelius tried to approach, the dungaroo used up its energy trying to attack. Finally, it was too weak to do anything but die, and Cornelius had performed an emergency surgery, right there in the open marshes, in the fading evening light, to try and save it. The operation had revealed intestines blackened with poisonous chemicals— for weeks, its food supply had been poisoned by runoff from a newly opened paint factory. They might have saved it even a few hours earlier, by applying a paste of charcoal and ground birch, or even removing the dead bits of intestine and patching them together with tissue from the dungaroo's own tail, which would regenerate over time.

But the agonized dungaroo did not know how to tell the difference between what brought pain and what offered relief, and so it had died.

Once, a diggle had lashed out and missed cutting Cornelius's throat by inches, when he was only trying to set a bone. A growrk had taken a chunk out of his ankle. Digbert the dragon had set his hair ablaze; thank

God Digbert was nearly blind by then, as they were sure he'd been aiming lower.

And yet weeks later, Digbert whimpered when Cornelius left the room. The diggle ate carefully from Cornelius's palm, mindful of every one of its razor-sharp scales. And the growrk, the one that had taken a chunk out of his ankle, had until its peaceful death from old age slept wrapped around Cornelius's head like a turban, with its long, heavy, deadly tail draped protectively around his chest.

"Monsters feed off many things. Pain. Greed. Fear. But hearts, all hearts, hunger for only one. Feed hearts with love, and many of them—most of them, in fact— make a *miraculous* recovery." Professor Natter was speaking directly to Cordelia now, and at last a single word drew to shore, out of the wave of all her memories and fears. It broke across her consciousness. It was, for a second, as large as the whole ocean.

"And the best news of all?" Professor Natter's smile split his face into radiance. Cordelia couldn't believe she had found him ugly at first. "*Unlike* in the case of the common zuppy, there is absolutely *no* blood required."

"Wait a second." Gregory straightened up in his chair. "How do you know what a zuppy eats?"

"How do you know what a zuppy *is*?" Elizabeth chimed in. "Cordelia didn't say a word about them."

Elizabeth and Gregory were right. She had named werewolves and pixies and goblins. But not zuppies.

Professor Natter's smile was on the march: by now, it had conquered half his face.

"I told you I'd never seen a werewolf, and that's true," he said. "But I never said I hadn't seen *any* living species of the kingdom Prodigia. The scars on my cheek were made by a bullet, true." He held up his left hand, showing off four long fingers, and the stump where a thumb had once been. "But you haven't yet asked what happened to my hand."

CHAPTER
23

"It was a hufflebottom," Professor Natter said cheerfully, after a moment of short, shocked silence. "Served me right, too, for waking it up from a deep hibernation."

Inwardly, Cordelia cringed. He was lucky he'd gotten away with losing only one finger; hufflebottoms were notoriously grumpy when their sleep was interrupted, much less their yearly hibernation. She said so.

"Oh, I know that now. It was idiotic. Reckless. Keep in mind, though, I was only a kid myself. This was in 1851, '52, maybe. My father, you see, fancied himself a bit of a naturalist. Amateur, of course. He'd brought the family over from Ireland during the potato famine. It almost killed him to give up the family farm, but once it stopped yielding, he had no choice. Went to work in a mill not far from Burlington. But he never lost his love for the land he remembered, and all the creatures that cohabited it. Gnomes, of course, both garden variety and a rare and very localized species. Irish dragons—the Scottish call them Scottish dragons, of course, which is absurd; they're green from head to tail, for God's sake!—and all sorts of diggles. Then there are the leprechauns. . . ."

"*Leprechauns?*" Cordelia repeated. Leprechauns were still hotly debated, and even her mother had left them uncategorized. The few naturalists who'd accepted the existence of monsters as a biological fact still argued about how to categorize them, or whether any relationship existed between species at all. Cordelia's mother had advanced arguments for three competing theories about leprechauns: one, that "leprechaun" was a distinct and single species; two, that it was a genus comprising many different species, some only loosely related; three, that it was simply a misnomer, a term applied incorrectly to a kind of localized goblin found almost exclusively in Ireland. The problem was, leprechauns were almost impossible to study: masters of concealment, vastly wealthy, and far smarter than the average human.

Professor Natter looked suddenly stern. "There's a great deal of evidence to support the idea that the entire famine was a leprechaun offensive, to retaliate against the politicians who had reneged on promises of land conservation. Fascinating theory. I've long thought there's a book there. But the leprechauns would never allow it. They've got their long, bony fingers in every newspaper and publisher in the world, and a fantastic publicity arm. That pot-of-gold twaddle? It's all spin. The leprechauns wouldn't give a penny to a piggy bank. . . ."

"The hufflebottom," Gregory prompted. "You were telling us about the hufflebottom."

"Quite right, young man. But I'm afraid there's not much more to the story. Like I said—I was young, and eager, and uneducated. America has a completely different ecosystem of monsters. And much of what my father taught me was just hearsay and superstition. For example, he was simply *wrong* about the burrowing habits of the diggle . . . for years, I was actually scouting for gophers. Keep in mind, this was twenty years before the first— the *only*—comprehensive work on the world's known monster species was even published. . . ." He stood up and, turning to the wall of books behind him, danced his fingers from title to title. "Brilliant work. Life-changing. I know I have a copy somewhere . . . aha!"

But even before he had turned to pass it over for inspection, Cordelia recognized it by the deep maroon color of its spine, and the wink of the gold-stamped letters there.

"That's my *mother's* book," she said. "*A Guide to Monsters and Their Habitats,* the abridged edition."

"Let me see that." Elizabeth sprang to her feet and snatched it from Professor Natter's hand. He barely noticed. He was staring at Cordelia, openmouthed.

"You're—you're Elizabeth Clay's daughter? Cornelius's little girl?"

Now it was Cordelia's turn to stare. "You know my father?"

"Knew him," Professor Natter corrected her. "And only very briefly, I'm afraid. We attended a symposium about the origin and expression of all that we deem monstrous. Mr. Darwin himself was the keynote. Great man. No pretense at all. Won't publicly throw his hat into the ring about the question of monsters, won't even say they exist, only that he hasn't himself found evidence. Bull-honk, of course. The man's been more places than most people can pronounce. . . ."

Elizabeth had the book balanced carefully on her lap and took great care not to crack the spine. Cordelia noticed that she wiped her fingers, too, before she turned the pages. She felt a surge of old affection, and also of concern. Elizabeth needed to know what she was.

Even if she would hate Cordelia forever, because she'd been the one to tell her.

Gregory was frowning over Elizabeth's shoulder. "If you ask me, the words look like they could use a little breathing room. Too many of them crammed together. Don't see any bridge, either."

"Not 'bridge,'" Elizabeth said, without looking up. "Abridged means the book has been shortened."

"Shortened?" Gregory's face turned the chalky gray of Cabal's fur. "You mean to say she didn't use up all the words there are right there in those pages? You mean to say there are *more* of them out there?" He looked around fearfully, as if a storm of vocabulary might be hiding in the corners, waiting to attack.

Elizabeth finally looked up with a huff of impatience. "You really must learn to read, Gregory. You must learn properly. You can't go through your life illiterate."

"I'm no ill-idiot," Gregory said, looking offended. "I'm no kind of idiot at all."

"I didn't say you were an idiot, you idiot," Elizabeth said. Then she rolled her eyes. "Illiterate means you can't read. But I *suppose* I wouldn't mind teaching you. . . ."

Gregory, for once, had nothing to say. But his face lit up like one of the electric lamps in New York City, bright with sudden warmth. Elizabeth hunched over the book again and pretended not to notice. But she was smiling—and not just secretly this time.

Cordelia turned her attention back to Professor Natter.

"... *in vino veritas*, as they say ... After we warmed him up a bit over dinner, he dropped the act and admitted to deliberate omission. Can't say I blame him. Half the world was already calling him crazy when they weren't calling for his head. 'There are people,' he'd said, 'important people, experts, even—who refuse to believe all humans are related. They're claiming different origins. But really they're claiming different kinds of human—some, of course, better than others.'"

Cordelia thought of the letter she'd found, and felt a chill.

"He was quite broken up over it. 'They won't even believe that all humans belong to the same family tree,' he told me. 'How do you think they'd feel if I'd dropped in the molting slug, or the three-headed sea serpent, or the Scandinavian trolls, too? I'd be laughed out of the country. No one would believe a word I'd written. No one would want to believe they have the Loch Ness monster for a cousin.'"

"He was exaggerating," Cordelia said sternly. "The species *Gargantua reptaurae* is only very, very, very distantly related to any of the mammalian species." Then, suddenly, she was walloped by a realization so enormous, it sent the whole room spinning. "Wait ... But that means Mr. Darwin believes what my mother did. He believes that monsters evolved just like any other species did. Just like *all* of them did. He believes that we're all related."

"Well, of course he believes that," Professor Natter said. "It's the only rational thing to believe. Life doesn't just sprout up like a potato. Life is mind-bogglingly finicky. It's a soufflé, but made of everything that exists. Plants and moss, trees and mushrooms. People and slugs, gigantic or otherwise. One ingredient missing, one minute too long or too short, and the whole thing collapses. The chance of life originating is less likely than the chance that a grain, scattered in the Sahara desert, will be selected by the only beetle that exists, as the only grain of sand it selects, and that this beetle will be carried by a wind across the surface of the entire universe and dropped on our world into a forest of a hundred million needles that exists only for the time it takes to blink, and dropped at exactly the right time that the grain of sand passes through the eye of the exactly right needle from a distance of two miles, and a millionth of a second later that the needle is then swept up by a single bird that has been migrating across the whole world and happened to arrive at exactly the right time to choose the needle, and that this bird will then wing over the oceans—all of them—circling the world incessantly, only to, at the precise right moment at the exact right angle, aim this needle so that it passes through a single bubble, the size of a grain of sand, traveling to the surface from the mouth of the only fish in the entire world. Now multiply by the chance that this broken bubble must join at the precise right time the precise right current the width of a thread, and that this current, cast out across a thousand miles blindly, must out of all the places it can land touch precisely on the only dry land in a world full of water, and that this land is the size of a grain of sand. Can you imagine all that? Good. That is step one. Only one hundred million steps to go."

"Hang on," Gregory interjected. "That's not a real number."

"Yes, it is," Elizabeth said. "And even bigger ones than that."

Gregory shook his head and muttered, "Leprechauns are *one* thing. . . ."

Professor Natter smiled. "The point is," he said, "the fact that life originated at *all* is a prayer next to impossible. What are the chances that it could have happened *several* times, separately, without reference or connection?" He shook his head. "It's one thing to believe the impossible; it's another to insist on it. Impossible things turn out to be true all the time. But it's absurd to take a true thing and insist it *become* impossible. That, my dear, is called insanity."

There was a beat of silence. Cordelia cleared her throat. "My mother wanted to prove that every living thing is connected," she said. "She had almost collected all the evidence she needed. Only one piece of the puzzle was missing. Proof of a single species, extinct ten million years ago." She looked down at her hands, knitted tightly in her lap. "She died looking for it."

It was the first time she had ever said the word out loud. It fell across the room like a heavy curtain. But somehow, Cordelia felt a little, tiny bit lighter. Like she'd been carrying the horrible weight of its meaning her whole life, and now she'd given a little bit over to someone else.

"I heard," Professor Natter said. "I'm so sorry."

Those words, too, settled down over all of them. Simple. Plain. But warm too. Honest.

"Your parents and I corresponded for a while. We kept running into each other at events, lectures, readings—the community of people interested in the topic was small to begin with, and it grew smaller every year. As Mr. Darwin's theory of the origin of life gained more and more support, the category of species he'd deliberately excluded was similarly deleted from our scientific reality. Those who still doubted his theories were the same ones who believed that only certain kinds of life were meant to be here, and others were perversions. They believed in monsters, and in their total destruction, until the vast majority of the minority of people who believe in monsters were the same ones who wanted to kill them altogether."

"Like SNP," Elizabeth said. "The Society for National Protection," she clarified, when Professor Natter raised his eyebrows. "They came after all of Cordelia's live-in monsters. And they took her father along for good measure."

Professor Natter turned to Cordelia, and in a second all his softness had gone. "Explain," he said. But the word was as sharp and final as a door closed in anger.

There was no reason to lie, so Cordelia took a deep breath and now, for the third time, confessed. Once again, she was at the end of the story before she fished the mangled bit of letter from her pocket and gave it to Professor Natter to inspect.

"Elizabeth thinks that squiggly bit might be an *S*," Cordelia said. "SNP."

"They say they want a safe America," Elizabeth said. "But they don't. They just want one where they're the ones who get a say. They want control."

"They're afraid," Professor Natter murmured. He was still clutching the letter. Cordelia saw his fingers had begun to tremble. "They feel unsafe . . . if the threat is outside . . . if it can be conquered . . ." He looked up, but his eyes were fogged by some inner thought. "So obvious . . . I wonder . . . could it be that . . . ?" Suddenly, he roused himself, shaking off whatever memory had gripped him. "Well. It doesn't matter now. What matters is that we find him as soon as possible. What matters is that we stop him before he does something terrible."

Thinking he was speaking of her father, Cordelia straightened up a bit and angled her nose the way Elizabeth always did when she was offended by something, which was most of the time. "My father would never do anything terrible," she said. "He would never hurt anyone—or anything."

Professor Natter was already on his feet and shoving his arms into his winter coat. He glanced over, looking mildly irritated to see Cordelia and the others still seated. "Your father? I wasn't talking about *him*. I was talking about *Byron*." He knuckled on a wide-brimmed hat and turned for the door. But seeing that Gregory, Cordelia, and Elizabeth were staring at him in puzzlement, he threw up his hands.

"Byron Newton-Plancke. That first little squiggle isn't an *S*, it's part of a capital *B*. Oh for heaven's sake," he cried out, when the name inspired no reaction.

"You're as bad as my students. Don't you ever read the newspapers?"

"You can read the newspapers?" Gregory asked. "I thought they were mostly for blankets, and birdcages."

"Newspapers are for old people," Elizabeth said. "Besides, my governess says that knowing too much will give me wrinkles."

"And? What's your excuse?" Professor Natter glared at Cordelia.

Cordelia fidgeted. She realized she didn't have one, exactly. Or rather, she had a lot of them, but she was ashamed to speak any of them out loud. *We don't go out during the day. We try not to worry about what's happening in the world. Our world is inside. Our world is the monsters. Things we know. Familiar things.*

Our world is ours alone.

It's safe. In our world, we know how to fix what's broken.

And Mother's library stays closed, so we never have to see that the room has long been empty.

In our world, time has stopped, and we are the ones stopping it.

You see, we are afraid of the world outside, because we can't control it.

Cordelia couldn't say a single one of those things out loud, because all of them spoke in a voice she now knew was very dangerous—the same voice that called for immigrants to go back to where they had come from, and shouted for monsters to die.

"I—I don't have one," she stuttered finally.

Professor Natter looked as if he wished desperately that he could enroll them at the university, only for the pleasure of flunking them immediately. "Byron Newton-Plancke is one of the wealthiest men in New England. He has also just announced his presidential candidacy. A long shot, and only recently it would have seemed impossible. Not so long ago, his ideas were considered either crackpot, or evil, or both.

"You see, Byron Newton-Plancke claims proof that life originated not at a single source, and not from multiple sources, but from two distinct sets of evolutionary roots. One tree is essentially a version of what Mr. Darwin's official theories suggest, with a very important distinction.

"The second tree, you see, is one that started with a single deformity and grew to encompass every monster we know. It is similar to its counterpart in only one way. Both trees—one that gave birth to life, and one a deformity of it—resulted in the evolution of humans. Or so it seems to us—falsely.

"In fact, the real crux of Byron Newton-Plancke's argument is this: a good number, perhaps even a vast number, of the people we call humans *are not humans at all*. They look like humans, and they dress like humans. But they are simply monsters, several generations removed from having fangs, but no less dangerous. They belong not to the tree of life—but to the damaged roots of the thing that exists to destroy it."

Now Professor Natter's voice sounded very far away. Or maybe Cordelia was far away. She felt as if she were listening from the bottom of a tunnel that grew longer and colder and darker with every word.

"It is time, Byron Newton-Plancke believes, to uproot the threat that has for too long sucked water from the tree of life, and sunlight from its branches. It is time to kill off the disease before it spreads.

"That is why we have to hurry. It isn't just *monsters* that Plancke claims must be destroyed. The monsters are just proof—that monsters are real, that their descendants are real, that we must all go on the hunt. Plancke intends to tell us all the secret ways they can be spotted. *Scientifically*, of course.

"Then people must track down all the monsters, and all the diseased perversions that evolved from them. The real humans, the whole ones, *the ones who are supposed to be here*, must track down every last seed of these horrible imitations of humanity. They must be uprooted, every one.

"They must be destroyed, every one.

"Otherwise, we will never be safe.

"It is, after all, evil to kill people. But it is *right* to kill monsters, so that people are protected.

"And though one may look almost exactly like the other, nowadays Byron Newton-Plancke is the world's expert. And he will tell everyone—the *real* everyone, I mean, the only ones who count—just exactly what to look for.

"Then the weeding must begin, and will continue, until all the true humans, the ones who deserve to be here, are the only ones left in the garden, and have nothing left to fear."

CHAPTER
24

Less than thirty minutes later found Cordelia, Gregory, Elizabeth, and the professor—who was, luckily, delighted by the company of the three monsters in their care—bumping together in a hansom cab on the way to the docks.

"I kept a filch for a pet before I knew what to call it," he said, looking absolutely blissful when Icky squeaked a few farts into his lap. "A sort of a stray, he was. Kept sneaking to the door for wormroot cakes, when I thought I would lure a growrk. That's what I meant about my dad, and how confused he was. Turns out growrks don't even *like* wormroot cakes."

"What's wrong with Cabal?" Elizabeth piped up as another rut in the road jolted them all six inches out of their seats. "He looks pale."

"He always looks pale," Gregory said. "It's because he's dead."

"No," Elizabeth insisted. "Usually he's white-pale. Now he's gray-pale." Another jolt knocked her head against the carriage ceiling. "I hope he's not going to be—"

But at that second, Cabal reversed the contents of his stomach onto her shoes, and she began to scream.

Almost immediately, his normal pallor returned.

"Look at that," Gregory said, while Elizabeth continued wailing. "He's feeling normal-dead already."

The smell of fish announced the harbor long before it came into view. Seagulls rose in swarms above the thinning trees, and the forest slowly ran into enormous colonies of rocks, and the whitecaps breaking between them.

The harbor teemed with longshoremen and fishermen, merchants and traders, and inspectors and smugglers posing as officials. Just off the coast, dozens of whalers and schooners, masts pointed confusedly at one another, were rocked by the waves.

Cordelia's heart was flapping wildly, like an unlashed sail. It would take at least three days to get to Boston, if the weather held. Professor Natter was certain Byron

Newton-Plancke intended to put the monsters on display before he killed them.

But what if he was wrong?

And what possible use could he have for her father?

The road finally gave up its pretense and melted into a churn of mud that flowed down to the docks. Elizabeth climbed out of the cab, still spluttering about her shoes, only to step directly into a giant mound of horse manure. She stood, trembling with mute fury, as Gregory leapt down after her.

"Aw, cheer up. It could be worse. You could've planted *both* feet."

And Gregory, demonstrating, stomped around a bit to show her—splattering an unfortunate sampling of the bad luck on her coat.

Cordelia hopped the short distance to the ground, keeping well clear of the manure. She had to coax Icky from Professor Natter's arms; the filch clung so hard to Professor Natter's shirtfront, the separation effort nearly plunged the professor facedown into the mud. He caught himself only by bracing hard against the ground with his walking stick, and at last, very slowly, he managed the dismount. But at the last second, he lost his balance again, and Cordelia reached out to grab him.

"I'm all right," he said. But he was panting. "Nothing to it."

Cordelia could feel his fingers, knotty with age, crush hers in their grip. And she realized, with a sinking feeling, that it would be wrong to ask him to accompany them all the way to Boston. He had his work here, with his students, to attend to. And he had already done more than his fair share. He had fought monsters all his life. He had given half his face up to the fight.

His place was here, among his books, where the battlefield was drawn in printed letters on the page.

"You can't come with us, Professor," she said. "I can't let you."

Professor Natter's eyebrows gave a ferocious leap. "Don't be absurd," he said, and nudged Cordelia aside with his walking stick. "Of course I'm coming with you. You can't stand up to Newton-Plancke alone."

"We've made it this far," Cordelia said. But Professor Natter was old, and obviously tired. He had earned his right to his books, and his comfortable office, and his hot chocolate. Marshmallows, too. He had fought bravely in the war; this was Cordelia's battle. "We made it all the way to New York from Boston. We made it here in a hot-air balloon. We gave a pair of lions the slip. We can handle Newton-Plancke."

"We can?" Gregory whispered.

"Yes," Cordelia said, with confidence she didn't feel. She turned back to Professor Natter. "You have your students, and your work with the university," she finished.

Professor Natter shooed off those concerns. "Stopping Plancke is far more important," he said. "So step aside, please, before I write you up for disobedience."

"No." Cordelia stepped in front of him again when he tried to get around her. For a second, the old man glowered at her so fiercely, she almost shrank back. But she forced herself to hold his gaze.

And finally, his expression softened. "You're just like your mother, you know," he said quietly. "A real firecracker. Stubborn as an ox, and brave as a lion."

Cordelia was momentarily speechless. She had never thought of herself as especially brave. She had been afraid since the moment she'd closed and locked the door of Clay Manor behind her. She'd been afraid even before then—afraid to go to school, afraid their secret would be discovered, afraid of a world full of menacing strangers, their faces blurred by her imagination into shadow.

But all that time, she had ignored the real danger—not that people would discover the Clays' monsters, but that they would invent their own.

"She would be so proud of you," Professor Natter said, and pretended not to notice Cordelia swipe her eyes. "You're wrong, by the way, that your mother's greatest work was never finished. She's standing right here in front of me." Then: "I want you to see this."

He removed the copy of *A Guide to Monsters and Their Habits* from his satchel. Cordelia hadn't even seen him tuck it away. Flipping open to the title page, he indicated several neat lines of faded cursive, writing as familiar to Cordelia as the lines that creased her father's face.

"She'd promised she would sign a copy for me when the book was published. You were just a few months old. But she didn't forget."

Cordelia blinked away the tears blurring her vision and read:

To my good friend Sam,

Every life is a miracle, no matter what we name it. Ours is named Cordelia.

Affectionately,
Elizabeth

This time, Professor Natter discreetly nudged a hand-kerchief from his pocket, and didn't even flinch when Cordelia returned it, soaking wet, a moment later. But he wouldn't take the book when she tried to return it.

"Keep it," he said.

Cordelia shook her head. "It was meant for you," she said. "We have a whole stack in the library, anyway. . . ."

And, as if stirred up on the memory of ink and paper rustling, an idea came to Cordelia.

"There is one thing you can do to help, you know," she said. The idea grew louder, and sharper, and wrote its way into a spark of excitement. "My mother never got to finish her book," Cordelia said. "She never found the proof she needed. Maybe . . . maybe you can."

"I wish I could," he said. "But I'm not the right person to ask. I was only ever an amateur, a hobbyist. You need an expert—"

"There *are* no experts," Cordelia said, a little more loudly than she'd intended. "There aren't any experts, because the truth my mom saw doesn't exist yet. You can make it true. You can find what she was looking for. You can at least try."

Almost imperceptibly, he nodded.

Cordelia's relief broke in waves in her chest. "I don't know everything," she said. "Only what my father told me. He said that for years my mother had been trying to track proof of the *Omnia morpheus*—the common shape-shifter. She thought the shape-shifter explained the gaps left in the evolutionary tree. Trouble is, we could have proof of a hundred thousand shape-shifters and never know it. If they die in the form of another kind of creature . . ."

"Then the proof they leave behind is of the disguise. I understand."

Cordelia nodded. "But she thought she'd finally, finally caught a break. She'd been writing to people all over the world: biologists, anthropologists, archeologists. And finally, someone wrote back. There were rumors of a fossil found in the jungle. A 'cursed stone,' the locals called it, that kept twisting and changing. . . ."

"In the jungle?" Professor Natter's eyebrows scurried a little closer together. "That's where this fossil was actually discovered?"

She nodded. "Somewhere in Brazil."

Another half centimeter, and his eyebrows merged into a single knit. "You're *sure* about that?"

"Of course I'm sure," she said, a little impatiently. "My father saw her onto the boat two days later. And the telegram that came with the news was from São Paulo."

He shook his head. "I don't want you to get your hopes up. . . ."

"That's all right," she said. "Impossible things are true all the time."

CHAPTER
25

"Now what?" Elizabeth said, after they'd said goodbye to Professor Natter.

"Now we find a boat," Cordelia said, and instinctively touched her hand to a folded stack of money in her coat pocket—*not*, of course, the pocket singed by the dragon's constant snoring.

The professor had insisted on giving them enough to pay their way onto one of the southbound whalers. But there was a small problem: hardly any ships were headed south, and the few that intended to put in at Boston Harbor had no room for passengers. They made their way painstakingly from one end of the wharves to the other, trying to negotiate for passage. But in all instances, the answer was the same.

"Save your money, girlie. Got no space for you," the captain or first mate would say, glowering down on them. "Don't take pets, neither. That's an ugly dog you got. And what's that other thing—a lizard? I'll give you two dollars for the lizard. That way 'e can help catch spiders on deck."

"He's not a lizard," Elizabeth burst out, the third time someone made the same mistake. "He's a dra—" Until Cordelia elbowed her in the ribs, and she fell silent.

One by one, the ships took off from port, floating away into the mist and drizzle until they were nothing but ghostly silhouettes. Soon there were only four ships left in the harbor; then two; then only one.

The rain continued falling. Cordelia was wet, and cold, and miserable.

"You're making a mistake!" she yelled, sloshing into the waves, as the final ship—their last hope—floated proudly off to sea, masts pointing to the sky like an accusation. Then, changing tactics: "Please come back! Please! Don't leave us!" But it was no use. She screamed herself hoarse as the waves battered her ankles and weighed down her trouser legs, making each step a chore. And still the ship drew farther and farther away, until it was swallowed by the billowing fog. Cordelia's voice echoed back to her across the surface of the roiling water.

Please. Please. Please.

"Come on, Cordelia." Gregory waded into the shallows and put an arm around her. "Let it go."

The water surged at her ankles, kicking back salt spray and sea foam. She wished she could call up a behemoth from the depths, as drowning sailors had once done; they might lash ropes to the backs of the *Gargantuan oceanus* and ride all the way to Boston. But those days were over. Their last remaining relative, the *Minius oceanus*, was roughly the size of a flounder and lived primarily in the shallow waters of the Caribbean. The last ship was vanishing, dissipating like a mirage—and with it, their only hope.

"Hey," Elizabeth said. "What about that ship?" She lifted a finger to point, and Cordelia noted a wart cluster—one of the more embarrassing symptoms of goblin pubescence. But now didn't seem like the time to point it out.

"*Is* that a ship?" Gregory asked, scrunching up his nose. "Looks more like a shipwreck."

He was right. Only now did Cordelia notice the remaining ship, a haphazard heap of timber and sail, listing in the waves at the very end of the wharves. It was half the size of the other ships that had sailed off, and twice as ugly.

"You won't be wanting to waste your time on that ship." The voice, which seemed to materialize from thin air, made Cordelia yelp. But it was just a fisherman, squatting on an overturned crate and gutting sardines from a bucket.

"Why not?" Cordelia and Gregory sloshed out of the water, careful to stay at a good distance from the man and his fish knife.

The man shrugged. "She's cursed," he said casually, as if it should have been obvious. "Got ghosts in the floorboards. At night you can hear 'em wailing."

"Ghosts?" Elizabeth repeated, paling.

The fisherman nodded. "No man ever took a haunted ship out to sea and lived to tell the tale. Captain Wincombe hasn't set out of port in months. Not since October at least."

"Well, thanks very much," Elizabeth said. She grabbed hold of Gregory's elbow, seized Cordelia's hands, and piloted them in the opposite direction. "I guess we'll just have to find some other way to—"

"Wait," Cordelia said, and pulled away from her grip. Her mind was racing. Goblins were real, obviously, and had been intermingling with humans for so long they showed hardly any visible characteristics of their ancestry, except for the occasional wart cluster or a strange proclivity to roll around in the mud.

Gremlins were real, and more common than anyone knew. They existed in every part of the world, perfectly camouflaged; in every part of the world, they lived for nothing so much as stealing keys and important papers and socks. Socks, especially.

Specters were real. Specters weren't even really specters. They were simply a translucent species of the two-legged wailer, a birdlike creature distantly related to the dinosaurs.

But ghosts weren't real. At least, no one had ever proven it. And Cordelia's father knew plenty who had tried.

A handful of young animals, especially dogs, were susceptible to a viral infection that kept their brains alive even after their hearts had stopped. Like Cabal, they could be revived and nourished.

Otherwise, dead was dead.

"We'd like to talk to Captain Wincombe," she announced.

Gregory looked startled. "We would?" he asked.

"We wouldn't," Elizabeth said firmly.

"Try the Gull and Tackle." The fisherman gestured toward a salt-stained shack, which loomed like a deformed mushroom at the end of the pier.

"You heard what the man said," Elizabeth whispered, as they started off. Gregory hurried to keep up, shepherding Cabal and Icky along. The dragon followed a few feet behind, pecking at invisible crumbs. "No haunted ship that sets sail on the seas returns."

"There's no such thing as ghosts," Cordelia said. "Besides, do you have a better idea?"

The inside of the Gull and Tackle was even more dismal than the outside. Battered, water-warped tables were huddled together beneath a fog of tobacco smoke, like refugees taking comfort in the middle of a storm. The haze was so thick that the few customers were transformed into shapeless lumps. At least the darkness would keep Cabal, the dragon, and the filch from attracting any attention.

Gregory cleared his throat. "We're looking for Captain Wincombe," he announced into the gloomy silence. No one spoke. "Do you know where we can find him?"

They were met only with a rustling laugh, hollow as the sound of autumn leaves. This came from a pile of filthy rags, heaped into the rough silhouette of a person, sitting at a corner table.

"You won't find him here," the pile of rags said. "You won't find *him* anywhere."

Then the pile of rags swept off her hat, shook out a wild tangle of curls, and angled her face toward the light. Cordelia was momentarily speechless. She'd never known a woman to captain her own ship. But evidence of the ocean was written all over her face: in the weather-carved look of her skin, in the wind-tossed mess of her curls, in her black and glittering eyes, the color of a nighttime ocean.

"State your business and be off," Wincombe said briskly.

Cordelia took this as an invitation to approach, and herded Gregory and Elizabeth along with her to the table. "We'd like to ask you about passage on your ship."

"There is no passage," Captain Wincombe said. "'Cause there is no ship. A ship that doesn't sail ain't nothing but floating firewood. And no one sails the *Medusa*. She's come down with ghosts. Contagious with ghosts, she is."

Elizabeth made a gurgling sound. Icky ducked behind her legs. Cordelia shot them both a dirty look.

Then she turned back to Captain Wincombe. "When did the hauntings begin?" she asked.

"It was last summer when I first heard 'em. We'd just pulled through a bad hurricane south of the Carolinas. I remember because at first I took all the knocking and shrieking for water damage." She shook her head. "But we couldn't find a hole to spit through, and it only got worse. All night long, I heard 'em wailing, a sound fit to drive a cuckoo clock crazy. Sometimes it sounded like a hundred fists pounding the walls. Then they started coming after the crew. Tore all my skivvies to shreds one time. Plucked my first mate clean of eyebrows another. That ship is cursed."

Captain Wincombe hadn't invited them to sit, but Cordelia took a seat across from her anyway.

"If I can get rid of your ghosts, will you take us down to Boston?"

Wincombe let out a scrape of laughter again. "If you can get rid of my ghosts, girlie, I'll take you to the end of the world."

"Good. Then we have a deal." Cordelia stood up, extended her hand for a shake, and tried not to wince at the force of Wincombe's grip.

"Are you out of your mind?" Elizabeth whispered to Cordelia, as they followed Wincombe out of the Gull and Tackle, toward the ancient boat listing sadly in the waves. From here, the ship did look haunted: its decks blackened, its sails sad and sagging, full of holes, and lichen crawling up the hull, mottling the figurehead of a mermaid. "Since when did you become an expert on ghosts?"

"I'm not. I told you, there's no such thing," Cordelia said. "But Wincombe doesn't have ghosts. She has *pixies*."

CHAPTER
26

Cordelia had lost count of how many pixies she and her father had captured, and treated, over the years. Because they lived in cramped colonies and were known for their explosive tempers and their habit of spitting, licking, punching, and even biting their opponents, illness spread among them quickly.

It took her only an hour to make a simple trap from a length of rope, an empty whiskey barrel, and a bit of plywood she scavenged from the galley. It was likely the pixies were the South American variety, which often migrated north at the start of the sweltering summer; they had either been blown onto the ship by hurricane winds or had deliberately taken shelter there and simply gotten comfortable. The fact that they were setting up for the long haul was confirmed, she thought, by all the pounding and wailing, and by the fact that they'd gone after both underthings and eyebrows.

It would soon be mating season, and they were no doubt decorating extensively for at least one wedding.

It took Cordelia nearly another hour to convince Elizabeth to sacrifice several inches of her curls to the cause, to make a lure. Pixies loved human hair and used it for bunting, carpet, elaborate garlands, and even decorative accessories. But they loved curls most of all. Cordelia would need a good heaping pile of them to attract the attention of the group. Nothing brought a pixie colony together like the fight about how spoils should be divided.

"If I end up looking like a shorn poodle, I'll toss in *your* eyebrows for free," Elizabeth said, after finally submitting. But once a cascade of golden curls was lying at her feet, she marveled aloud how much lighter her head felt. And afterward, she kept swishing her hair back and forth across her shoulders and admiring her reflection in the back of a large cooking spoon.

"I look like an absolute urchin," she said. "My mother will faint when she sees me." But the idea seemed to cheer her enormously. Cordelia couldn't help but wonder how Elizabeth's mother would react when Elizabeth grew bony ridges on her spine and knuckles, if she could get worked up about a simple haircut.

She had to tell Elizabeth the truth.

By now, the sun was setting. Soon the pixies would wake, and the smell of strange intruders in the galley would draw them out to explore.

"Do me a favor, Gregory," Cordelia said. "Go and tell Wincombe that it won't be long before we've chased off all the angry spirits. Make sure the crew is ready to sail immediately."

"Aye, aye, Captain," he said, touching his fingers to his hat in a salute.

His footsteps soon echoed into silence, and Elizabeth and Cordelia were left alone. At least, they were alone except for Icky, Cabal, and the dragon, of course. But they could hardly be counted on for conversation.

There was a long beat of awkward silence. Cordelia was still trying to work out the nicest way to tell a girl that she was, in fact, part-goblin, when Elizabeth spoke up.

"I have something to tell you," she said.

Cordelia took a deep breath. "I have something to tell you too."

"I'll go first," Elizabeth said. "Mine is important."

"Let me go first," Cordelia said. "Mine is important too."

"It's not a competition, Cordelia," Elizabeth snapped.

"Why don't we *both* go at the same time, then," Cordelia said.

"Fine." Elizabeth tried to toss her hair, only to remember that she didn't have enough hair to toss anymore. "On the count of three. One . . . two . . . *three*."

"I'm part-goblin."

"You're part-goblin."

For a second, both girls stared at each other, stunned. Then both said, at the same time, "You *knew*?"

"Of course I knew." Elizabeth was the first to recover and speak. "I found out years ago, after we stumbled in on my great-aunt Gertrude in her nest. I mean, I didn't know she was my great-aunt Gertrude when we found her, obviously . . . although I *did* think it was weird that she was using all the nicest guest pillows for a bed. . . ."

"Why didn't you tell me?" Cordelia asked.

Elizabeth's eyes nearly popped out altogether. "Why do you *think*? My family was already getting hounded. There were reporters at our door, and crazies threatening fire, and then the SNP came barreling in and tried to smoke her right onto their pitchforks. Thankfully, my dad had tunneled an escape route beneath the garden. . . . She's fine now," Elizabeth added. "Remarried, and living in a four-bedroom hole in Arlington, Virginia. Sends up hideous Christmas knits every year.

The last one had beetles in it." She shuddered. "We were terrified someone would find out we were . . . *you know . . .*"

Monsters. The word hung between them in the silence. But even unspoken, it carried power—echoes of violence, of hatred, of cages and isolation.

"My father would have lost his job. My family would have lost everything. No. We had to be sure no one would know. We had to be sure no one would poke around and begin asking questions. That's why," she finished, "my parents said I shouldn't speak to you again."

Cordelia felt the words like the punch of a fist. "They . . . ?"

"They were worried that you would ask too many questions, or get suspicious. You might wonder how she'd managed to survive under the garden for so long, or remember the guest pillows the next time you slept over. Or you would someday notice the green at my mother's roots, or the length of her hands and feet. . . . She made it through her teenage years without ever showing, luckily. But a size-fourteen shoe might still raise eyebrows. I was too ashamed, anyway. . . ."

"There's no reason to be ashamed," Cordelia said. "Most people have a goblin or two *somewhere* in their family tree."

"Yeah, but not beneath their *actual* trees," Elizabeth snapped. "I thought for sure you wouldn't want to be my friend anymore. Especially after I found out I was related to that . . ."

She trailed off with a helpless gesture.

"She is especially warty," Cordelia said synpathetically. "Even for a goblin."

Elizabeth nodded miserably. "You lied to me too, you know. You told me your father was a veterinarian."

"Technically, that's true," Cordelia pointed out.

"Sure. But you left out some *pretty important details*." Elizabeth's eyes flashed yellow again, and this time stayed that way for several long seconds. "If I'd known you were knocking around with dragons and— and hufflepins—"

"Hufflebottoms," Cordelia corrected her.

"—I would have told you the truth. And we could have stayed friends. *Real* friends." Elizabeth looked down again, knotting her hands in her lap. "We moved houses. My mom insisted I grow my hair long and start wearing stupid frilly dresses everywhere, so I'd look like a walking wedding cake. I had to pretend to like St. George's Academy—"

"Wait." Of all the things Elizabeth had admitted, Cordelia thought this was the most surprising of all. "You don't like St. George's Academy?"

She might as well have asked if Elizabeth liked getting stuck with hot pokers.

"Like it?" Elizabeth repeated. "I hate it. I've *always*

hated it. The teachers only teach us nonsense, like how to sew a hemline straight or make conversation at a party. The girls are a bunch of pack animals—if they catch even a whiff of weakness, or difference, or weirdness, it's goodbye to your intestines." She shook her head disgustedly. "I had to act like they did, and dress like they did, and speak like they did. I started to think like they did, sometimes. And then I would remember why all the pretending, and remember it was so that no one like the girls I called 'friends' would scream about the beastly terror in their watercolor class. So none of them would find out what I was, and hate me for it. So no one would."

Cordelia felt a wrench of pity twist around her stomach. She couldn't imagine how lonely Elizabeth's life had been, for years now. She knew what it was like to carry a secret, of course—a big one. But although she'd learned to see the outside world as a threat to monsters—although she'd expected the monsters would be misunderstood and hated—she had never seen the outside world as a personal threat. She had never believed that *she* was the monster—and that everyone, everywhere, would surely hate her for it.

If she'd only been brave enough to tell Elizabeth the truth about her father, and the monsters, Elizabeth might never have believed it, either.

"But someone *did* find out. Actually—more like

some*many*. A whole organization, in fact."

"The SNP," Cordelia said, understanding.

Elizabeth nodded. "They've had their eye on my family ever since my great-aunt Gertrude had to flee in her underpants. They've had their eye on *me*." She bit her lower lip with three rows of teeth. "My parents were hoping the goblin wouldn't show. That I'd take after my mother—she hardly shows at all, really—and not my aunt and her side. My cousin Millicent," she added, "was greening at just ten years old. By eleven she'd developed a taste for spiders. Can you imagine, Cord? *She eats spiders*. Sometimes she takes them with tea!"

It had been years since Elizabeth had called Cordelia by that nickname, Cord. Cordelia had almost forgotten the sound of it. It spread with all the warmth of hot chocolate.

It bobbed with all the floating joy of marshmallows.

"I'm not afraid of spiders," Elizabeth finished. "I'm afraid to like them. I'm afraid one day I'll look at a creepy-crawly and think, 'Now that I think about it, it *has* been several hours since I ate lunch.'"

Although the idea of Elizabeth—with her flouncy dresses, and (formerly) flouncy curls—snacking mindlessly on daddy longlegs might have been comical, Elizabeth looked so miserable that Cordelia couldn't find any humor in it. She thought about telling Elizabeth that spiders were actually full of protein and nutrients, but it didn't seem, somehow, like the right thing to say.

"My father puts mustard on his toast like jam," Cordelia said. "Sardines too. Spiders can't be worse than that."

Elizabeth attempted to smile, and failed. "The SNP is giving cash rewards for help purging Boston of evil. Signs of unnatural possession include discoloration of the skin, yellow eyes, and dental crowding." She shook her head miserably. "I'd been hiding the signs for months, even from my parents. But the night before my birthday, I found . . ."

She tugged down the collar of her dress, and Cordelia swallowed a sharp inhale. The skin at her neck and shoulders had cracked already, revealing an underskin the color and texture of baked mud. That, too, would someday molt, into one of a hundred vibrant colors of the adult goblin's skin.

"I *had* to run away," Elizabeth said. "I couldn't face my parents' disappointment. I couldn't stand to stay and ruin the life they'd worked so hard to protect. I set off for the train station, thinking old Gertrude might take me in. But when I saw you and Gregory . . ."

"You followed us," Cordelia finished for her. Gregory had been right after all. There *had* been someone on their tail, all the way from Boston.

Elizabeth knitted her hands so tightly in her lap,

another row of warts bloomed briefly on her knuckles. "I'm sorry," she said. "I should have trusted you. I should have trusted you years ago."

"And I should have told you the truth," Cordelia said.

A lie, she thought, was a little like building a fence around somebody else's house, as if it might protect anyone from breaking into yours.

"I thought you hated me," she blurted out suddenly. "I thought I wasn't good enough for you."

"And I thought I wasn't good enough for you," Elizabeth said, so quietly Cordelia nearly missed it. When she looked up, her eyes were full of tears, and the vivid green of summer leaves. Her cheeks too. Several warts of strong feeling broke out suddenly on her nose.

She was a goblin. She was Lizzie.

She was the bravest, most beautiful girl Cordelia had ever seen.

"I missed you," Elizabeth whispered.

"I missed you too," Cordelia said, squeezing the words out through the enormity of all her feeling. "So much."

Elizabeth smiled, even as huge tears, dark like moss, dampened her lap. "It isn't a competition, Cord."

Then Elizabeth fell onto Cordelia, or Cordelia leapt for her, and the girl who was part-goblin and the monster-keeper's daughter laughed and cried and hugged and became best friends again. They stayed that way so long that Cabal grew jealous and squirmed into Elizabeth's lap, and then Icky got agitated and began to tug at Cordelia's hair, and then the dragon grew protective and began snapping at Icky.

They might have stayed that way forever—or at least, for hours—were it not for the sudden whirring of soft wings that announced the pixies' arrival.

CHAPTER
27

There were six of them, dark-winged, easily mistaken for moths from a distance.

Until, that is, they started screaming outrage from inside the barrel Cordelia had used for a trap.

"What are they saying?" Elizabeth inched a little closer to the barrel, then jumped backward when it gave an angry wobble.

"You don't want to know," Cordelia said. A common joke among monsterologists was that pixies had 567 words, and only three were appropriate for the dinner table.

Gregory was heartbroken when he returned and found the pixies already captured, and all the action over. But he cheered up when Cordelia asked him to help her with the transfer of the pixies into a birdcage Elizabeth had found in the captain's berth, a sensitive operation that required precision and a strong tolerance of nibbled fingers.

Cordelia showed Gregory how to distinguish between the males and females by the color of the fur that grew all over their bodies, fine as silk. The males were much more vividly colored—in this case, blue and green. The females had tawny fur and beige-and-black-striped wings.

Gregory, it turned out, was a quick study. With no prompting, he had picked out the matron of the clan, identifiable by a secondary set of wings—plucked, no doubt, off the body of her predecessor—secured to her back by a chemical secretion that Cordelia's father had never been able to replicate.

"Didn't see the wings," he said, when Cordelia congratulated him. "I just saw her shrilling all the rest of 'em around."

Captain Wincombe and her skeleton crew—grown miserable after months of stumping around with nothing but solid land around them—agreed to set sail immediately, even though it was only an hour until midnight, and the weather was unfavorable. After they'd let out the sails and turned south toward Massachusetts, the crew got to work scrubbing the deck and chasing cobwebs out of the corners, cleaning out the berths, and driving the shadows from belowdecks with dozens of lanterns, smoking off their whale fat. Wincombe lashed the bird-cage to an iron hook in the mess, narrowly avoiding a nip on the nose when she leaned in for a better view.

"Blow me from the ballast. *Pixies*." Wincombe shook her head. "I thought pixies was just make-believe. Garden twiddle, pastel colors, you know."

"You're thinking of fairies," Cordelia said, as the enraged pixies lunged for Wincombe, shrieking, gnashing their teeth. "And they're totally different species. Pixies are related much more closely to bats, actually."

Wincombe sniffed as if it didn't surprise her. "Don't like them, either," she said.

She told them that the journey would take almost three full days, assuming there were no squalls. Cordelia simply prayed that would be quick enough. After a dinner of hardtack and oyster stew, Cordelia, Gregory, and Elizabeth settled down in one of the cabins. Icky curled up at Elizabeth's feet and belched a quiet bass rhythm that underscored the slushing of the waves and the creaking of the ship as it rose and fell inside of them. Cabal, who'd made due with just a few drops of blood from the nearly empty pipette, snored loudly on his back. And the dragon turned lopsided circles in the air, testing out his wing, which was almost fully healed. His shadow turned circles with him, tripled in size across the ceiling.

It was surprisingly peaceful there, in the narrow room, with the wind singing in the sails and the waves rocking them to sleep and the creaking of the ancient wood.

Cordelia slept for nearly sixteen hours and dreamed of absolutely nothing.

The weather had held. The wind had turned strong. They would soon close in on Boston—and Cordelia's thoughts turned to revenge.

CHAPTER
28

Byron Newton-Plancke had inherited his father's vast chain of pharmacies, and the wealth that went along with it. A portion of the family estate, sprawled across twenty lavish acres just a few miles outside of Boston, was a dedicated museum of natural history, and boasted the largest private collection of fossilized and biological relics in the world. On rare days, the museum was open to the general public. For the most part, however, Plancke kept the doors barred to everyone but special patrons and invited guests.

Cordelia learned all this from the *No Trespassing* sign hung neatly from the heavy iron padlock on the gates.

Thanks to Professor Natter, they had paid for a hansom cab to take them out to the estate, surprised to find that the driver knew the way without any address.

"You've got crowds going just to get a peek of him through a window four hundred yards away," he said. "And bigwigs, too, kinda names you only see in the paper. Governors and deans and book writers and all kinds of swanks. Well. I guess they want to get in good now, just in case he *does* become president. . . ." The driver leaned over to spit from his perch. "I hope he doesn't, though. Saw him once or twice. Somethin' the matter with his eyes. Never seem to be lookin' in the same direction."

It was just after eight o'clock in the morning when they arrived, and brittle cold. Cordelia was sorry to see the old man and his carriage go, rattling and bumping back down the road. She couldn't help but feel that they were being abandoned at the end of the world, although the idea was absurd. Several reporters had beaten them there and tried to argue, unsuccessfully, with the patrolling guards for admittance. Cordelia gestured the others into the dense trees just across the road, where they would have a clear view of the gates.

"No press on the premises today." Only one of the guards spoke. The other three remained in the guard-house, blank and indistinguishable as enormous knobs of clay. "No exceptions."

Undeterred, the reporters began to fire off questions.

"Is it true that the governor has been invited to tour?"

"Is it true that he has the endorsement of the police commissioner?"

"Is it true he has another book in the works?"

"The book's finished," the guard corrected him. "Mr. Newton-Plancke is expecting his publisher today, in fact. Now clear off, or I'll have you hauled in for harassment."

The Newton-Plancke estate was patched with snow, and above the swell of the winter gardens, the mansion spread vastly across the hill. A scud of clouds bustled busily across the blue sky.

A beautiful day. A beautiful place.

But Cordelia couldn't shake the impression of something dark and evil waiting for them just beyond the gates. She could *feel* it, like the squelch of sewage beneath a boot. The monsters seemed to feel it too. Icky kept squirming in Elizabeth's arms, and Cabal's fur stood up on his spine. The dragon, already too big now for Cordelia's pocket, had settled on her shoulder, and every so often hissed an agitation of smoke.

Stay calm, Cordelia told herself. She had gone up against ghouls and flesh-eating chupacabras; she had once taken a piggyback ride on a werewolf, whose breath had still smelled of blood.

She could do this. *They* could do it.

They had to.

"How will we get in?" Elizabeth whispered.

"The guard said that Plancke is expecting his publisher today," Cordelia said. Somewhere in that beautiful prison of stone and marble, a terrible plot had taken root, spreading poisonous ideas about monsters and men. "I say we go along for the ride."

Breakfast was a bag of old pretzels, bartered from a baker selling down by the docks for one of Elizabeth's hairpins, which she no longer needed. It was very cold in the trees, especially when the wind picked up. But the overhanging evergreens kept them nicely concealed.

Around noon, they heard the rattle of an approaching carriage, and a muffled shout from the guardhouse. Cordelia stood up quickly, trying to stamp the feeling back into her toes. She knew from the size of the coach, and the sleekness of the horses pulling it, that this must be Plancke's visitor from the publishing house.

"Come on," she said, as the driver slowed outside the gates. "Now's our chance."

As the guards busied themselves with the padlock, and heaving open the heavy iron gates, Cordelia, Gregory, and Elizabeth—each of them holding tight to one of the monsters—sprinted the short distance to the carriage and ducked beneath the rear boot just before the driver cracked his whip to urge the horses forward again. Clinging tight to the leather thoroughbraces that girded the underside of the carriage, squeezed together between the enormous hammered wheels, they scuttled forward with the motion of the horses, passing straight through the gates and leaving the guardhouse behind.

Soon the drive twisted sharply around a stand of thick fir trees, taking them out of view of the guardhouse. At a silent gesture from Cordelia, all three of them released their hold on the thoroughbraces and let the carriage roll on without them up the hill to the main entrance. They ducked into the trees, being careful to avoid the crunchy bits of snow that might betray their presence, scouting for a secondary entrance.

The shadow of the mansion soon engulfed them, and they were close enough to see the coach release its sole passenger—a plump little man who looked exactly like an overgrown baby, stuffed into a two-small suit and given a cigar for a pacifier.

Suddenly, Elizabeth hissed in a breath. "That's him," she said. "Newton-Plancke. Coming down the stairs."

A shiver of dread moved down Cordelia's spine. Newton-Plancke's face looked vaguely familiar—she had, she thought, seen him before in the newspapers her father occasionally used for the pixies' bedding— although from a distance it was difficult to make out more than the impression of a normal man, pulled like a length of taffy into the longest, thinnest person Cordelia had ever seen. His face was long. His nose was long. His mouth was long, and played drooping support to a long mustache and an even longer beard. His neck and arms and fingers were long. His legs, too. She was reminded, as he jogged down the stairs to greet his visitor, of the jointed appendages of a spider.

Plancke exchanged a few words with the new arrival and disappeared inside. A moment later, Cordelia saw the lights come on in what she assumed was a drawing room. They must have settled down in the part of the estate that served as Plancke's private residence, because signs at the top of the drive pointed museum visitors to the wing on the opposite side of the building.

"Let's see if we can find a way in through the museum," she said. "That's where he'll be showing the monsters, anyway."

Luckily, the estate was stippled with trees and greenhouses, miniature follies and fountains, and statues dedicated to the achievements of previous

Newton-Planckes (most of them invented, Cordelia was sure), so they had no shortage of hiding places as they made their way across the estate.

"I didn't know that Roger Newton-Plancke patented the steam engine," Elizabeth whispered, as they ducked behind an enormous statue of yet another long and evil-looking ancestor squeezing a miniature train in one triumphant fist.

"That's because he didn't," Cordelia whispered back. "Any more than Elliot Newton-Plancke invented the sock. Now come on."

To their relief, there were no guards posted at the entrance of the museum, although another sign indicated its closure to the public.

But the doors were, unsurprisingly, locked.

"What now?" Elizabeth said, with a huff of frustration that flushed her freckles green.

Cordelia shook her head. The lower windows were barred, and she saw no way up to the upper floors. Icky could climb, of course. . . . But what would he do once he got inside, if he got inside? He would likely follow the smell of food to the kitchens, or get hysterical and knock down some priceless exhibit.

Gregory was bent double, puzzling over the lock. "This one's fiddly for picking," he muttered. "Too bad we don't have a torch. . . ." Then he straightened up suddenly, eyes flashing. "That's it. That's how we get in. We'll torch the lock. Flimsy bit of metal like that, shouldn't take more than a few seconds."

"But we don't have a torch," Elizabeth said testily. "You said so yourself."

He gave her a smirk that Elizabeth herself couldn't have beaten. "True. But we got a *dragon*." And he plucked the dragon from Cordelia's shoulder, gave him a tickle, and neatly ducked the trajectory of fire.

The lock was melted, and the doors opened within seconds.

Just like that, Gregory, Cordelia, and Elizabeth were inside Byron Newton-Plancke's Museum of Natural and Unnatural History.

CHAPTER 29

They stood for a second in the foyer, waiting for their eyes to adjust to the dark. An empty welcome desk advertised the price of admission at ten cents.

"Hall of Prehistoric Evolution, Hall of Biological Curiosities, Hall of Anthropological History . . ." Elizabeth read off the signs that pointed the way to different exhibits that encircled the entrance hall. "Where are we supposed to begin?"

Cordelia shook her head. Something felt wrong. It was too quiet, too still, too *dark*. There was no whir of pixie wings, no chatter of excited diggles, no slosh of squelch feet in the muddy water that formed their habitat. Only a cavernous silence that echoed back every footstep and rustle, only louder.

But perhaps Byron Newton-Plancke had found a way to keep them quiet. . . .

She didn't want to think about what else he might have done.

"We'll start with Biological Curiosities and search the rooms one by one," Cordelia said. She knew it would be faster to split up, but she couldn't bear to be alone in the gloom and silence, with the wet slick of fear moving down her back.

They passed from exhibit to exhibit, past the skeletal remains of ancient species and the vivid reconstructions of extinct predators glowering from dioramas. Past murky jars of three-eyed fish and dead jellyfish, giant walls of butterflies and insects pinned into place, taxidermy snakes and fossil remnants.

But no monsters.

With every passing minute, the knot of anxiety in Cordelia's stomach grew bigger. Where were the monsters? She was sure they weren't wrong about Byron Newton-Plancke. She was sure this wasn't another dead end.

So where were they?

When they were satisfied they'd explored every corner

of the ground floor, they headed upstairs. By now, Cordelia had lost track of how much time had passed. Ten minutes? Thirty? The shadowed halls seemed to suction not just light, but time. And the longer they stayed, the greater the chances they would be discovered.

The second-floor landing fanned left and right, into the Hall of Prehistoric Evolution and the Hall of Anthropological History. Between them, a sweeping set of velvet curtains pooled fabric on the floor. Then the fabric rippled slightly and discharged a marble into the open.

Immediately, Cabal lunged.

"Cabal, no." Gregory tried to grab hold of his collar, but Cabal was too fast. The marble skittered beneath the curtains when he walloped it with a paw, and Cabal went under them after it.

"Cabal!" Gregory leapt forward and swept the curtains apart.

Cordelia sucked in a breath. Icky whimpered.

Cabal was gone—vanished into the dark mouth of a concealed exhibit hall, roped off from visitors with a sign that marked it as *Incomplete*.

But the newly painted letters stenciled above the entrance made its purpose clear.

Hall of Monsters.

A mounted placard on the wall welcomed visitors to:

THE WORLD'S FIRST COMPREHENSIVE
HISTORICAL COLLECTION OF MONSTROSITY,
TRACING THE EVOLUTION OF MONSTERS FROM
THEIR PREHISTORIC ORIGINS TO THE DIVERSITY
OF THEIR MODERN FORMS. PLEASE USE CAUTION
WHEN APPROACHING LIVE SPECIMENS.

With a growing sense of horror, Cordelia, Gregory, and Elizabeth moved into the soupy dark of a vast hall, five times the size of any of the others. Cabal was sniffing around the base of a towering mural that dominated the center of the room. Even in the dark, Cordelia recognized the twisted shape of what looked like two inverted trees, side by side, and the neat lettering beneath them. One inscription read *The Origin of Species*.

And written beneath, the dark one, the twistier one, the uglier one: *The Origin of Monsters*.

It was the only thing in the room—besides the long, skeletal rows of empty iron cages.

Elizabeth sucked in a deep breath. Gregory whispered a bad word he had only just learned from Captain Wincombe. Cabal began growling.

"Hush," Cordelia said. But he only growled louder and made a sudden leap toward the marble he'd been chasing before, which promptly rolled behind one of the cages, shooting into the narrow space that separated it from the wall. Cabal tried to squeeze in after it, but had to settle for swiping with a paw.

"Be quiet, Cabal," Cordelia said urgently, as Cabal's barking became louder and more frenzied.

"He's going to get us killed," Elizabeth said in a shrill, terrified voice.

"Stop it," Cordelia said. She dropped to her knees just as Cabal managed to dislodge the cage a few more inches from the wall and disappeared. She reached for him and missed. Instead, her hand came down on something puddled on the floor—something slimy and very cold. She jerked back immediately and saw a long trail of green goo coating her palm. For a moment she simply stared, bewildered.

She had seen that goo before.

She had seen it on the floor of her father's bedroom.

Time seemed to slow down, and awareness gathered on the edges of Cordelia's consciousness like waves swelling in the ocean before a storm. Still on her knees, she pivoted the cage out from the wall a little more, so that she too could squeeze behind it.

Cabal was in a crouch, growling terribly at the marble, with all the fur standing along his spine. Suddenly he turned, whimpering, and fled into the open.

The marble retreated another few inches into the shadows.

But not before Cordelia had seen that it was not a marble. Not at all.

It was an eyeball. A *moving* eyeball, with a pale blue iris and a pupil as dark as ink.

Suddenly, it zoomed into the open, missing her by inches, leaving a trail of thick slime behind it.

Cordelia opened her mouth to scream. But she didn't need to; Elizabeth screamed for her, then abruptly went silent, even as the dragon started screeching.

Hands gripped Cordelia's ankles. She tried to turn. A heavy burlap sack was thrown over her head, and there was a starburst explosion of pain at her temples, then darkness.

CHAPTER
30

"Well, well, well. Cordelia Clay, what a pleasure. I must admit, I've been wanting to meet you for quite a long time."

Cordelia's brain felt as if it had been swirled around in a stewpot and then sloshed haphazardly back into her head. She was in one of the exhibit hall's steel cages. Gregory and Elizabeth had been enclosed in cages of their own; so had Cabal, Icky, and the dragon. The dragon, additionally, had been muzzled, and his wings clipped to the floor by means of small iron rings.

Cordelia struggled to sit up, moaning at the throbbing

pressure in her forehead.

Up close, Byron Newton-Plancke gave even more the impression of a man made up of old elastic, stretched one too many times. And Cordelia saw, at once, that their cabdriver had been right—there was something wrong with his eyes.

First of all, he had none.

Or rather—he had no eyes in his *face*, just gaping red sockets.

The eyes in question were on the floor, separated by at least four feet. One of them rolled closer to her cage bars, and she drew back instinctively.

"Don't be afraid . . . yet," Newton-Plancke said. "They can look, but they can never touch." He laughed at his own joke. The second eye rolled slightly, as if it didn't find its limitations very funny.

Then both eyes swiveled in her direction. "Pretty girl," he said. "Though I don't see much resemblance to your mother."

Cordelia's heart seemed to freeze in her chest. A terrible feeling slid from her neck to the base of her spine.

"My mother?" she whispered.

Newton-Plancke twitched his long, thin lips into a smile. "A smart woman," he said casually. "Had a promising career ahead of her—at least, until she met your father and became consumed by her *ridiculous* idea of a single evolutionary tree. I tried many times to point out the error of her thinking. But she was too stubborn. . . ."

Now Cordelia's heartbeat punched back on, and she fought against a sudden breathlessness. "You—you knew my mother?"

"We ran, for a time, in similar circles," he said. "Her early work showed promise, I admit." Cordelia remembered, in a flash, what Professor Natter had told her: the group of monster experts and hobbyists was small, and tightly knit. But Cordelia didn't believe for a second that any group, big or small, would have welcomed Byron Newton-Plancke as a member.

Probably he had slimed his way in. He clearly had practice.

"But after she made herself a laughingstock . . ." Newton-Plancke shrugged. "Well, like I said. I tried to warn her. Her ideas were more than absurd. They were *dangerous*. Just imagine the idea of monsters being *normal*, of monsters being *necessary*. It's a threat to civilized society as we know it! Luckily, there was no danger that she would be believed . . . not after the failure of her first book. It was a sad thing, really, for a woman of such promise. Overnight, no one would touch her, much less her nonsensical theories. . . ."

In a moment, Cordelia's fear tightened into hatred. "It was you," she said. "You were the one who got all her books yanked from the libraries and bookstores. You were the one who got her banned from speaking, from publishing."

"Of course," he said simply, without regret. As Cordelia watched, disgusted, both eyes rolled quickly back to his feet, leaving small, slick trails of green slime behind them. He bent down to retrieve them, then worked them back into his face with a sickening squeaking sound, like a wet finger around the rim of a glass. "What else could I do?"

Cordelia noticed that he had mispositioned his eyes. His left eye was rolling ever so slightly toward the bridge of his nose. He had monster blood, obviously, and was likely descended from a long-ago line of . . . what? Not goblins, certainly. Trolls, perhaps? But no troll species she could think of came with detachable eyes; many hardly used their eyes at all, and navigated mostly by smell. And she understood, all at once, why Newton-Plancke was on a mission to purge monsters and their descendants from the world.

It was like her father had always said: Fear is the real monster. It breeds by making monsters, and the monsters make more fear.

"You're afraid," she said, and was pleased to see the words wipe the smirk from Plancke's face. "You're terrified you'll be found out for what you are. For *whatever* you are."

"Quiet," he snapped, and Cordelia felt sure she was right. Who would possibly suspect him of being a monster, when he had dedicated his life to rooting them out? "Or I'll have your tongue cut out for dog feed."

Cordelia didn't doubt it. Even though she would have liked to torture and insult him, to see him squirm, she knew she would only enrage him, and put the others in even more danger. She tucked her tongue firmly behind her teeth so it wouldn't betray her better judgment.

Byron Newton-Plancke then pivoted to face Elizabeth. As he scanned her filthy dress and ragged mess of curls, his face twisted into an ugly sneer. "Let me guess," he said. "Poor little rich girl on a runaway adventure. What happened? Do Mommy and Daddy ignore you? Do they stick you away with the governess and refuse to give you kisses? Are they *embarrassed* by you?" Even his laugh was stretched thin, a hysterical giggle that soon died in his throat.

"Shut up," Elizabeth said. Anger was darkening her cheeks to green. Cordelia wanted to shout a warning. But of course, Elizabeth couldn't help it.

It was too late, anyway. Plancke jerked backward when the warts began to pop angrily at her hairline, as if goblins were contagious. "I see," he said, as his lips curled back over his teeth in a sneer. "Well, no wonder they're embarrassed. Ugly little brute. Although I suppose it was their fault, for having you in the first place."

"Yeah, well, at least she can keep her eyes in her face," Gregory fired back at him as Elizabeth ducked her head, blinking away tears. Cordelia longed to reach out a hand and comfort her. She knew Plancke might feed that to the dogs, too, and might have risked it anyway. But the cages were too far apart.

"True," Plancke said icily, turning now to Gregory. "But she's the one in the cage, isn't she? An unfortunate position to be in," he added, "although perhaps for you it is quite the upgrade from your usual accommodations." He leaned a little closer and sniffed. Then he drew back with a look of disgust. "Just as I thought. You reek of orphan, you know. A boy no one will miss. Don't bother to contradict me"—this, as Gregory opened his mouth to protest—"I can smell it on you. The desperation. The sad, cloying desire to be liked. Is that why you volunteered to come with Cordelia on her misadventure?"

Gregory's eyes were burning. He lifted his chin. "Cordelia's my friend," he said. "She helped me, and so I helped her."

"And then she 'helped' you into quite a pickle," Plancke said. "So I suppose her 'friendship' came with a price tag."

"I don't know about that." Gregory shrugged. "Buying friends is your line of work."

The effect was immediate. Newton-Plancke's face

twisted so suddenly into a rage, his eyes popped—literally—and he barely managed to push them back in place. "I have more friends than you have breaths left in your body!" he shrieked. "I have so many friends, I've lost count of how many friends I've lost count of!"

"And how many of them would sit in a cage just to keep you company?" Gregory fired back.

"Shut up!" In his anger, Plancke seemed to bloat. His eyes bulged in his face, and his head ballooned on his neck. "Shut up! Or I'll cut you up into so many pieces, even the dogs won't have use for you!"

Cordelia's fear turned to fury. It was because of people like Byron Newton-Plancke that Elizabeth had carried the burden of loneliness and worry along with her all these years. It was people like Byron Newton-Plancke who imagined monsters everywhere, insisted monsters *be* everywhere, just to have an answer for the gnawing fear inside them.

"All right, then. Go ahead. You can start with me." Cordelia grabbed hold of the bars and shook; not because she thought it would do any good, but because she needed to push something, to squeeze something, to work the anger out of her palms. "If you're so desperate to kill us, why waste time?"

"*Cordelia,*" Elizabeth whispered sharply.

Newton-Plancke's fit of temper had passed. He turned to Cordelia with a look of some amusement. "I assure you that your time here will be *well* worth it. But since you are so eager to get down to business . . ."

He came closer, and closer. Cordelia noticed that he didn't seem to walk so much as ooze, or glide, and she thought of those long trails of slime. What *was* this man?

Finally, his shadow fell across her, and all her bravery withered. His eyes were colorless, dead-looking. His skin was the marbled white of bad cheese.

"Tell me, Cordelia." His fingers were so long, he threaded one easily through the bars to lift her chin, even after she scooted away from him. "Where are the monsters?"

CHAPTER
31

Cordelia felt as if the question had turned solid and blown a hole through her chest. "What do you mean?"

"The monsters, Cordelia. The only private collection of monsters in the world. The world's only private collection of monsters, representing more than a dozen species. So many different kinds of living horror, here, right in Boston. Proof of evolution gone horribly awry. Proof of life gone terribly wrong." He withdrew his finger slowly, letting her feel the sharpness of his fingernail. "Where are they?"

It was Elizabeth who spoke. She'd given in to the surge of goblin and was almost completely green. Warts ran down the length of her nose, dividing it exactly in the middle. "Very funny," she said. "You've obviously had lots of practice playing dumb."

Plancke kept one eye on Cordelia and spun the other one in Elizabeth's direction to glare. "I will ask you again nicely." His voice was very quiet, but Cordelia wasn't fooled. She could hear the anger pulled tight underneath it. "Then the question will be very painful—for you. Where. Are. The. Monsters?"

Panic was building inside Cordelia, pressing at her stomach and throat. "You tell me," she fired back. "*You're* the one who stole them. You're the one who's got my dad locked up somewhere. You're the one playing games."

Plancke jerked backward, as though touched by an electric shock. For a moment, he said nothing. His eyes roved every inch of her face, and she imagined that they left her covered with a film of slime.

Then he gave a short sigh and turned away from her. "I see," he murmured, frowning. "How foolish I've been. You were unaware . . . that is, he never told you . . ." Producing a pair of glasses from one coat pocket and a handkerchief from another, he began to polish the lenses. "Well. It's no matter now. There's more than one way to skin a cat. We will draw him out, from wherever he's been lurking."

Cordelia swallowed. Her mouth was as dry as dust. "Are you saying . . . are you truly saying . . . you have no idea where my father is? Where the monsters are?"

Newton-Plancke brought the glasses to his mouth and gave a little huff to mist them. "How could I?" he said unconcernedly. "I had been keeping an eye on them—literally—for quite some time. I even wrote him a letter, hoping he might see reason once he realized all of the *benefits* that his cooperation might buy. Unfortunately, it seems he decided on a most *un*reasonable course of action." Having polished his glasses carefully with a silk handkerchief, he repositioned them on his nose. "By the time I arrived—under the legal authority of the governor's office, and with the full support of the Boston Police—your father had made off with them."

Cordelia felt as if the ground was spinning beneath her. "I don't understand," she whispered. Her *father* had taken the monsters? But why? And where?

And why hadn't he brought Cordelia with him?

"Surely you see, child. It's the only thing that makes sense. It had been many years, of course, since our last . . . *run-in*. I wish I could say it was a pleasant one." Newton-Plancke's lips curled back over gums the gray-pink of a dead salmon. Even his *teeth* were long. "Your father and I exchanged some very nasty words. He even, I'm ashamed to say, managed to throw in a punch."

"He should've thrown in a few more, for good measure," Gregory muttered.

Newton-Plancke ignored him. His eyes were fixed on Cordelia. "He might have killed me then," he said. "He wanted to. I could tell. All because I'd said to be careful *proof* of his wife's love for monsters wasn't growing in her belly . . . after all, she was seven months pregnant then. . . ."

"You're a monster," Cordelia spat.

Suddenly, he drew closer again. "Say it again," he said.

"You're a monster," she said, a little louder. Then louder again: "You're a monster! You're a monster!"

"Go on," Newton-Plancke said. "Let it out. You'll feel better."

"You're a monster!" She was screaming now. Now the fire was inside of her, scorching her insides, clawing up her throat and burning through her mouth. "My father should have killed you when he had a chance!"

Unexpectedly, a wide grin split his face. He reminded her in that moment of a jack-o'-lantern, behind which some maniacal fire was burning. "You see?" he said. "You see how *good* it feels—to scream, to point your finger, to say *die*?"

Cordelia realized, in that second, that he'd tricked her.

He bent down, so they were eye to eye. "Your mother intervened that night to save me," he said softly. "She told your father to leave me. She even, I believe, made him apologize for getting blood on my shirt. *Vince malum bono*, she said. Good overcomes evil. . . ."

Cordelia recognized the words from the frontispiece of her mother's unfinished book. Now the fire had turned to a kind of sickness. She didn't feel well. She felt as if she needed to throw up.

"She even offered me her hand. . . ."

"Stop." She couldn't listen anymore. "Stop it."

For the first time ever, she was gripped by hatred for her mother. How could she have been so stupid? How could she have loved monsters—any monsters, all monsters—more than she loved the people who really needed her protection? How could she have loved evil, more than she did its victims?

"That's exactly what I told her," Newton-Plancke said. "But it was just another one of her misguided ideas, and she was as stubborn about it as all the others. My philosophy has always been *Vincere est vivere*— to conquer is to live. In fact, I was just having a lively debate with my publisher about whether or not it should subtitle my next book. You see, Cordelia . . ." A strange ripple pulled his face, for a moment, into a hundred other faces—dimly familiar, people she had seen at the pharmacist, in the park, on the street. "I know better than anyone that monsters can be very, very dangerous. That is why, for years, I let your father go on collecting proof. I waited until he had all the evidence I needed."

The room was spinning into dark. Or it had disappeared, and Cordelia was spinning, down into the darkness of Newton-Plancke's eyes, where she could see the past distorted. The only known domestic collection of monsters in the world. More than two dozen species. Here, in Boston.

They'd been so stupid. All along, they'd been doing Newton-Plancke's work.

"I waited until I would be able to use it for good. For the country. For the world. There must be rules, you see. There must be *right* . . ."

Now, he slotted all ten fingers into the cage, between the bars. As she watched, his fingers *grew*, flowed like narrow rivulets of skin toward her face.

". . . or else how would you know that you aren't *wrong*?"

Cordelia skittered backward, choking on a scream. But there was nowhere to go. Soon the fingers were at her jaw and pinning her gaze to his.

"You do have her eyes, you know," he said. He passed

a long, slick finger over her cheek, and Cordelia fell into the hole of fear in her stomach. Then, in a different voice: "I want you to know I regret what I had to do," he said. "I tried to avoid it. It was her fault. She gave me no choice. It had become a matter of survival. She was trying to expose me, you understand, even if she didn't know it. . . ."

"What—what are you talking about?" Cordelia's voice sounded as if it came from far away.

"It gave me no pleasure to kill your mother," Newton-Plancke said simply. And in a second, with a terrible, wet, suctioning sound, he retracted his fingers—and Cordelia, at last, knew what he was.

"A morpheus," she whispered. "You're . . . you're a morpheus."

"Your father taught you well." He stood up. He neatened his shirt and coat, readjusted his sleeves. "Now you see, I think, why I had to do it. Your mother had already written several prominent universities to claim she'd even tracked down fossil evidence. . . ."

"In Brazil," Cordelia said. "That's why she went."

"An absurd gambit," Newton-Plancke said sharply. "She knew better than to believe the morpheus would possibly leave evidence in *Brazil*. I should have seen right through her trap."

A question tickled the very back of Cordelia's mind.

A *doubt*. But she couldn't make it take shape. "Her . . . trap?"

"I'm afraid I wasn't thinking clearly. I was too focused on making sure her evidence—if she *had* any—would never become public. It might have ruined everything." He turned away with a shrug. "Stupid woman. Perhaps she'd thought to weaken me. But I was still strong enough to kill her."

He made hardly a sound as he oozed across the exhibit hall toward a door marked *Private—No Trespassing*. Cordelia assumed the museum abutted his living quarters directly. "I look forward to seeing your father again. Soon, I should imagine, now that my whisperers have begun their work. Your father is a wanted man, you know. It is quite criminal to leave a twelve-year-old child unattended. And Boston is a civilized city."

Cordelia finally understood. He would lure her father out—using Cordelia as bait.

At the door, he paused to look back at her. "I hope we can put all that unpleasantness behind us. After all, I am quite grateful to him. I will be president because of him."

He smiled. "And you, of course." Then, casually, as he slipped through the door: "I hope you don't mind the dark."

And with that, he slammed the door shut.

CHAPTER
32

Time seemed to stretch interminably. Moonlight reached across the exhibit hall with long, pale fingers, like the frigid reach of Newton-Plancke's hands.

Cordelia's mind was turning so quickly, she felt dizzy even sitting down.

Newton-Plancke had reminded her of something . . . something she had read . . . something important . . .

Cordelia closed her eyes. She saw, in a flash, Professor Natter leaning heavily on his walking stick down by the docks. She saw his eyebrows drawn into a single, dense cloud. . . .

In the jungle? Even in her memory, she saw his eyebrows leap. *You're sure?*

"Give it up," Elizabeth grunted. "You don't have the key, anyway."

"But if I could just *reach*—" Gregory panted.

"Elizabeth's right," Cordelia said. Her voice echoed. "We'll never get out of here without the key."

"We may never get out of here *at all*," Elizabeth said quietly.

There was a moment of heavy silence. They all knew what she said was true. At last Gregory gave up and sat down with a sigh. Cordelia's throat was tight. All her fault. This was all her fault.

"I'm sorry," she blurted. It was easier to apologize in the dark. Easier to talk, really, when she didn't have to see the way that Gregory and Elizabeth were looking at her. "This is all my fault. If it weren't for me, we wouldn't be in this mess."

"That's all right," Gregory said.

"No." Cordelia shook her head. "No, it isn't all right. I nearly got us killed a half-dozen times. And now . . ." *And now all hope is lost,* she added silently.

"I'm sorry too," Gregory said, after a moment. Cordelia turned to him. "Why are *you* sorry?"

"Just because," he said, shrugging. "You shouldn't have to be sorry all on your own."

Cordelia felt her throat squeeze up to the size of a pea. She wanted to reach out and hug Gregory. But of course, the cage bars prevented it. There was another moment of silence. Elizabeth cleared her throat.

"I'm sorry too," she said.

Cordelia was so startled she forgot, temporarily, to feel awful. "What are *you* sorry for?"

"For lying," Elizabeth said. "And for being so horrible. And for being, well . . ." She held open her hands, which were swollen to double their normal size, and blinked her yellow eyes mournfully at them. *"This."*

"You aren't *this*," Cordelia said. "You aren't anything. You're *you*. And that's nothing to be sorry about."

"Besides, the green looks good on you," Gregory said cheerfully. "Goes with your haircut."

Cordelia felt it then—something shifting, growing, knitting together between them in the dark, something delicate as silk, invisible as wind. They were changing. They were *changed*. Cordelia had spent so long trying to keep everything exactly the way it was. But about this, too, she'd been wrong.

It was so cold in the exhibit hall, their breath seized on the air. Soon Cordelia's fingers were numb, and Elizabeth's shivering was so bad that her three sets of teeth chattered together.

"You'd think a big-timer like Plancke could afford

a bit of heat," Gregory said, hugging his knees to his chest. "But it's always the rich ones don't like to spend a dime. . . ."

"It isn't that," Cordelia said. She plunged her fists into her pockets and was surprised to feel her mother's little oval stone had made it past Newton-Plancke's inspection of their pockets, perhaps because it had slipped underneath the empty bag of pretzels. The rest of her tools were gone. "It's because of what he is. The morpheus despises the heat. Imagine how it feels to be melting, if you're actually in danger of—"

She broke off, gasping.

"What?" Gregory said. "What is it?"

"—*in danger of melting,*" she finished in a whisper. "No morpheus would ever dream of living in the jungle. . . ."

"The jungle?" Gregory frowned. "Who said anything about a jungle?"

"My mother sailed to Brazil before she died. She claimed she was looking for fossil evidence of a morpheus. But she can't have been. She knew better. Heat and moisture weaken the morpheus's shape and make it much harder for it to take a lasting form." Cordelia was breathless with excitement. Now she understood what Newton-Plancke meant by *trap.* "She must have been trying to lure Newton-Plancke to go after her, to a place where he would be weak enough to . . ."

But she trailed off. Weak enough to trap? To reason with? Surely she hadn't been planning to kill him. . . .

And just as quickly as her excitement came, it left. Whatever she'd been planning to do hadn't worked. In the end, he had beaten her at her own game.

Just like he had beaten Cordelia.

Like he would no doubt beat her father.

It was like Plancke had said: even weak, he was strong enough. Stronger than they were, certainly.

She had the funny oval stone in her hands now, this little relic of her mother's life—meaningless and beautiful and easily mistaken for any other, but for the etchings on its surface. Lives, too, were like that. Insignificant, beautiful only to the people who looked closely enough.

Who would miss her mother, if Cordelia and her father were gone? Who would think about her?

Had her mother been thinking of Cordelia when she died?

She was crying without meaning to. The tears were hot on her cheeks, and fell so hard and fast she didn't bother to try and stop them. Who got to say what was beautiful and what wasn't, who was important and who didn't belong, which lives had value, and which ones more value? Whose lives disappeared like stones down a well, forgotten and ignored, dismissed and vilified, because they simply weren't the right shape? If only certain stars got to shine in the night sky, wouldn't the sky be a little uglier? Wouldn't it be missing pieces?

The stone was now dark with tears, and warm from her grip. She'd been squeezing so tightly, she'd even left the imprint of her fingers on its surface. . . .

Cordelia blinked. *She'd left the imprint of her fingers on its surface.* Even its shape was different now—no longer oval, but tubular and flesh-colored, and sized exactly for her cupped hand. But when she opened her fingers, it pooled immediately across her palm. . . .

She dropped it with a cry and saw it wink, and harden into sharp edges, and flush the exact color of steel.

"What is it, Cordelia?" Gregory said.

"Don't tell me it's a spider," Elizabeth said. "I haven't eaten anything for hours, and I don't want to be tempted."

"Cordelia had the last pretzel," Gregory said. "But she might let you lick the salt. . . ."

"It's not a spider," Cordelia said wonderingly. "It's a fossil." She flipped the small panel of metal into her hand and saw it take on the color and shape of her hand again. "It's a *morpheus* fossil. My mother had it all along."

"I thought you said—" Gregory began.

Cordelia interrupted him. "I don't understand it,

either," she said. "But I'm sure. And look. See how it changes? See how it fills in the shape of whatever it touches? Water relaxes the morpheus's shape. I must have soaked it while I was crying. And my hand was hot. . . ."

"Cordelia." Elizabeth's voice was suddenly high with excitement. "What about a key?"

Cordelia looked over at her, confused. "What *about* a key?"

Elizabeth was on her knees, gripping the bars of her cage. "Will it take on the shape of a key? A key fitted *exactly* to a very complicated lock?"

Suddenly, Cordelia understood.

With trembling fingers, she stretched an arm through the bars of the cage and tried to reach for the lock on the cage door. The angle was so awkward, she could barely get the fossil up to the keyhole.

"Come on," she whispered. "Come on."

Gregory and Elizabeth were watching her intently. Cordelia held her breath. The fossil had taken on the shape of a finger. She nudged it a little closer. . . .

And nearly lost her grip, as one end of the fossil narrowed into the keyhole, and twisted around the bolts, and hardened into shape.

Cordelia barely had to turn before she heard a *click*, and was free.

Both Gregory and Elizabeth shouted when Cordelia tumbled out into the open. Cabal began to bark, and Icky to whine, until Cordelia hushed both of them.

"Hurry, Cordelia," Elizabeth said. As if she needed to be told.

She rubbed the fossil in her palms to warm it and ran to Gregory's cage. But just as soon as she'd fed it into the lock, she heard the *swish* of curtains behind her.

Then a familiar voice called to her. "Cordelia?"

She barely had time to turn around before her father was in front of her, sweeping her into his arms. "Thank God I found you," he said, his voice choked up with feeling. "Everything's okay now. You're okay now."

He set her down. As her tears started falling again—a sudden release of fear and relief and love—he found her cheek with one rough hand. His beard was untrimmed and his fingernails ragged, but he smelled exactly the same, like pipe smoke and bergamot.

"Don't cry. You're safe. I'm here now."

Just as quickly, Cordelia's relief turned to horror. Her father was *here*. This was what Newton-Plancke had wanted all along. It was what he'd *counted* on.

She pulled away, swiping at her cheeks with both hands. "You can't stay here," she said, panic cresting suddenly inside her.

"Sounds like a great plan." Gregory, impatient,

reached out to maneuver the cage door open. "All in favor of a quick exit . . . ?" He wriggled free and rolled to his feet.

Cordelia was still trying to push her father toward the curtains. "You don't understand. Plancke is waiting for you. It's a trap. He was only using me as bait. He knows you're here, you're not safe, you have to—"

She didn't get any further. The room was suddenly flooded with light, and Plancke, wearing a dressing gown and slippers and holding a very large, very sharp knife, was illumined.

"Cornelius," he said pleasantly. "I was very much hoping you'd show up."

CHAPTER
33

Cornelius pivoted slowly to face Plancke. His face grew hard, as if it had been recast in stone. "Byron," he said. His voice, too, was stony. "And I was hoping never to see you again."

"Don't say that," Plancke said cheerfully. He had a tasseled stool tucked under one arm, and in the slippers and dressing gown, he looked like the madcap host of a weekend party. "Old friends are so important. Come, have a seat." He flipped the stool to the ground and patted the seat cushion. "Let's chat. Catch up on old times." Cornelius didn't move, and Newton-Plancke grinned, displaying his long teeth. "Come, come, Cornelius. Don't be stubborn. It's very impolite to refuse your host."

Still, Cornelius didn't move.

"*Now.*" Newton-Plancke dropped all pretense of cordiality. His voice was suddenly full of venom, and he advanced a step forward. "And no one gets hurt. Otherwise . . ." He twirled the knife in one hand.

Slowly, never taking his eyes off Newton-Plancke, Cornelius moved toward the stool. Plancke tracked his movements with the knife, until Cornelius was seated in front of him. Only then did Plancke lower the knife, though Cordelia noted that he was still gripping the handle tightly.

"Let's get right to it, shall we?" he said. "Where are the monsters, Cornelius?"

Cordelia could see beads of sweat on her father's face. But when Cornelius spoke, his voice was steady.

"You know I'll never tell you," Cornelius said.

Cordelia felt a rush of love for him, so strong it nearly doubled her over. He looked thinner than she remembered him—his cheekbones seemed to be whittled out of ancient wood, and his eyes were sunk deeply in his weather-beaten face—but his expression was still one of determined strength. This was the man who had pinned full-grown growrks to the floor to extract splinters from their massive paws; the man who had stayed up all night to save a bleeding cockatrice, which had become impaled on an old fence and lost several quarts of blood; the man who still found time to make Cordelia chicken soup from scratch when she was sick, to tickle her and tell her stories before bed.

Newton-Plancke's mouth thinned to a smile. In one step he had pressed the blade to Cornelius's throat. "You know what I'm capable of, I think. Don't make Elizabeth's mistake."

"Let go of him!" Cordelia cried out. She was so full of anger, so full of fury, that her feet moved all on their own. She was charging Newton-Plancke, ignoring the ricochet of shouting, ignoring the knife, ignoring the danger, ignoring everything but the fire of rage in her chest. She saw Plancke look up in surprise—

"Cordelia, no!" Her father flung out his arm before she could leap at Plancke, and caught her in the chest. She tumbled backward, landing hard on the marble floor. "Stay away! Do you hear me? Stay away!"

"Listen to your father, girl," Newton-Plancke said casually. "Don't worry. I won't cut his throat. How would he talk then? No, no." He turned back to Cornelius, seizing him by the hair. He ran the blade lightly down from Cornelius's throat all the way to his right hand, which was gripping the stool. "We'll save your throat for dessert. But a finger," he said, "will serve quite nicely as an appetizer."

He raised the blade. Time seemed to freeze. Cordelia wanted to cry, "Stop!" but the word gummed in her throat.

"Don't hurt him!" Elizabeth shouted suddenly. "I know where the monsters are! Just don't hurt him!"

Newton-Plancke paused, knife raised above his head. Cordelia was so stunned, it took her a moment to speak.

"Don't be stupid, Elizabeth," she said, her voice quivering. Then, in a louder voice: "She knows nothing."

"Cordelia's telling the truth," Cornelius said. "Leave the girl alone."

But it was too late. Plancke had already turned to Elizabeth. Elizabeth shrank backward, as if she wished to press herself into nonexistence.

"Don't play with me, girl." Sensing movement behind him, Plancke cupped a hand to his face. To Cordelia's horror, he pursed his lips and exhaled, and his left eyeball popped out into his outstretched palm. When he set it down, it promptly slithered over the marble until it reached Cornelius's feet.

"Just in case you have any ideas of escape," Plancke said with a nasty chuckle, without taking his remaining eye off Elizabeth. "Remember I have eyes in the back of my head. Or anywhere, really, I need them to be."

In two strides, Plancke had crossed the room to Elizabeth's cage. He produced a set of keys from his dressing gown and unlatched the cage that contained Elizabeth. Then he reached inside and grabbed her by her blond curls. Elizabeth kicked, aiming for his face, but Plancke merely tightened his grip on her and dragged her out into the open.

"Get off her, you slimy lug!" Gregory yelled.

Before Cornelius could start from his chair, Plancke spoke sharply to him: "Don't move, or I'll cut off the little girl's ears." Cornelius stared at the eyeball at his feet with distaste as it oozed a little closer to his toes.

"You're a monster." The words were in Cordelia's throat, on her tongue, before she could stop them.

"We've been over this already," he snapped, holding the knife close to Elizabeth's throat. "I'm a morpheus, remember? The only living member of a prehistoric species—"

"Lucky for you." Suddenly the fog of anger and fear lifted, and Cordelia understood. "That's the only part that even gets *close* to being human. You're a morpheus, sure. *And* you're a monster."

Plancke froze. He let go of Elizabeth. She fell to her knees, whimpering.

Cornelius's face had gone totally white. "Hush, Cordelia," he said. "Hold your tongue."

Still, Cordelia didn't stop. "I feel bad for you, really. You've been wrong all these years. You think if you find cages for all the monsters in the world, then the monster inside of you will finally be defeated." The current of understanding was still bearing her forward, holding her up, protecting her. "That's why you hate monsters," she said. "That's why you want to show everybody how *much* you hate them. That's why you want to point your finger at other people and say, *you*. It isn't even that you're afraid to be discovered. It's so that the mirror might stop pointing back at you. It's so that your sickness and hatred can stop whispering, *me*."

"Shut up." Newton-Plancke's voice was a whisper, but those two syllables contained the force and venom of all his hatred. "Just *shut up*."

"You've been feeding the wrong monster all this time," Cordelia said. "And now you'll never be free. You can turn into as many shapes as you want, but you'll never find one that isn't a horror."

He lunged at her, roaring with fury. Elizabeth shot out a leg and caught him in the shin, and he lost his balance, taking her down at the knees. Cordelia scurried backward as Plancke reached for her again—

—just as Cornelius landed on top of him.

"Help!" Plancke screeched, as he struggled to buck Cornelius from his back. "Someone! Anyone! Help!"

Almost immediately, Cordelia heard the drumming of quick footsteps from Plancke's living quarters. "The door, Elizabeth!" she cried. "Latch the door!"

Elizabeth scrambled to her feet and threw herself against the door, latching it just as a fist began pounding on it from the other side. Cordelia could just make out muffled shouting.

Plancke and Cornelius were still wrestling, struggling for control of the knife, grunting and sweating. Plancke had the advantage; then Cornelius; then Plancke again. Plancke raised the knife, roaring with fury, and struck. But Cornelius deflected him, grabbing Plancke by the throat. The knife thudded to the floor and skated across the marble.

Pinning Plancke to the ground, Cornelius plunged a hand inside Plancke's robe and found his key ring.

Boom. The door shuddered as though someone was taking a battering ram to it from the other side. Elizabeth yelped. She had thrown her back against the door, but now her feet were slipping on the marble.

"Catch!" Cornelius lobbed the keys to Gregory, who hurried to the dragon's cage. It only took him moments to open the cage door and free the dragon of his muzzle. He started next on the dragon's wing clips.

The momentary distraction had cost Cornelius the advantage. Plancke got an elbow free and clocked Cornelius in the chin.

"That," he said, shoving Cornelius off him, "is for old times' sake." Then, as he stood, he aimed a kick at Cornelius's head.

Cordelia screamed as Cornelius slumped, dazed, to the ground. She saw Plancke turn for the knife. As Plancke's eyeball rolled in her direction, bare and accusatory, she punted it toward the corner. Plancke screamed.

And Cordelia ran.

She was fifteen feet from the knife . . . then ten . . .

Plancke was closer, but half-blind, and still breathless from the fight. Still, he was going to reach it before her. . . .

Then the dragon swooped, screaming, in front of him, and aimed a blast of flame that Plancke ducked only at the last minute.

"Stupid *beast*." He swung a fist hard, catching the dragon mid-belly, and knocking him from the air.

Cordelia snatched up the knife and saw the dragon, dazed, trying to stand up. Icky was free now. . . . Gregory was at Cabal's cage. . . . But he was shaking so badly, he kept dropping the keys. . . .

Plancke was advancing on Cordelia, one eye a red wound, and the other gleaming with hatred. He was smiling.

"Stay where you are," Cordelia said, gripping the knife in two sweaty palms.

Another gigantic *boom* sounded, vibrating the door on its hinges, rattling the flimsy lock. "Gregory," Elizabeth gasped out. Even with most of her goblin showing, and her shoulders thickened with scales, she was no match for the force on the other side of the door. "Help me."

Gregory finally got the key in the lock and twisted. Cabal bounded out, barking, and followed Gregory as he dashed across the room. When Gregory hurled himself against the door next to Elizabeth, Cabal nudged up next to him.

And still, Plancke came. He seemed to stretch with every step, carving into the sickle shape of a crescent moon, until he almost reached the ceiling.

"Stay where you are, I said!" Cordelia was practically screaming. "Not another inch!"

"You remind me more and more of your mother," Plancke said. "You have the same scream. . . ."

Cordelia lunged for him without thinking. She slashed with the knife and struck him in the arm. Still, he managed to get hold of her jacket collar, and for a second she was pinioned in his grip.

"Gotcha!" he cried.

She managed to get her arms free of the sleeves. But before she could run, he swept a leg behind her knees and flipped her backward. She lost her hold on the knife. When she grabbed for it, he planted his slipper on the handle—and kicked it down the length of the exhibit hall. Her jacket, he simply cast aside into a corner.

"Perhaps you're right, about what makes me a monster." It wasn't blood that welled from the wound, but a dark green slime. Plancke hardly seemed to notice. "But you know what makes me a morpheus?"

There was a split second when his image seemed to shimmer, like hot air over a distant road.

"The shape of other lives. Other people. Other creatures." Then he wasn't Plancke anymore, but a Plancke mask made of wax, dripping onto the floor. When he spoke again, his voice was horribly distorted. "Even *dragons*."

Then he was a Plancke puddle, still bearing traces of the man's reflection. Finally he was nothing but a dark pool of evil-smelling slime, sliding out of the crumpled dressing gown and abandoned slippers, gathering together like a grounded cloud.

Gathering, and growing. And growing.

And growing.

CHAPTER
34

Where there had once been a man, there was now a vast dragon with black-tipped scales; enormous, curved fangs; and a tail ridged with heavy spikes. Cordelia and her father huddled next to Elizabeth and Gregory near the door. Cabal and Icky cowered at their feet. The baby dragon shrank back as the shadow of its enormous double swallowed up the corners of the room, exhaling hot, stinking air from nostrils the size of tree trunks. The only indication that the dragon wasn't natural—that it was Plancke in a different form—was the blank mass of scarred skin stretching across the space where his left eye should have been.

"Everyone stay calm," Cornelius said, herding Elizabeth, Gregory, and Cordelia behind him, as if he could shield them from Plancke's wrath. "Stick close to me."

No sooner had he finished speaking than the dragon-that-was-Plancke curled his lips back over his fangs and spat out a rushing stream of flame. The morpheus might have weakened in the heat, but his choice of shape more than compensated: it would take an oven the size of the whole museum to melt him down now.

"Down, down! Get down!" Cornelius cried.

Everyone was screaming. Elizabeth and Gregory scattered, and Cordelia felt her father push her to her knees. She rolled a few feet, blinking smoke from her eyes. The air stank of ash and sulfur. Fire had engulfed the door and a portion of the ceiling; there were more distant shouts, and the banging from the hallway went temporarily silent.

Cordelia had landed underneath the dragon's swollen stomach. She could see the diamond pattern of his hide, his squat, powerful legs, and his thick tail lashing across the room, splintering plaster from the walls and crashing cages to the floor. She could feel the heat from his massive body, the *whoosh* of air every time the dragon swiveled his head or adjusted his position.

They were all trapped. They needed a weapon.

The *knife*.

Cordelia, still on her hands and knees, pivoted in every direction, ducking to avoid getting clobbered by the dragon's tail. The smoke made it hard to see.

She swiped at her eyes carelessly, pushing back her sweaty strands of hair. *Whoosh*. She spotted the knife lying only a few feet away on the floor. As the dragon once again reared back and aimed a burst of fire at Cornelius—who escaped only by ducking behind the center mural—Cordelia lunged for the knife. Gripping the handle with both hands, she rolled onto her back and thrust the knife upward, as hard as she could, into the exposed belly of the beast.

The dragon stiffened. Smoke flared from his nostrils, as he swiveled his head to face her, his single eye glinting with malice. The knife was embedded deeply in his flesh, but Cordelia saw that the monster wasn't bleeding. Instead, a sticky, gooey slime was oozing from his wound, and Cordelia scrambled out of the way to avoid getting spattered. It was the same slime she had seen in her father's room; the same slime the eyeball left in its wake; the same slime a slug might puddle on a stone floor, after its back had been sprinkled with salt.

The idea hit her like a punch to the stomach: Byron Newton-Plancke was mostly water. Easily heated. Easily blurred by wet.

And fatally allergic to salt, which would evaporate it into its true shape.

"Cordelia, watch out!" Gregory shouted just in time. She dove as the dragon exhaled a wall of fire and smoke. She somersaulted into the corner, bumping her head on the wall. Sitting up, she shook her head to clear the stars from her vision.

The dragon's yellow eye hovered right in front of her, reflecting a terrified Cordelia cowering at its center. The dragon's nostrils quivered with pleasure. Every time he exhaled, Cordelia felt as if she were being blasted by air from a hot oven. With his crooked teeth exposed, the dragon looked as if he was smiling.

She couldn't move. She couldn't breathe. She couldn't think. Dimly, she was aware of her father shouting, of Gregory calling her name, of Elizabeth telling her to get out of the way. But there was nowhere to go. She was trapped.

It was over.

Cordelia squeezed her eyes shut as the dragon sucked in an enormous breath—

But instead of the expected blast of heat, she felt the dragon jerk backward. Looking up, she saw Icky—cowardly Icky—clinging determinedly to the dragon's nose, letting off an explosive artillery of farts.

Cordelia rocketed to her feet. Doubling over to pass underneath the belly of the monster, she sprinted for her jacket. Someone—Gregory?—called to her to watch out.

Whoosh. Once again, the dragon turned its eye on Cordelia. She was so close. . . .

She dove as a stream of fire incinerated the wall behind her. She landed hard behind the cage, using it as a makeshift shield against the shimmering heat as she reached for the jacket that Plancke had cast off into a corner. From a pocket she rooted out the paper bag that had once contained the pretzels. She dug a fist into the bag and withdrew a handful of salt, praying it would be enough.

And as the dragon's head rose, rose, rose over the top of the cage, his yellow eye like a sun just rising, steam issuing from his massive nostrils, she threw.

The salt landed directly in his eye. The dragon drew back, roaring with pain. Cordelia tossed another handful, straight up the dragon's nostrils. For a terrifying second, nothing else happened, and Cordelia's heart stopped: they were lost.

Then there was a sizzling sound, like bacon in a fryer. The dragon blinked. Then he began to melt.

His eye went first, oozing and popping, transforming into the same bubbling slime that had oozed from Plancke's wounds. Then his snout, and his gigantic, quivering nostrils, began to blur—melting, melting, pouring away, so that even when Plancke attempted one last burst of flame, the fire itself transformed into liquid, splattering the walls and ceiling and dousing the remaining flames.

And as Byron-Newton Plancke puddled, shriveled, and collapsed, he started to howl. The sound was so loud and so horrible, Cordelia covered her ears. But the smaller he got, the fainter the noise became.

Until at last, when he was no larger than a house cat drowning in a pile of slime, the sound was tolerable again; and when he was no bigger than a mouse, the howl was no louder than a faint whistle.

And finally, Plancke the morpheus assumed his true form: a long, sluglike creature the size of a child's finger, marbled with a complex pattern of veins, like the one her mother had found, fossilized into stone.

For a long moment, no one spoke. Gregory was panting. Elizabeth was shaking so hard her knees were knocking together with a hard, wooden clanging. She had broken out in warts all over.

Cordelia didn't even try to stand up. She was flooded with exhaustion, suddenly; she felt as if her body had been replaced with iron.

Cornelius adjusted his glasses, which were perched crookedly on his nose. "Well," he said. "Well." He limped a little closer and stared down at the sluglike morpheus with distaste. He raised his boot. "Now that he's been salted . . ."

"Don't," Cordelia cried out. Cornelius looked at her in surprise. "Don't," she repeated. "Let him live this way, as himself. Put him in a jar, and set the jar next to a mirror, and let him live with his reflection. That's punishment enough, isn't it?"

"You're sure?" Cornelius asked quietly.

Cordelia nodded. "It's like Mom thought," she said. "*Good overcomes evil.* Then the evil has no one to blame for its evil. Right?"

Cornelius stared at her. Tears dampened his eyes. Then he pulled her tight into a hug. "That's right," he said. Then he released her and turned his attention back to Byron Newton-Plancke, in his true form.

"We'll need to find some kind of container . . . ," he began.

In a way, they did, a minute later, when Elizabeth, still gripped in an explosive outbreak of goblin, spotted the slug on the floor—and instinctively darted out a long, pink tongue to snatch it up.

A horrified Elizabeth clapped both hands to her mouth. There was a beat of silence.

Then Elizabeth cried out, *"Slugs?"*

Gregory patted her on the arm. "At least it's not a spider," he said.

CHAPTER
35

Less than six weeks later, on the day before the grand reopening of Clay Home for Veterinary Services, a passerby might have startled at the strange grunts, bumps, groans, and creaks emanating from the open windows of the house known as Clay Manor. This stranger might then jump, hearing a cheerful voice from the garden, only to see Mrs. Emily Perkins, founder of the New Collective School, waving cheerfully with a garden spade.

And then, a moment later, the door would burst open, and Cornelius Clay would emerge to cart a ratty armchair to the growing stack of furniture on the corner, earmarked for the dump. Or a sweet-looking girl with an unfortunate haircut would float by in one of the windows, holding a paintbrush and complaining that Gregory, whoever he was, had chosen the wrong color.

And the passerby would hurry on, embarrassed for having been caught spying.

The same scene had been replayed for many weeks. Since late January, Clay Manor had been full of the drumming of feet up and down the stairs, shouted conversation, and furniture bumping through the doorways. The rhythm of a hammer was almost constant, as was the rhythmic *shush* of paint on the walls. And laughter. Almost always, laughter.

What was *missing* from Clay Manor were the screeches and squawks, the wailing, the animal grunts and growls.

What was missing, in fact, were the monsters.

"I still don't see why you had to give them *up*," Gregory grumbled, even as Cornelius and Cordelia wedged a dresser into the corner of his new room. The walls had been patched and painted sky blue. The floors repaired and refinished. No one would guess that mushrooms had ever grown in the corner.

"You still have Cabal," Cordelia pointed out.

"Cabal's different," Gregory said dismissively. Down

in the garden, Cabal began barking, as if he'd overheard and taken offense. Cordelia went to the window and watched him rooting around the planting beds, while Mrs. Perkins's husband tried to shoo him away from the beds. Elizabeth and her mother were kneeling side by side, carefully tamping down the earth around a trellis meant for climbing roses. The garden was already taking shape under their care. Goblins were known for their green thumbs. Literally.

"Professor Natter says you can visit Icky whenever you want," Cornelius said, carefully centering a lamp on the dresser. The professor had come to visit not long after they'd escaped Plancke, and his bond with the filch, a double of his favorite childhood pet, was undeniable.

"But what about all the others?" Gregory said. "I don't mind sharing a room with a squelch, even if it *is* molting. . . ."

"We miss the monsters too," Cornelius said, laying a hand on Gregory's shoulder. "But what we were doing—keeping them here, locked up in the house—it wasn't right. Monsters belong to the world. They belong *in* the world. We had no right to keep them here."

"But what if something happens?" Gregory persisted. "What if they get hunted down, or caged up, or—?"

"We can't stop all the evil in the world," Cornelius interrupted him. "We can only make sure we don't repeat it. A cage is a cage, even if it has a roof. Even if you name it 'protection.' Now go on," he added, tousling Gregory's hair. "There's still plenty to do before the grand reopening of Clay Veterinary. *Especially* since someone's been spreading a rumor that I can perform miracles, like bringing dogs back from the dead. . . ."

"People say all kinds of twaddle," Gregory said, flushing a deep red. "Come on, Cordelia." He seized Cordelia's hand and yanked her toward the stairs.

They slid down the polished banisters, Gregory's favorite new trick, and landed with a soft thump on the new carpet that ran the length of the first floor hallway—all of it courtesy of the New Collective, a school founded by Mrs. Perkins for "project-based education and learning," for students who did not fit traditional models of schooling. So far, forty-five people had enrolled for the fall, and while the ground floor would be dedicated primarily to Cornelius's practice, the upper floors were slowly being converted into classrooms and project centers.

But the school's heart, its center, its *library*, was almost complete.

Cabal was still barking, and Mr. Perkins was shouting something about his trouser leg.

"I'll get him," Gregory said. "Before he tries to sample blood straight from the source."

"Good idea," Cordelia said.

He dashed down the hall. Moments later, she heard the kitchen door wheeze open and bang shut.

She stood for a moment, enjoying the rare stillness. The rustle of paper made her turn. The windows were open in her mother's former library, and a breeze turned the pages of the large books, open for display on the lower shelves.

She passed into the room, both familiar and unrecognizable. Gone was her mother's desk. Gone was the crib. Gone were the heavy curtains. Sunlight spilled over the bookshelves, now filled with not only her mother's collection of scientific treatises, but other books Mrs. Perkins had selected for the school—plays and poems, historical volumes, dictionaries, foreign language primers. Still, her mother's first book was among them—and some of her collection of natural objects too.

Not the fossilized morpheus, though. They'd lost that during the scrum with Newton-Plancke.

But in the end, perhaps, it didn't matter very much.

Cordelia moved to the glass-topped table at the center of the room, where the first bound copy of her mother's now-finished manuscript, featuring an introduction and conclusion by Professor Natter, was proudly displayed. She turned again to the tree of life: a river of ink, flowing from a single source into dizzying rivulets of being, into everything that exists and has existed.

She placed a finger on the blank space, where the morpheus was meant to be.

It was funny, how the pattern was so clear, as soon as she was staring down the length of her finger. The veins of life on either side of it looked just like the pattern she'd seen cross-hatched in the fossil. Like you could twist them all together around her finger, and make a coil.

Two coils, actually. Each coil coiled, and coiled around the other. Like a double staircase, winding upward toward infinity.

Cordelia closed her eyes and heard her mother's voice come in, carried by the wind, alive everywhere.

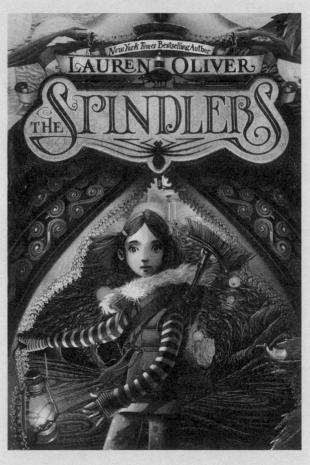

Chapter 1

Patrick

THE CHANGELING, AND THE
LETTERS SPELLED IN CEREAL

One night when Liza went to bed, Patrick was her chubby, stubby, candy-grubbing and pancake-loving younger brother, who irritated and amused her both, and the next morning, when she woke up, he was not.

She could not describe the difference. He looked the same, and was wearing the same pair of ratty space-alien pajamas, with the same fat toe sticking out of the hole in the left foot of his red socks, and he came down the stairs exactly the same way the real

Patrick would have done: *bump*, *bump*, *bump*, sliding on his rump.

But he was not the same.

In fact, he was quite, quite different.

It was something in the way he looked at her: It was as though someone had reached behind his eyes and wrung away all the sparkle. He walked quietly—too quietly—to the table, sat nicely in his chair, and placed a napkin on his lap.

The real Patrick never used a napkin.

Nobody else noticed a thing. Mrs. Elston, Liza's mother, continued sorting through the stack of bills on the kitchen table, making occasional noises of unhappiness. Liza's father continued passing in and out of the room, his tie unknotted and wearing only one sock, muttering distractedly to himself.

The fake-Patrick picked up his spoon and gave Liza a look that chilled her to her very center.

Then the fake-Patrick began to eat his cereal, methodically, slowly, fishing all the alphabet letters out of his Alpha-Bits one by one and lining them up along the rim of his bowl.

Liza's heart sank. She knew, at that moment, what had happened, as well as she knew that the sky was up and the ground was down and if you turned around fast enough in a circle and then stood still, the world would keep turning the circle for you.

Patrick's soul had been taken by the spindlers. And they had left this thing, this not-younger-brother, in its place.

"Mom," she said, and then, when her mother did not immediately respond, tried again a little louder. "Mom."

"Mmm?" Mrs. Elston jumped. She squinted at Liza for a moment, the same way she had looked at the instruction sheet that came along with the Easy-Assemble Coffee Table in Mahogany, the one she had had to return to the store after she could not figure out how to screw the legs on.

"Patrick's being weird," Liza said.

Mrs. Elston stared blankly at her daughter. Then she whirled around, suddenly, to her husband. "Did you ever pay the electric bill?"

Mr. Elston didn't seem to hear her. "Have you seen my glasses?" he asked, lifting the fruit bowl and peering underneath it.

"They're on your head."

"Not *those* glasses. My reading glasses."

Mrs. Elston sighed. "It says this is our final notice. I don't remember a first notice. Didn't we pay the electric bill? I could have sworn . . ."

"I can't go to work without my glasses!" Mr.

3

Elston opened the refrigerator, stared at its contents, closed the refrigerator, and rushed out of the room.

Across the table, the fake-Patrick began rearranging the cereal letters on the outside of his bowl. He spelled out three words: I H-A-T-E Y-O-U. Then he folded his hands and stared at her with that strangely vacant look, as though the black part of his eyes had eaten up all the color.

Liza's insides shivered again. She slid off her chair and went over to her mother. She tugged at the sleeve of her mother's nightgown, which had a small coffee stain at its elbow. "Mommy."

"Yes, princess?" she asked distractedly.

"Patrick's freaking me out."

"Patrick," Mrs. Elston said, without looking up from her notepad, on which she was now scribbling various figures. "Stop bothering your sister."

Here's what the real Patrick would have done: He would have stuck out his tongue, or thrown his napkin at Liza in retaliation, or he would have said, "It's her *face* that's the bother."

But this impostor did none of those things. The impostor just stared quietly at Liza and smiled. His teeth looked very white.

"Mom—" Liza insisted, and her mother sighed

and threw down her pencil with so much force that it bounced.

"*Please*, Liza," she said, with barely concealed impatience. "Can't you see that I'm busy? Why don't you go outside and play for a bit?"

Liza knew better than to argue with her mother when she was in a mood. So she went outside. It was a hot and hazy morning—far too hot for late April. She was hoping to see one of the neighbors out doing something—watering a plant, walking a dog—but it was very still. Liza almost never saw the neighbors. It was not that kind of neighborhood. She didn't even know most of their names: only Mrs. Costenblatt, who was so old she looked exactly like a prune.

Today, as on most days, Mrs. Costenblatt was sitting on her porch, rocking, and fanning herself with one of the Chinese delivery menus that were often stuck—mysteriously, invisibly, in the middle of the night—under the front door.

"Hello," she called out to Liza, and waved.

"Hello," Liza called back. She liked Mrs. Costenblatt, even though Mrs. Costenblatt hardly ever moved except to rock in her chair, and could not be counted on to do anything interesting.

"Would you like a glass of lemonade?" Mrs. Costenblatt called out. "Or a cookie?" She offered

Liza lemonade and a cookie every time they saw each other, unless it was winter, in which case she offered hot chocolate and a cookie. Mrs. Costenblatt liked to rock even in cold weather, and she would appear on her porch so bundled in blankets and scarves, she looked like an overstuffed coatrack.

"Not today, thank you," Liza said regretfully, as she always did. She was not allowed to accept things to eat or drink from Non-Family Members. Liza often wished the rule applied to Family Members instead. She would much rather have had one of Mrs. Costenblatt's cookies than her aunt Virginia's tuna casserole.

She wondered whether she should tell Mrs. Costenblatt about Patrick, but decided against it. Two weeks earlier, at recess, when she had tried to tell Christina Millicent and Emma Wong about the spindlers and the constant threat they posed, they had laughed at her and called her a liar. Mrs. Costenblatt was a good listener—partly, Liza thought, because she couldn't hear very well—but Liza didn't want to risk it.

There was only one thing that Liza hated more than liars, and that was being accused of being one.

At one edge of the yard, a pile of pinecones had

been neatly stacked. Liza had arranged them this way only yesterday, thinking that she and Patrick might play a round of Pinecone Bowling in the morning. But of course she could not play with the false Patrick; he would no doubt find a way to cheat.

She had a sudden, wrenching, fierce desire for Anna, her old babysitter, to come home. She would have played Pinecone Bowling. In fact, she had invented it.

Last fall Anna had gone away to college, which meant that she had moved and couldn't babysit anymore, and instead Liza and Patrick were left with Mandy, who always chewed her gum too loudly and didn't like to play games—she didn't like anything, really, except talking on the phone. Anna had come over to babysit several times during her Christmas vacation, but on her spring break she had gone away with her friends. Liza and Patrick had gotten a water-warped postcard from her, but most of the writing had been too blurry to read.

In addition to the postcard she had sent from the beach, she had sent two letters from college, and a white sweatshirt with a fierce-looking bear on the front, explaining in the attached note that it was her school's mascot. Patrick had cried like a baby when it turned out the sweatshirt was in Liza's size, and she had finally lent it to him. He had promptly spilled tomato sauce on it, and she'd refused to speak to him for an entire day.

Liza knew it was stupid, but sometimes she fantasized that Anna would turn up again and confess her deepest secret: that Liza and Patrick were, in fact, her siblings, and they had all been torn apart by some horrible event when they were little and forced into different families.

Liza's fantasies were a little hazy after that point, but she thought that somehow she, Anna, and Patrick would end up on a long journey together, hunting down some of the magical creatures Anna had always told them about, like gnomes and nimphids (who were beautiful but bad-tempered).

Liza sighed. Anna would also have known what to do about the spindlers. She was, after all, the person who had first told Liza and Patrick about them. She was the one who had warned them about the strange spider creatures and had told them what they must do to be protected.

Liza scanned the yard for gnomes, but saw nothing. Only last week, Patrick—the real Patrick—had spotted one scampering into the rhododendron.

"Look, Liza!" he had cried out, and she had turned just in time to see a hard, brown hide, which was as cracked and weathered as a leather purse.

It was too hot for the gnomes today, Liza decided. Anna had told Liza they preferred cool climates.

Liza pressed her face up against the small fir tree that stood next to the birdbath, inhaling deeply. It was easier to see the magic through its branches, she found. The scratchy needles poked deeply into her skin, and she stood and squinted through the layers of green. Looking at the world through the fir tree meant seeing only the essential things: the vivid green of the grass, dew glistening on petals, a robin flicking its tail, a squirrel rustling through the rhododendron, a miracle of life and growth that forever pulsed under the ordinariness.

And, of course, it was only when looking through the tree that you could make a wish and have it come true—Anna had also told them that.

Liza spoke a wish quietly into the scratchy branches.

We will not repeat it. Everyone knows that only wishes that are kept secret will ever come true. But know this: The wish was about Patrick.

Liza heard a step behind her. She turned and saw the Patrick-who-was-not-Patrick standing on the front porch, watching her.

Liza sucked in a deep breath, gathered her courage, and said, "You are not my brother."

Not-Patrick stared at her with flat blue eyes. "Yes, I am," he said calmly.

"You aren't."

"Am too."

"Prove it," Liza said, crossing her arms, and she tried to think of a question whose answer only the real Patrick would know. She was quiet for a bit. At last she asked, "When you are playing hide-and-seek on a rainy day, what is the best hiding space?"

"Behind the bookcase in the basement," not-Patrick answered automatically. "In the crawl space that smells like mold."

Liza was disappointed. He had gotten it right; this fake-Patrick was obviously smarter than she gave him credit for—smarter, she wouldn't wonder, than the real Patrick. (Though that wasn't saying much. Only a week ago the real Patrick had tried to turn the basement into a swimming pool by flooding the sink! Absurd.) Maybe she needed to ask a harder question.

"What must you do every night before you go to sleep?" Liza said, eyeing the not-Patrick narrowly to see whether there was any hesitation or shiftiness in his answer.

But he responded promptly, drawing a big X across his chest, "You must cross yourself once from shoulder to hip and say out loud, 'Sweep, sweep, bring me sleep. Clear the webs from my room with the bristliest broom.'"

Liza was stunned. She had been sure—positive!—that the question would baffle not-Patrick, but his answer was correct, and he stood looking at her with an expression of triumph. When Anna had first discovered the spindlers, she had invented this rhyme as a way of keeping the spindlers at bay while they slept. Everyone knows there is nothing a spider fears more than a broom, and someone sweeping with it, and the broom charm had, in fact, protected them for years.

Patrick—the real Patrick—must have forgotten to say the broom charm last night before he went to sleep. He and Liza had been fighting—Patrick had accused her of stealing his favorite socks, which were blue and embroidered with turtles, as though she would ever have worn anything so ridiculous— and Liza called him paranoid, and when he did not know what that meant, he stormed into his room and slammed the door.

He was distracted; that must be why he had not said the broom charm. Liza felt a heavy rush of guilt. It was her fault, at least partially.

And so the spindlers had gotten him: They had dropped down from the ceiling on their glistening webs of shadowed darkness and dropped their silken threads in his ear, and extracted his soul slowly, like a fisherman coaxing a trout from the water on a taut nylon fishing line. In its place they deposited their eggs; then they withdrew to their shadowed, dark corners and their underground lairs with his soul bound closely in silver thread.

And the soulless shell would wake the next morning, and walk, and talk, as not-Patrick was walking and talking.

But eventually, the soulless shell would crumble to dust, and a thousand spindlers—nested and grown—would burst forth, like a lizard hatching from an egg. And distraught parents would wake up, believing their children to have been kidnapped while they slept, and they would appear tearfully on television, begging for their children's safe return, when really the spindlers were to blame.

Liza felt a sudden tightness in her throat.

"You see!" not-Patrick crowed. "I told you. I *am* your brother."

Then Liza was struck by an idea.

"Come here," she said to not-Patrick, and even though she was filled with revulsion by the closeness of this imitation, this cold and cardboard thing, she forced herself to stand still as he approached.

Suddenly she lunged for him and began tickling his stomach.

The real Patrick was extraordinarily ticklish and would have screamed with laughter and tried to shove Liza off and begged for mercy. Liza loved the sound of Patrick's laugh. It came in short, explosive bursts, as though each time he was relearning how to do it.

This Patrick stood still, watching her dully. "What are you doing?" he asked.

Liza pulled away. She then had the same feeling she'd had several years ago, when she had swung too high and too fast on the swings at the playground, and the world teetered underneath her: a feeling of triumph but also of terror. She knew it. This Patrick was not the real Patrick. And that meant that the soul of the real Patrick had been bound up in silver thread and carried deep underground, and that inside the body of not-Patrick, insects were nesting.

Liza drew herself up to her full four feet four inches. "I am not afraid of you," she said to not-Patrick, but she was of course speaking to all those infant spindlers sleeping soundly in their thousands of soft eggs, somewhere deep inside his chest. And of course she *was* afraid. She was more afraid than she had ever been in her life. "I will find my real brother, and I will bring him back."

And then she spun quickly on her heel and stalked off toward the house, so not-Patrick and the tiny monsters he carried inside him would not see that she was shaking.